I0550199

Heroes of the Empire

Doom

Michael P. Andre

No part of this publication may be reproduced, stored, or transmitted in any form or by any means in a retrieval system, or electronic, mechanical, photocopying, recording, or otherwise, without the written consent of the author and publisher, Michael P Andre or a licence from the Canadian Copyright Licensing Agency (Access Copyright).
For an Access Copyright licence, visit www.accesscopyright.ca or call toll free to 1-800-893-5777.

Copyright © 2018 Michael P. Andre
All rights reserved.
ISBN 978-0-9937384-4-9 (Paperback)
ISBN 978-0-9937384-5-6 (e-book)

DEDICATION

I would like to dedicate this to my wife and family.

ACKNOWLEDGEMENTS

I would like to thank Saima, Denis, and my sister, Joanne for their editing skills and Amazon for their cover picture.

OTHER BOOKS BY THIS AUTHOR

First Born of the Moon and Other Stories

Healer and More Stories

TABLE OF CONTENTS

INTRODUCTION

I am a historian, although your historians would not agree but I assure you I am.

Your Oxford dictionary defines a 'historian' as a 'writer of history', or a 'person learned in history' and defines 'history' as a 'continuous methodical record of important and public events'. Those events happened in the past. I do exactly that.

However, your historians would challenge me by saying my events are in the future, so it is not history but fiction. On the other hand, if a person were to come from the far future, as I have, to your period, and record the events of that time accurately and faithfully as it is known to him or her, then he or she would be writing history, only to you it would appear to be from the future.

From where I come is not important. From what time I come, is of no consequence. I bring forth to you from my past the glorious exploits and achievements of the women and men of your future, so that you too, can stand tall as a representative of mankind, of that ruddy being that goes by the genus, Homo, and the species, sapiens; the body collective that will spread itself within one arm of the Milky Way galaxy and create your future.

I came to this time and spent the good part of my lifetime learning your language and your ways to bring your future history to you because you are now ready. You have grown and matured from the time of the club, the spear, the arrow, the gun, the cannon, the plane, and the atomic bomb. You are now ready to hear of these events; stories of hope, of love and great heroes of your glorious future. Hopefully, they will inspire you and make you proud not only of what you have done but of what you will do.

Ignore what your historians would say. These stories are real, the people are real. This is a biography of very heroic people in your future.

PROLOGUE

The event you are about to read takes place in the relatively early era in the young life of Earth's empire. On one arm of the galaxy arching through space is the home of millions of stars shared by trillions of people. The empire has spread like a giant balloon with a greater concentration of beings at the centre while, near the edge, exploration parties rush out relentlessly into the void to find new planets to spread their seed.

In this near void, in many cases, lawlessness reigned supreme. The general rule was that there was no interference in the formation of planets. They were left to develop naturally. As the populations grew in these new worlds, order eventually followed. When this failed to happen, and the people called for assistance, the empire would send help. To preserve this independence of development and not give the appearance of interference, neither police nor armies were sent, just one lone person in most cases. The emperor or empress sent out their special agents.

These agents were handpicked for their integrity and skills in the martial arts or other areas; men, or women, who became judges, juries, and executioners. These agents, of course, were not just present in the outer territories; they were called in whenever and wherever their special talents were needed.

This is the fourth and last notable event of one of the greatest of them. It begins on the extreme edge of one sector of the empire.

1

The captain returned to the bridge after reading the secret message sent to him from sector base 139-84.

"Captain on the bridge," rang out from the computer's realistic-sounding voice track. The other officers stood up to acknowledge his presence. He uploaded the ship's new heading into the system. His first officer wandered over to him and gazed at him questioningly.

"Meeting in the wardroom in fifteen minutes," the captain said aloud then left the bridge.

Fifteen minutes later, everyone sat patiently in the room anxious to hear what the captain had to say. So far, their yearlong mission of patrolling this sector of the known galaxy had been totally uneventful, perhaps even boring. The news that a message had been sent to their captain had raised their interest that maybe there was something of note they were going to do now.

Their patrol ship, a small cruiser, was an older model that had spent many faithful years of service in this sector. Almost all crew treated their craft more like one of the gang rather than a machine at their service. The craft served many functions beyond just providing necessities like food, water, and a way to get them from one point to another. It was also a way of entertaining the crew with games, as well as something neutral to talk to in their long and lonely hours on patrol, particularly at night. This ship had a crew of twelve.

The captain stepped into the cabin and everyone stood up. When he seated himself, the crew sat down again.

"I received a message a while ago from sector base 139-84," the captain began. "I've read it several times to try to understand exactly what the issue is. I don't even think anyone on the base knows what happened. In short, a "P" class vessel with five people on board was exploring the fringe in 139-101 when everyone on board just died."

The crew members sat up in their chairs.

"Cabin breach?" the first officer asked, suggesting the cabin had lost its air pressure.

"That's what I first thought," the captain responded, "but it appears not to be the cause. The ship is responding to communications and there does not appear to be any breach in the hull. The air pressure is normal. Everything was normal, then everyone's hearts just stopped beating, all at the same time."

"Did they get hit by something?"

"Not."

"Were the ship's shields on?"

"Just on running." That meant normal shielding was in operation to protect the ship against damage from impacts by meteorites and other space debris."

"How about a blast of solar radiation?" asked the engineer.

"No, none reported," answered the captain.

It was quiet for a few minutes. Everyone was in deep thought.

The captain continued. "We have about two days before we get there. They were pretty well in the middle of nowhere. We're not sure what we'll find, so keep alert. I've programmed for us to arrive some distance from the stricken craft, so we can scan around a bit before we move in for a closer look. The lifeless ship reports no foreign objects, vessels, or anything like that nearby, so I don't think we'll encounter another life form, at least nothing we've encountered before."

"Maybe we can find out what killed them when I do an autopsy," the doctor mused aloud.

"Maybe," the captain responded.

"What about the ship?" the chief engineer piped up. "Is it still in good running order? Is it still on its original trajectory?"

"It's fully functional," returned the captain. "The base has taken it over and brought it to a full stop until we can determine our next steps. They don't want it to enter our territory if it might be a hazard of some sort. They will be turning the ship over to us tomorrow, so we can investigate to our heart's content. You can get all your questions answered then. I recommend everyone get back to their duties and think about everything we need to do. I also want to run several emergency drills to make sure everyone is reminded of emergency protocols and processes to follow. I have no idea what happened there and I don't want anything to happen to us. I also want an all-systems check of our ship, particularly our scanners. Let's be ready for anything."

Three hours later, the captain called a meeting with the engineer and the doctor.

When they were seated in the captain's quarters, he lowered the view screen and they were presented to a team of four doctors and the head engineer of the base. They were then shown a video of the interior of a "P" class ship. One person was taking a nap, while the other four were performing routine activities. Suddenly, the three seated persons sat rigid in their chairs, then slumped forward on the panel in front of them. The standing person's face grew pale and blank then he slumped to the floor. The sleeping person's monitor is straight-lined. Everything happened at the same time.

The commander, a rear admiral of the base, opened the conversation. "What you have seen, ladies and gentlemen, is what happened in the stricken ship slightly before, during, and after the event. Now let's have a look at it several times with all the ship's monitors visible, so you can determine if there's anything that might indicate what happened. We've run it many times ourselves but maybe someone on your ship can notice anything we missed."

The video was shown again with all the ship's monitoring devices around the periphery of the video. The video was shown another three times so everyone had time to examine all the gauges, screens, etc.

The commander asked, "Now what did you see?"

The patrol ship's engineer said, "Everything looked normal to me, except for the slight nudge of an energy surge in the power gauge, although I noticed there was a slight dip before the surge."

There was a hubbub in the base's council chambers. The video was run again and put through slow motion action, focussed on the power gauge.

"You're right," stated the commander. "We didn't notice that, although it may be irrelevant."

The base's chief engineer stated that it was not unusual for something like that to occur during a surge.

"Is there anything else?" the commander continued.

The patrol ship's engineer stated, "Nothing from me. There was nothing on the long or near-range scanners that showed there was anything nearby that would have attacked it. They also didn't appear to have hit anything."

The patrol ship's doctor added, "It was almost as if the crew was turned off by a switch. It didn't look like a mass heart attack or a stroke. From looking at their faces, they just appeared to stop living. I don't think it was a disease or anything like that – a disease would not work that way, so it's not a plague of some sort."

There was silence for several seconds.

"Well, all interesting observations," the commander noted. "We'll keep investigating at this end but we still have nothing much to go on. We'll set things up so you can take full control of the ship and do whatever you feel necessary to dig into this further but don't take any risks. What happened to them might happen to you. We still don't know what to expect from this."

The meeting closed.

Twenty hours later, the crew had control of the other ship and had it send them reams of information about its status before and after the event. After analysing all the information, they were no more knowledgeable than they were before. They were all still stumped.

Ten hours later, the captain called another meeting of the team.

"I know you guys are a little frustrated with the results you have. Is there anything more you can glean from the facts?" the captain asked.

"Could a power surge harm the crew in any way?" the first officer asked the engineer.

"It's highly unlikely, especially one as minor as the one that occurred."

"Can we rule out any natural occurrence?" the captain probed.

"As far as I can see," responded the doctor, "people just don't go down like that. They gag, they writhe; they don't just turn off like that. They were like puppets where the puppeteer dropped the strings. I have no idea how that happened."

"No other ideas?" the captain asked again.

There was silence.

"We're nearing the site, so I want everyone on high alert for the next few hours."

Everyone but the first officer and captain left the room.

"We've been on many missions in our years on duty together. Most of the time we've had lots of boredom, sometimes we've had tragedies and missions of mercy and I've never seen you as I see you now. You look worried," the first officer said.

"Whatever we've experienced before was known. We knew what it was and what we needed to do. I've never experienced anything like this before. When we get to the stricken ship, I don't have a clue what to do when I get there. Do I just hook up the ship and bring it in so the bodies can be buried? Do I sit there and see what happens? I have no idea. If I keep our distance, how far should I stay? What is safe, and what isn't? Is what killed everyone on board still there?"

"But you don't know if it's anything. If it was something, wouldn't we detect it?'

"That's what I mean. We don't have a clue what we're up against. Maybe it shouldn't be us here but a battleship that can deal with any eventuality."

"Maybe we're exactly what should be here. If it's dangerous, we're a minimal loss."

"Yeah, the shooting ducks, the guinea pigs. . ."

"But it's our job."

"Hopefully, this turns out to be nothing." The captain sighed. "I was also thinking about why this had to happen now. I'm planning to retire in a couple of years."

"You never told me."

"It's been in the past year that I've thought about it. I thought I'd leave any announcement until next year.

"I'll keep your little secret."

"Thanks, I want the crew to be thinking about the job and not about my leaving. So many of us have been together a long time . . . Thinking about the crew – any issues arising, like nervousness about this mission?"

"Well, they're talking about it but they're confident in your leadership. They feel safe with you on board."

"Little do they know, I'm more nervous about what I'll do than they are."

"Well, you've pulled us out of a lot of tight situations."

"Hmmm . . ."

The two of them left the room to get some rest before they arrived at their destination.

The captain, though, got no sleep.

The next morning, they could feel the slight tug of deceleration of the ship and soon could see by the monitor they were motionless.

"What's our status?" asked the captain when he entered the bridge.

The computer's voice track responded, "Ship at full stop. Location one point 1,000,000 kilometres from target."

There was complete silence for about ten minutes until the nurse could not stand the oppressiveness of it anymore. "Well, what are we doing?"

"We're just sitting here," answered the captain.

There was more silence.

The captain continued. "I've parked us here, so we can see if there is any reaction to our arrival. As you can see, I've put the ship's field up at full strength which should repel just about anything. Our probing and scanning will be more intense than that of the Class "P" unit, so we should see if anything moves, makes noise, blinks, or anything detectable, even 1,000,000 kilometres away. I'm guessing this will be a safe distance to have a look at the other ship."

The crew was smiling. They liked his approach.

2

The captain tapped lightly on the door.

"What is it?" came a woman's voice from inside.

"It's Captain Weyburn, Admiral."

"Oh . . . Just a minute, I'll be right out."

In less than a minute, the door opened and a tall lanky woman stepped out into the passageway. She adjusted her uniform a bit, as she began walking to the council chamber.

"Sorry, I lost track of time, Captain," she lied, and the captain knew it. She had dozed off while resting after having many discussions with her team about the incident in 139-101, and following up with a full report to imperial headquarters. She had raised the issue to that level and would pay the price if this turned out to be nothing.

Sector base 139-84 was a relatively new installation, only ten years old and set up as a forward base in their newly developed part of the empire. It orbited an old red star in a small nebula cluster; ideal for protection in case of attack and would also be difficult to detect, if you did not know it was there. It served not only military purposes but also as a transit station for passengers and freight.

Commodore Kerchov had been promoted to Rear Admiral here as its first commanding officer. She had asked for several renewals to extend her stay but was now being promoted in six months to lead a space fleet in another sector of the empire. Ten years greatly exceeded the term in any one place for military personnel. She had mixed feelings about the promotion. She had grown comfortable here and had secretly liked the lack of any crises in this sector. It had been exceedingly boring and she liked that.

This was the only incident of any note she had had to deal with and she was not amused. She was hoping this would turn out to be nothing important, even if she would get chided by her seniors and peers for her overreaction.

They arrived at the council chamber door. Their presence caused the door to open and the computer announced her arrival. She waited until everyone was standing and she entered, walked over to her chair at the head of the table, and sat down. The captain followed her in. There was a little hubbub while everyone got re-seated. She secretly loved the pomp and ceremony of the military discipline. She glanced over at Captain Weyburn and caught his little smirk. She was beginning to hate the captain. She sensed that he always seemed to know what she was thinking. She did not know why she thought that. Sometimes she considered her imagination was getting the better of her, and it was getting worse. Times like this made her glad she was moving on. Maybe that was why the military kept moving people around.

She refocused herself.

"Okay, from the chronometer, the patrol ship should have arrived at its destination?"

"Yes, Admiral," another captain said.

"Fill me in."

"The ship has stopped about one point 1,000,000 kilometres away from the Class "P" vessel."

"That's being overly cautious but I can't say I blame the captain of the patrol vehicle," the admiral stated.

"They are just sitting there. They have full shields up and are scanning around their area, with a special focus on the vessel."

"How long are they going to sit there?"

"I don't know. We're letting them take charge at this point. The captain's the point man."

Everyone sat and waited, concentrating on the scene in the patrol ship and its monitors on another screen. They had a third screen up with different shots of the Class "P" vessel with its instruments being monitored.

"I don't want to assume all this is being recorded," the admiral probed.

"Definitely."

"Good."

She twiddled her thumbs for a few minutes then said, "Well, there isn't much going on. I think I'll go for a walk." She had had a long day and was afraid she would doze off. "Let me know if anything else happens."

She got up, and everybody else did too, until she left the room. The officers sat down except for Captain Weyburn who left a few seconds later.

One captain turned to the one next to him and said quietly, "Weyburn's got his nerve, don't you think?"

The other replied with a whisper, "A rather large fish to catch. He'd better keep his pants on for this one though. We know what happens to anyone who fools with her."

In the hallway, the admiral walked slowly for about five minutes while she thought about what she had seen so far. Occasionally, she passed someone who saluted her as she went by. Suddenly, she stopped and whirled around. About ten meters behind her, she spotted Captain Weyburn.

"Since when do I get a shadow?" she demanded.

"I thought I'd see if you were okay. You've had a long day today."

"Does that warrant what you're doing? If I needed security, I'd call an MP."

"How about stopping for a coffee – on me?"

She paused for a few seconds. "I'd like to talk to you about a few things, anyway, so yes."

They walked for about five more minutes until they stopped at the officer's mess. She entered and all the seated officers stood up. The captain pulled out the chair at a table near one corner of the mess and she seated herself. He sat on the other side of the small table. The rest of the officers sat down and resumed their conversations. He called the server over and ordered two coffees.

He turned to her and asked. "You like that don't you?"

"Like what?" she queried.

"The formality all the time."

"You mean people getting up for me every time I enter a room?"

"Yeah."

"Why do you say that?" She reddened.

"I can see it in your reactions."

"That's what I want to talk to you about. I'm a straight-out person and I have noticed that in the last few months – and it might have been going on longer than that – you're always staring at me. I find it annoying and I want you to stop. There's no law against it but I would prefer you respect my wishes. I could give you a tough time if you don't."

"I've been on this base now about five years and have developed a profound respect for you. I know you have a fine reputation in the forces – very competent, and I've developed a great interest in you."

"What do you mean?" She squinted slightly.

"Well, your character; you're an interesting study. I don't know if you've looked at my record but you would find that I worked my way up from the ranks. I'm a military person. I love the forces for the fellowship, for the respect everyone has for the other members, for the thrill, the pride, for satisfaction, and because I'm good at it. I'm a fighter.

"You, though, are different. You're not here for the fight – you love the pageantry, the respect you get, and the feeling of power."

"You'd better watch what you say," she warned with a frown.

"There, we're alike. We're tell-it-like-it-is people."

"Am I that transparent?" She cocked her head to the side.

"No, you hide it well."

"I've had front-line experience too, buster. You don't get to be an admiral with your nose in the books."

"I didn't say you had no experience. I said you don't love the fighting part of it."

"I don't think anyone loves killing people. It's just part of the job – or do you love killing?"

"Not particularly but sometimes it has to be done. It's either the other person or me and I don't want me to be at the short end of the stick. No one in your family was in the military, why did you pick that as your career?"

"Boy, you do your research, don't you? You're so smart, you tell me," She responded defiantly.

"You're not a recluse and have made a name for yourself in your own right. Being in the limelight, your history is known, so why did you join the forces?"

"It's none of your business. Maybe it's just what you said, for the pomp and ceremony, or maybe I'm old fashioned and miss when men opened doors and gave up their seats for a woman," she replied mockingly.

There were a few seconds of silence. It was the captain's turn to cock his head to the side. "Somehow, in you, I see a small-town girl trying to be a big-city woman."

She just glared at him with her forehead and nose all wrinkled up, ready to put a fist in the middle of that smart-assed face of his.

"I know all about you." She forced herself to keep her voice low, so the other officers would not hear what she was saying but she was making her point. "I know everybody who comes aboard my base. It's my business. I know how hard it is to be commissioned from the ranks. I respect that. You've done some remarkable feats in your career but you've also got yourself into hot water several times; incidents that almost dropped you several ranks. You can't seem to stay away from the ladies. You are what I view as, the typical alpha male."

He blushed slightly. "Well, I've never said I was a saint but I'm a little older and wiser now . . ."

"Well, it's just to let you know, that I'm on to you and I'm not interested in becoming one of your trophies. You've set your sights a little too high this time. You've become very close to putting yourself in the brig. You throw country bumpkin remarks at me and I'll walk all over you. I'm the boss around here and you'd better remember that," she remarked angrily.

"I'm sorry you've taken my interest in you that way. I honestly have no wishes for any conquest, as you've put it. I have a lot of respect for you. I hope that, in time, you can put my history behind you. I've tried to do that. I don't want anything to get in the way of our just being friends."

Suddenly, their conversation was interrupted by a call over the communications system. "Admiral, please attend the council chamber."

They both got up and raced to the room to see what the news was.

The door opened for her and she quickly entered the room, saying loudly, "Please remain seated."

One of the captains blurted out, "They're all dead, all twelve of them!"

The chief engineer gave a briefing. "Forty-eight minutes after the ship parked near the Class "P" vessel, all the crew died where they sat or stood. There were no instrument changes, other than a repeat of the power surge in the patrol vessel immediately before it happened. There was nothing else – no tell-tale sign that anything had happened and no movement of anything between the vessels."

"So, we learned nothing new?" the admiral confirmed.

"Well, we did learn one new thing. Whatever it is can move at least a million kilometres an hour."

Another engineer piped up, "The object if it is an object, may have already travelled closer to the location of the patrol craft before it arrived."

The chief engineer countered, "That's true but it would not have known where the patrol ship was going to stop, so what you say is possible but the probability is rather low. We've already seen the event several times, so here it is again for you, Admiral."

After she had seen the playback, she just sat there quietly with everyone else in the room.

"Those were twelve good people," the admiral said as her voice cracked. "I'll recommend they receive a posthumous commendation for their act of bravery."

Everyone turned toward her. She was trying to hold her composure. She dared not say anything else.

Captain Weyburn cut into the silence. "There is not much more we can do for now. With your permission, Admiral, I recommend we break off for the present, so we can consider what we've seen and come up with some options for action. Meanwhile, I'll prepare briefings for you to send to update headquarters about what happened. Communications: prepare a message we may have to send out to anyone even remotely close to the problem area. We may want to activate the plague-ship warning on both the stricken ships."

The admiral gathered all the calmness she could muster and said firmly, "Dismissed."

Everyone except the admiral and Captain Weyburn got up and filed out of the room. The door closed.

"May I stay behind, ma'am."

"Yes."

"You almost didn't make it there," the captain said quietly.

"Yes, thanks for pulling me out of that. It would have been embarrassing to break down in front of the other officers. It's just, here I am, the most powerful person in this sector and I feel so helpless. I've got patrol craft, cruisers, destroyers, several battleships, and what do I do with them in a case like this? I couldn't help the crews of those two vessels. I can send no reprisals and I don't think I can do anything to stop this 'thing' from harassing us further. I'm not without sympathy."

They sat in silence for several minutes.

"Well, we've had our sympathy," the captain said. "Unfortunately, as you say, you are the most powerful person in this sector and we now have to consider our next moves."

The admiral took a deep breath and replied, "Yes . . . so it is . . ."

First thing the next morning, she held a meeting with her senior officers to discuss their options.

"Good morning, everyone, I know you're shocked at what happened yesterday. A lot of you may have gotten little, if any, sleep but I hope, during that time, you've thought of some options. This killer is still outside of our territory, that's a good thing but in time, it may find its way into more populous areas, so we have to find out more about it and find a way of either moving it away from us or destroying it. Let's do a little brainstorming to start giving us some ideas. The lieutenant will keep track of them and we'll be recording this meeting."

After they had listed some options, they began to analyse them.

One option was to do nothing and hope the killer went off in another direction. Everyone thought this to be unlikely. It seemed to be moving, at present, to ships with people aboard.

Another thought was to evacuate and quarantine a large area around the stricken ships, so the thing would have a huge jump to another source of life, hoping the gap would be too large to jump. This was also ruled out. It would be wise to evacuate a large space but they could not count on it to stay in the current area, as it must have had to cover a large gap to get where it was. There was no known life beyond the area attacked by this thing.

They could try to blast it with a nuclear or antimatter torpedo but there was a risk in that. It might destroy it but they could not be sure where it was. It might not be near the blast, or worse, they could hit it and have it break into smaller parts that would spread even faster over the empire. They could not be sure there was just one of these things. Perhaps this was an advanced unit and there were hundreds of others heading toward their territory.

One person thought they could try to lure it away from the empire's territory by having a ship travel at a distance from the derelicts but close enough to be noticeable and speed off in a direction away from the border, however, how would one know if the marauder was following the ship?

In the end, they thought they would try a decoy to lure it away from their territory and consider vaporising it with a torpedo if it did not work. This option would require the imperial headquarters' approval.

In the meantime, their communication officers had prepared a news article on the incident to inform citizens of the occurrence of this event. They felt they could conceal it no further. They knew it might cause some discomfort to people in the area but it might encourage them to move out of the area to reduce the number of people that may have to be evacuated if the thing continued to move toward more populated areas.

They also prepared a communiqué to cancel travel into a designated zone around the area and to reduce movement only to essential approved travel, so the passenger vehicles could be commandeered to evacuate people from the stations and planets too close to the thing.

The meeting was closed and the people were dismissed.

Captain Weyburn went to his office and finished his report to send to headquarters under the name of the admiral for their information and decision if required. He also prepared a message to the captain of the cruiser 3849-3731 to try the decoy move and to two battleships to be battle-ready for any other eventuality. Messages to two adjacent sectors' base commanders were prepared to alert them to the need for help if required.

He sent the files to her and went to her office to see her.

The admiral looked over them quietly. "These are well done. I think this takes care of everything for now. If we don't solve this thing quickly, we're going to have some very unhappy people and then some very panicky people." She sighed.

Captain Weyburn responded sympathetically, "We have to prepare for anything. We need the help of the citizens. If we can't contain this thing we've encountered, the effect is going to spread quickly to other sectors. There is a risk of overreacting but what has happened until now is serious and may quickly become critical within a period of weeks."

She replied, "Get these sent out," then, more quietly, "This is like going to war."

"It just might be . . ."

3

Captain Wang finished his lunch while he simulated a famous battle from the recent past on his computer. He loved going through these simulations. He always wanted to be ready to do battle but as the years went by, he had become disillusioned with the military where he had found only boredom and a wasted life. The empire had been in a period of peace for many years now and he saw himself as an anachronism; a warrior in the wrong time. If only he had been in the war against the Sirians, or even way back in some of the ancient wars of Earth. He had read about almost all of them – warriors who had been carved in the annals of time: Mao, Paton, Rommel, Lee, Napoleon, Nelson, Genghis Khan, Caesar, Alexander, and so many others. He was just Captain Wang, captain of the space cruiser 3849-3731. It did not even have a name.

Suddenly, he spotted a blinking light in the corner of his screen.

"A coded message? Why am I being sent a coded message? What's going on that's so important?" he mumbled.

He clicked on the light. As the message was top secret, the computer read his retina and face to confirm his identity.

"Identity acknowledged," the computer responded.

The image on the monitor was that of the admiral, his commanding officer. He was quite surprised. Never did he have an admiral send him a message.

She started, "I need no introduction. I have an important mission for you; a possible suicide mission. We have encountered a strange phenomenon that has encroached on the edge of our territory and has killed all the crew of two small ships. What we would like you to do is follow the path and strategy we have attached with this message to get this thing to follow you away from our territory. We are hoping it will follow you and keep going along that path.

"The difficulty is that we cannot detect this thing with any of our sensors, so you won't know if it's following you or not. However, if it catches up to you, everyone on board will die, apparently instantly. That's why we thought you should treat this delicately with your crew. As this may end up in a tragedy, we are offering it as a voluntary mission. If you, or anyone of your crew, does not want to participate in it, you can refuse it, and any one of your crew can be let off at Sigovena, which you will pass by on the way to the starting point of your mission.

"The entire scenario has been pre-programmed and can be transferred into your autopilot. More information on this thing is in the second attachment to this message. Inform me within two hours of your decision.

"I send you my best wishes, and hope this thing will indeed follow you and you can outrun it."

The message ended.

He knew that, when headquarters offered anyone a voluntary mission, one could refuse it without penalty but it may affect one's chances of promotion. They were offered only when the chance for success was low and the risk to life was high.

He was not concerned with danger though. Finally, he had something of consequence to do and he would not turn down this opportunity. It might be the only dangerous mission he would ever get.

He went over the details in the attachment, which showed the actual scenes within the two stricken ships. For about thirty minutes, he just played the recordings repeatedly while he tried to decide his course of action. This was not a routine mission. There was no simulation for this scenario. There was no model. He wanted to fight someone but, in this case, what would he fight? If he was successful, though, whether he lived or not, it would be a remarkable thing he would have done for the empire. This would not be a spectacular battle, however; to him, it looked like an act of desperation.

He called his first officer through the communications system and told him to set up a meeting with the crew in five minutes in the wardroom.

He entered the wardroom and sat down. He plugged in the details of the mission and the scenes then waited as his crew of twenty-five persons arrived and sat down.

"Good afternoon, ladies and gentlemen," he began. "I received a message from the base about something strange that has occurred in our sector. I've looked at the event several times and can't determine exactly what happened. I'll show it to you shortly but headquarters has asked us to volunteer for a diversionary tactic.

"Something has killed the personnel of a "P" class vehicle and a patrol ship. They were killed instantly. The craft themselves were left entirely intact with no apparent damage. The oddest thing about all of this is, we have not been able to determine exactly what this thing is. Look at what happened, so you can get a feel of what we must do to deal with it, then I'd like to ask you if you would like to volunteer with me on this mission."

He showed everyone the scenarios in both ships.

After the show, there was complete silence.

The captain continued. "As you can see, this thing is completely invisible; undetectable by any sensors we have. As such, it may be a great peril to our citizens. Our mission is to tease this entity into coming after us then slowly we'll accelerate to try to outrun it and draw it as far away as we can from populated areas. First, though, we will swing around, so we come from an approach opposite to our territory to make it appear that is where our base is. There is no way we can determine if this thing takes the bait or not unless someone, somewhere, dies again, so we keep running until it moves somewhere else to kill somebody.

"If it does overcome us, the ship is on automatic to continue the journey with the hope that the thing stays with the ship as long as possible.

"We don't need everyone on board to perform this mission, so if anyone wants to leave, you are welcome to go. We pass by Sigovena on our way to our starting point and we can drop you off there. We have twenty hours before we pass by there and forty hours before our start point. We will have a meeting again about two hours before reaching that planet, so you can inform me of your intentions. My door will be open to answer any questions you may have. I have left all the information in our system for you to review. You may also discuss it among yourselves; however, this information is secret – restricted only to people within this ship. Does anyone have any questions right now?"

There was silence.

"In that case, you're dismissed, we head for Sigovena."

The captain sent off a message to the admiral accepting the task and that he would notify her, before he reached Sigovena, of exactly how many shipmates would also be participating.

He downloaded the mission's information into the autopilot, he authorised it, and they were off.

He did not care how many of the crew were going to help him. The ship was running the routine on autopilot, so he could even do it alone. He preferred that crew members volunteer to improve their chances of enticing the thing to his ship but was prepared to support any decision they made.

The time passed quickly. There were many small group discussions about what was happening and, by the time they got to Sigovena, everyone had decided to stay aboard. Most of the company on the vessel had been together for eight years or more and they had great confidence in their captain and the competence of the rest of the crew. They wanted to remain together no matter what happened. They had had quite a boring, uneventful career so far and this was a terrific opportunity to have something exciting to do. If they succeeded, they would go down in history as warriors.

The captain notified the admiral that the entire crew had proudly accepted the mission.

The ship flashed by Sigovena and continued its trek first through the fringes of the known territory then into uncharted territory. Almost two days later, the ship swung around heading toward the stricken area, getting within 5,0000,000 kilometres of it. The captain manually pushed the ship within 2,000,000 kilometres for greater temptation then continued the routine. They sat there for about two hours then slowly the ship swung around and began its journey back along its track away from human populations. As it travelled, it picked up speed.

Soon, they were millions of kilometres from the site and accelerating rapidly. The tension in the ship was high and remained high as they continued along their path.

4

"Have you heard the news bulletin today?" the head supervisor asked Lisa, his administrative assistant, as he walked into the office at the start of a new day.

"Yes, scary, isn't it? The news is spreading around the mine. You'll have to address it soon. We're not that far away from where it happened," Lisa responded.

"The first thing I'm going to do is get a video conference going with the other foremen and decide if there is any action, we should take because of this."

Jack Bayley worked for Galactic Exploration and Mining Inc, or as people called it, GEM. Almost twenty years ago, the company explored this planet and established seven mining operations in the most profitable areas on and beneath its surface. Jack was responsible for the mine over two kilometres beneath the surface.

The planet itself was devoid of life. It was too close to its star to have evolved life and had almost no atmosphere. Its surface temperature ranged from over two hundred degrees Celsius on the sunward side to minus 150 degrees on the dark side.

GEM had set up each of the mining sites as dome-shaped triple-lined buildings. The underground mine had a larger dome over the building and the shaft entrance so it had air throughout the entire enclosure. The company had created residences and recreation areas within the mine that expanded the useable area for the employees so that the site had sports fields and green rooms where the locals could grow fresh food. During the frequent days off, employees in the other sites could travel to that mine to enjoy its additional amenities.

Life there was generally pleasant. People signed up for ten-year periods, which could be extended. Almost all the inhabitants could make enough money in that time to retire on a habitable planet somewhere else in the empire. That kept most of the population quite young. Most people brought, or established, their families there, so excellent schools were provided. The population of the planet was over 3000 people including 800 children.

Because of the productivity of the mines, GEM had begun the groundwork for building a centrally located smelter. Up to now, the company had been pulling out the almost 100 per cent pure metal from the mines, leaving the tailings aside until it became feasible to process the less abundant ores. The plan was to double or triple the number of workers within ten years.

The news that there was a mysterious killer only a few solar systems away from them had created quite a buzz. It had everyone talking and many were wondering about what should be done. So far, this thing had not attacked any planets, which made them feel somewhat more comfortable but the local base commander had warned people about it and told everyone not to go near that area of space, and anyone inside should leave the area. Everyone was going to be kept informed about further developments.

Jack sent a message to the other six foremen and arranged for a videoconference with them. Thirty minutes later they were all assembled.

Jack opened the meeting. "Ladies and gentlemen, I guess even our pets have heard about the message we got earlier today. So far, we have not heard anything from GEM. They are probably as dumbfounded about this as we are. We have no real guidance from the base other than the word that we are just outside the designated evacuation zone, so I guess we are not in immediate danger and are on our own."

The foreman from mine three commented, "There have been many discussions at our site. Some people have asked if we should leave. Others have talked about temporarily moving over to the deep mine. If that thing does come here, we should have protection down there. The planet is loaded with heavy elements and must be dense enough to minimise the chance of penetration. We may be able to seal up the shaft to prevent the thing from penetrating down it. Also, some people don't think it will come here. Why would it attack a planet? We have no military significance. Maybe this thing is attacking because those vessels were encroaching on its territory, so, if we back off, it will back off, too."

Jack added, "We can hope so but I think we should let people decide for themselves. If some people want to leave for now, I think we should let them. We can move seven hundred people off right now, if they want, with GEM's transit vessel. I'm sure we can get GEM to send ships to get the others off. We should also be able to arrange to stay at the base or another planet for the time being. I know the company will not be happy with reducing production but they will understand our concerns. I'm willing to take everyone interested in our site. If we gather the food and other supplies from the other sites, everyone can stay down in the shaft for months."

The mine three foreman responded, "I think that's fair. The people who want to stay where they are and continue to work can just continue as they are and the rest can go into the deep mine or leave the planet. I'll pole my people and you can discuss it with yours. Let's get back together again in three hours."

Jack closed with, "So everyone can meet and discuss this, we'll have to suspend all operations and call a holiday for service personnel. I'll contact GEM and inform them of our meeting to get their support."

He cut the link with the others and turned to his assistant. "Notify everyone that today is a paid holiday and arrange a meeting with all the adults in our mines in thirty minutes. Let my wife know that she should pick up our daughter from school. I'll contact GEM and the base."

"Right away, Jack," she said as she hurried to her desk.

Jack called GEM's managers and informed them of the discussion they had had. The company was also discussing the issue and trying to decide what should be done. They were satisfied with the options discussed with the other sites and said they would support any decisions made. They would free up some company passenger ships to make them available to evacuate everyone if that was the decision on their end.

Jack also contacted a communications person at the base. It sounded wild over there. The only reason why he got through so quickly was because of the proximity of their planet to the danger zone. He explained their situation and asked if the base could provide a haven for anyone who wanted to leave during this time of uncertainty. The communications officer offered any help they could but if everyone wanted to leave, it would create too much of a logistics problem for them. They would take in as many people as they could and find refuge sites on other planets for the rest.

He sent a note off to the other foremen with the news and suggested things to say to their people, so they were all delivering the same message.

All was set. Now, it was just a matter of finding out what people wanted to do.

Jack walked to and entered the recreation room, which was the only area large enough to hold everyone. Meetings like this were not often held. Everyone had cooperated in setting up the chairs. There was a general hubbub in the room. Rather than bringing this site's surface people into the deep mine, they had set up a video link with them.

He called the meeting to order and proceeded to talk. "Welcome everyone. You all know why we're here, so we won't go into the details of what's going on. You've all heard the news bulletins and I know nothing more than you do in that regard. I'm aware of discussions that have taken place among you about any discomfort you feel as we're one of the closest populated sites to the marauding killer.

"I've had a meeting with the other foremen about your concerns and we offer you some choices. I've also talked to GEM and the military base communications person. For your information, the other mine sites are having similar meetings with their personnel.

"First, consider that we're outside the designated danger zone, although there are very few people who occupy that area. I understand your concern that we're one of the closest significantly populated planets in the affected area. It depends on which direction the marauder wants to go next. The press seems to think we may be a target because the patrol craft's ion trail leads back through this area. It's also probable the thing may follow the trail of the "P" class vessel, or go in any other random direction.

"That leaves us with what you'd like to do about it. We've considered three options. One is to go about our lives as we have until now and hope it doesn't come here. Another is to leave the planet and GEM will support anyone who would like to take that option, while the base will accommodate us in one way or another. The third is to accommodate anyone who would like to seal up in the deep mine and hope the killer, if it does come here, will not be able to penetrate it.

"Please discuss these options with your families and let Lisa know what you'd like to do. To act as quickly as possible, let her know your decisions within one hour. I'll be talking again with the other supervisors soon after that and we can proceed to accommodate your wishes.

"Thanks for coming. If you have any questions about this issue, I'll be in my office for the entire hour."

Only two people came to see him with questions; both were about how confident he was of the thing's inability to penetrate the mine. Jack could offer no opinion. He knew the thing could penetrate the shells of spacecraft but those were relatively thin and light. He could only hope the high-density material of the planet would provide some protection. He suggested they base their decision on assuming the shaft could be penetrated.

Jack went home to discuss what to do with his family. Jack had been one of the early immigrants to this planet. He had moved up from a worker to foreman quickly and had met his wife, Mary, here. They had two children, a boy three years old and a girl seven years old.

He sat down with Mary at their kitchen table while the children played in the next room.

He said quietly, "Well, we've heard from a lot of people on-site. I guess it's good we discuss what we're going to do. Most people have opted to stay at our mine site. I don't want to decide for us, Hun, so what are your thoughts?"

"We've made our home here. I know our long-term goal is to retire somewhere else, so we can see a green surface on a planet again and not just greenhouses but I think it's good to stay here to be with our friends and support them."

"Some have opted to leave."

"I know; I've been hearing the buzz. I think we should stick to our plan. We should be safe in the mine."

"Are you afraid?"

"Not really. We're together as a family and we can weather this storm. What do you think?"

"I'm a little nervous. I want to be honest with you. I just don't want to scare people by my leaving. I'm trying to be a calm model but inside I don't feel like that. I'm no hero. I feel like running."

"I'm not a hero either but if that thing can get down there, then everyone in the empire is doomed; nobody is safe and life won't be worth living. Nobody will be able to run forever."

"Hmmm, how stoic; I guess our decision is made."

When the seven foremen got together again in a video conference, they compared notes. About three hundred and fifty people wanted to leave, about six hundred and fifty people were prepared to stay on the surface, and the rest opted for the deep mine. Jack notified GEM and the base of the results of their meetings.

The rest of the day and the next morning were spent moving the people with their supplies to where they needed to be. The children went to school but had no formal classes as some of the teachers had opted to leave. This ensured they were managed while all these activities were being carried out.

The ship left the planet mid-morning. The last of the people opting for the deep mine was at the bottom of the shaft early in the afternoon. The remaining people on the surface congregated into four mines with the four foremen who opted to stay on the surface. The mines were selected based on being as far away from each other as possible, in the hope the marauder would miss one or more of them.

After they had moved all their supplies, beds, and other stores into the mine, Jack led a large work crew to seal the mine from the inside, while another work crew sealed it from the outside. They intended to seal the over two-kilometre mine shaft with a one-kilometre plug of highly packed rock filled with a high-density slurry of filling material, which would harden into a plug that would be as dense or denser than the surrounding rock. They had equipment inside to drill their way out. After two days of working around the clock, they were done.

The outside workers were moved to the four mine sites.

The populace had worked hard, so the foremen gave the workers a three-day holiday to rest and spend time with their families.

Jack's daughter was surprised and happy to be away from school.

She asked, "Why do we all have to stay in the mine now and why are there so many new people? Some of the kids at school were saying that we have to stay down here forever. Do we have to stay here forever?"

Jack chuckled. "You're full of questions, aren't you? No, we won't have to stay here forever but we plan to stay here for a while. We don't know how long yet. We can have a lot of fun here. We have lots of room even with the new people staying down here and we're taking three days of holidays then we'll go back to work and you to school."

"Ah," their son squealed disappointedly.

"What about the monsters?" their daughter asked.

Jack looked at Mary with a serious look on his face. "What monsters?"

"Some kids at school said monsters were coming to get us."

"What kind of monsters?"

"They didn't say. The monsters were just coming to get us so everyone came here to try to hide from them."

"Well, not everyone came."

"But we did and some people ran away, too."

"Well, I think we shouldn't worry about any monsters. Look at Mommy, she isn't afraid and you don't see the other people afraid. We're not going to be down here very long, and we're going to have a lot of fun. Don't you like having a few days off from school?"

"Yes."

"Then let's just have fun today and we'll see what other fun stuff we can do tomorrow."

Jack spent the day playing with the children and reading books to them. At the end of the day, they all piled into the king-sized bed together.

Their daughter said, "This is fun, we should do this all the time."

After the kids had fallen asleep, Jack could hear Mary quietly sobbing.

He wrapped his arms around her to soothe her.

He whispered close to her ear, "Thinking of changing your mind?"

"No," she whispered back.

"Afraid?"

"A little, I'm more afraid for the kids. If this doesn't work out, they won't have had much of a life . . ."

"But, if we sent them away, they'd be orphans."

"True."

"All we can do is hope it doesn't come here, or if it does, it'll leave us alone. It has other directions to choose from, so all we can do is wait it out."

"I can still cry for us."

He gave her a warm kiss and another hug.

The next day, all the parents arranged a series of team games and challenges along one end of a shaft, so the children could play team games and other running activities.

5

The admiral joined her officers and staff in the council chamber.

"So, what's the latest news?"

The commodore responded, "We now have a video and sound tie-in to the six closest populated planets and the cruiser. Everything is calm now. None of the planets have official names yet, so instead of a bunch of official designations, we've opted to give each one a simple number.

"Number one is a fairly large desolate planet principally consisting of ice. It is too far away from its star to be habitable. However, it has a large ice mining operation with 2,000 people.

"Number two is another large planet that is being developed for mining gold and other precious metals. Its atmosphere is principally ammonia, nitrogen, and methane. Its population is about five hundred people.

"Number three is slightly smaller, has almost no atmosphere and is quite close to its star. We're mining it for heavy metals. It's a particularly dense planet with 3,000 people.

"Number four is a beautiful green planet that is being developed for habitation. It has an appropriate size, temperature, and atmosphere to nurture life. Companies are in the process of building retirement facilities, hotels etcetera for the service, vacation, and recreation industries. It has evolved plant life but no known animal life, other than fish-like creatures. It has about 50,000 people. It's reasonably close to planet three but is the farthest from the designated danger area and the most populated of the six planets.

"Numbers five and six are in the same solar system. Both are uninhabitable but are currently being explored for mining. They are the closest planets to the stricken vessels. There are about 1500 people on them. That solar system is the farthest from our territorial border.

"To update the status, some people have left all the planets either in their vessels or in company ships but, for the most part, people have opted to stay. As far as we know, all six planets cannot be hit at the same time.

"We've analysed the scarce data we have on this thing but our findings are limited. We don't know its tracking mechanism, for example: does it 'sense' human life, does it follow any trail that may be around from our interstellar vessels, or does it have a way to determine maximum population density? We don't even know if there are more of these things around. What we do know is it kills quite quickly.

"If it follows trails, then planet three is the most likely target. If it's population density, then it's planet four. If it goes to the closest populated area then it is planets five and six. We're not even sure if it can attack a planet; maybe it restricts itself to spaceships.

"Our best guess is that it may strike planet three, as the stricken patrol ship passed by it on the way to its tragedy. It's also on the way to the most populated planet in the area, planet four. If it goes that way, then it's directly on the way to entering our territory.

"Now, for the actions we've taken in response; we've tried to be a little conservative as we don't know if anything else is going to happen and we don't want to overreact but we want to be prepared for any eventuality for the foreseeable future. What we've done is to commandeer about thirty passenger vessels from our sector and spread them out to be able to evacuate planets around the six closest planets. We've placed the bulk of them near planet four. Nearby sectors have offered to supply us with another thirty ships that can be sent to us within a few days if required. Headquarters have likewise offered us fifty vessels and they're on the way, in case we need them but they'll arrive over a period of a week or more as they'll be coming from all parts of the empire.

"Bottom line is, no other strikes have been made, most of the people remain on the planets under surveillance and the diversionary cruiser is at top speed racing away from our territory. We've prepared ourselves to evacuate the planets ahead of this menace as soon as we know where it's going next."

The admiral mulled over the facts and said, "No news about this killer is good news. Maybe it's gone away in another direction completely. There's no way to tell."

The commander added, "If it does attack planet three, then we couldn't have set up a better experimental trial."

"Why is that?"

"The foremen have divided the surface population of the mines ideally by spreading them out as far as possible over four locations. That'll help us determine how quickly it can knock out a planet and if it'll miss some parts of the population. They've also located some people in the deep mine. That will tell us if the thing can penetrate a dense object and how fast it can do it. If it cannot penetrate the mine, then we know we've got some protection against this killer. If it can do it, then we're going to be in a rather desperate situation.

"I have a bit more information of interest; one of our doctors has been monitoring the cabins of the patrol craft and "P" class ship and pointed out that the air quality of the ships is perfect."

"Isn't that good?" one of the captains asked.

"Not, if there's a bunch of rotting corpses on board."

"Oh?"

"The ships' air cleaning systems should be struggling to eliminate the terrible smell of the corpses. That can mean only one thing. There are no live bacteria in the cabin to rot the corpses. Therefore, when the thing killed the people, it killed everything else on the ship, including the bacteria or any other entity on it. If they had mice, they would be dead too. It sterilised the spaceships."

Everyone in the room went pale.

The admiral ordered that he contact the six planets to ask any of them who had live plants, to set up a camera, so the base could monitor the plants too.

For several minutes, the people in the room sat in total silence.

The admiral then added, "We all don't have to stay here waiting for something to happen. Nothing has happened for a couple of days now. This was just an update meeting. Let's get some rest and, if anything else happens, we'll notify you. Everyone but the commodore and his aide are dismissed."

Slowly, everyone got up and filed out of the room. The commodore and one of his lieutenants were scheduled to remain to monitor the planet's situation through the night, so they stayed. The admiral glanced around the room and spied Captain Weyburn still sitting in his chair.

"I said everyone is dismissed," she said bluntly.

The captain noticed she was looking at him and said, "Oh . . . sorry, Admiral, I thought you may have needed me. It's been pretty busy lately."

"We're not busy right now, are we? I suggested that everyone should get some rest or sleep when we can."

He said embarrassedly, "Yes, ma'am, sorry, ma'am." He stood up and left the room hurriedly.

She glanced over to the commodore. He turned to face the monitor screen. She got up and left to return to her cabin.

Captain Weyburn stopped at the mess for a light meal and a couple of beers. Shortly after he arrived, two captains walked in and asked if they could sit with him. For a while, they made light talk but drifted onto the issue at hand.

One of them said, "The situation doesn't look great. Everyone is waiting in anticipation of the killer's next move. Imagine, even killing bacteria."

"It's not surprising," Captain Weyburn responded. "Life is life."

"What do you think will happen?"

"The killer didn't move randomly from the "P" class vessel to the patrol ship, so it must have a way of detecting life in space because there was no vehicle trail between the two vessels involved. Using that as a base, if I was the thing, I would hit planet three, then four."

"Hum, sounds reasonable. Most people, and even the press, have lined up behind planet three."

The second captain changed the subject. "There's also a lot of talking about something else."

"Yes?"

"It's about you."

"Oh!" Captain Weyburn exclaimed with interest.

"We thought it was best for us to discuss it with you in case you get into trouble."

"I recommend that you get right to the point and stop talking around issues."

"Okay, it's evident to pretty well everyone that you're displaying some interest in the admiral."

"Is that so? Does she know?"

"We don't know. If she did, she would have marooned you on some asteroid around a barren star far outside our territorial limits. I'm guessing you know past attempts at trying to befriend her ended up disastrously for the potential suitors."

"I've been here as long as you have, and you're trying to make her out to be some type of monster, which she's not, so I'd appreciate it if you'd show her the respect she deserves. I also think she's quite capable of taking care of herself. You know me well. I guess that you think I engineered this conversation because I'm out to seduce her or something. Well, nothing is farther from the truth. I'm not about to commit a career-limiting move, so thanks for your advice and mind your own business. Right now, she needs our complete support and dedication, so focus on what's important."

Captain Weyburn got up and stomped off.

The first captain turned to the other, and commented, "Wow, he seemed miffed."

"I've been assigned with him on two other occasions. I'm not sure what to make of this. That's not his usual reaction."

"What do you mean?"

"Well, he would have given a sly smile and walked away, instead he seemed almost angry."

"He still gave himself away though. He didn't deny what we suspected. Even if he said he wasn't out to seduce her, his reaction indicated that something was happening."

"It's different though. I wonder if she has captured him." The second captain seemed puzzled.

"They're water and oil. From what some people say, she may not be interested in men at all, if you know what I mean. She's one of the best admirals I've met but she's cold as ice as far as men are concerned. How can you say she captured him?"

"Well, there's nothing certain one way or the other but she hasn't dumped him yet, has she?"

"I'll bet he makes a bad move and ends up being shipped out of here. Right now, I think she's too distracted with the crisis to bother with a low-priority issue like a wayward captain."

"I'm not sure. I'm puzzled about what's going on here but I'll agree with your idea about the current distraction. There are a lot of people worried about the killer. Nothing further has happened with it yet and I think the tension is getting to everyone."

"Let's get some shut-eye," the first captain said with a yawn.

At the same time as Captain Weyburn was having his discussion with the other captains, the admiral had settled into bed to try to get to sleep. She read for a few minutes then put down the book and shut off the light. Usually, she would drift off to sleep in a few minutes but today she could not sleep. Her thoughts were not just on the thing menacing her sector, which was reason enough, she was annoyed about a certain captain.

While there was this pause in action, she had to do something about him. The captain had not, to this day, broken any rules. He was becoming annoying, yes but he had been cautious, however, she could now move against him. She could take his remaining in the room after her dismissal order as insubordination. She was stretching the rules but she had her opportunity and she was quite sure he knew it, too. He was one of the best captains she had encountered and a brilliant person, so her reaction would have been a clear signal as to what he had done. She also had two witnesses, and they knew it, too.

This crisis was the worst time, however, to eliminate one of her best and most senior officers. She got up, turned on the light, grabbed her pad, opened it, and looked at his file. He was only three years older than she was. She sighed. She spent many minutes looking at his image. The image faded away as her screen timed out. She stared for a while at the blank screen then put her pad aside, got up, and looked out of her window at the stars. It looked so quiet out there. It was hard to believe, that in this void, there lurked such a murderous entity.

She had to get some sleep, so she crawled back into bed and tried to sleep but kept wondering what to do with Captain Weyburn. If he was not so annoying, perhaps she could learn to get along with him. Everything he did seemed to perturb her . . . She finally drifted off to sleep.

Meanwhile, Captain Weyburn wandered the corridors of the base wondering about what the two captains had said and what had happened in the council chamber. He was now making a fool of himself, and for what? What was wrong with him? Rumours were going around and he had tried to squelch them but they would not go away unless he did. Her reputation was paramount to him and his foolishness was already creating a stir. He was torn, though. If he left, he might never see her again.

He went to his room and sat down. He could not sleep. He checked his mail but there was nothing there. He read for a while, and finally, he nodded off to sleep with his face on his desk.

The uncomfortable position he was in woke him up after about an hour and he thought of going to bed to sleep, except he felt he had one more thing to do before he could rest. He would talk to the commodore to request a transfer. He brushed himself off and tidied himself for the occasion.

He left his room, walked over to the council chamber, and entered. The lieutenant was doing some work on his computer while the commodore played solitaire on his pad. The commodore raised his head with the sound of the door opening and closing.

"Anything I can do for you, Captain?" asked the commodore. "It's a little late to be wandering around."

"I wonder if I may talk with you, sir." He stood for several seconds. When there was no reaction, he added, "Alone, sir?"

"Oh, yes, yes, of course." He got off his chair and walked to a door that opened into a small ante-room.

Captain Weyburn followed him in. The door closed.

The two men sat down on opposite sides of a small table. The captain stumbled a bit over what he was going to say. "Sir, I've been thinking for a while now about getting a transfer. I've been here for about six years now and I know I put in for an extension and have two years to go but it may be best that I move on."

"You're not afraid of that monster we've got out there are you?"

"Of course not, I know it's a bad time, which makes it look like that but . . ."

The commodore cut him off. "You don't need an explanation for that question. You're likely the best man I've got. You're just distracted, that's all."

"Distracted?"

"Yeah, female distracted. You're a little old to be going around like an adolescent, aren't you?"

"Well, then, knowing my situation, sir, please grant my transfer."

"You know I can't grant your request; I can only recommend it. The admiral must sign it. What do you think she's going to say about it?"

"She'll be disappointed because she can't maroon me on some asteroid somewhere."

The commodore gave a light chuckle. "Maybe, when do you want to go?"

"Next ship out, if possible. In the end, it's up to you."

"Yes, good old operational requirements. Are you sure about this? You'll miss all the fun we're going to have."

"At least, I'll be out of your hair."

The commodore took a deep breath. "I'll get the form and let's fill it out, shall we?"

He disappeared for several minutes and returned with the computer pad. "Here, you complete the first section." He handed the pad to Captain Weyburn.

The captain gave his responses to the questions asked by the pad. He gave it to the commodore who verbally completed his area and forwarded it to the admiral's office.

The captain now wondered if she was going to sign it.

Suddenly, there was a knock on the door. The commodore stood up and let it open.

It was the lieutenant. "Come in and watch this, Commodore," he said excitedly.

There was a moment's hesitation until they realised what he was agog about.

They quickly entered the room to watch the rerun of the recording of the killer sweeping a planet. The captain noticed it was planet three.

"Captain, would you please alert the admiral and have her come here? Please be quiet, so we don't wake anyone up. I'd like to give her a private viewing first."

The commodore placed the tablet on a small table at one side of the room.

The captain was going to leave, instead, he hesitated and turned. "Are you sure, Commodore? Why don't we just buzz her?"

"Just go and get her."

As the captain left the room, the commodore smiled slightly.

At 02:30h Captain Weyburn tapped lightly on the admiral's door. There was no response. He tapped a little harder.

"What is it?" came a gritty response through the door.

"I've been asked by the commodore to request that you come to the council chamber."

"Oh? Is something up?"

"Yes, ma'am."

After a minute, the door opened and a bleary-looking woman stepped out. The bags under her eyes hung low. She was still pulling on her uniform. Her hair was still in its stately bun but there was loose hair visible.

"Why is it always you?" she asked in a hoarse voice.

"Why is it always me, what?"

"You're always the one who gets me up, brings messages, and comes up with ideas. Don't you ever sleep?"

He just smiled.

She glanced at him. He was still neat as a pin; unperturbed as ever. He so annoyed her. She felt like smacking him just for being there. Before going into the council chamber, she diverted into the washroom. In a few minutes, she walked out very refreshed and almost back in order.

He smiled again.

She noticed it and remarked, "What is this, a contest?"

"What?"

"Are you trying to out-dress me or something?"

"My, are we touchy today."

"It's in the middle of the night; I think it's deserved."

"Yes, ma'am." He smiled.

She clenched her fist and her teeth, walked to the door of the council chamber, and it opened before them.

The commodore and lieutenant greeted them dourly.

"Admiral," the commodore began, "the killer has struck again. I thought, as it's so late, I'd notify you first."

She sat down hard in a chair and covered her face in her hands. The men stayed standing.

After about two minutes she raised her head again and said, "What planet was it?"

"Planet three."

"They had children there, didn't they?"

"Yes, several hundred."

"That's the one with the mines, right?"

"Yes, I have the recording right here, so I'll play it for you. I'll show you the four surface mines and several locations in the underground mine. All the times are synchronised, so you'll see it happen exactly as it unfolded. You can see about ninety per cent of the people were asleep."

Within a few seconds, it was all over. One after the other the alert people dropped and the sleeping people's hearts stopped. The deep mine was no hindrance to the killer. It must have penetrated the rock as if it was not there. They could see from the monitors that pets and plants died with the people.

The admiral sat, shocked. The killer had spared no one. "Maybe we should have evacuated the planet?"

The commodore responded, "The people had the opportunity. At that time, we didn't know for certain where it was going to strike, or even if it was going to attack. The people made their own decisions. We were prepared to evacuate them all if they wanted it. It's not your fault."

"The children didn't choose. That monster killed innocent children . . ." She sat quietly for several seconds.

"It doesn't make sense to wake everyone," she added. "Activate our evacuation plan and wake up the people necessary to carry it out. I want everyone who wants to leave the planets in our new expanded danger zone the opportunity to do so but let's inform them of this later in the morning, so they can get the rest of their sleep. It will be a long day and we need the time to move the ships into place for the evacuation."

Captain Weyburn cut in. "I was just doing a quick calculation; we don't have enough ships. As that thing moves farther into the empire, we'll have to set some selection criteria. We won't be able to take everyone. We also can't force them to move, so some people will stay put and others may just commit suicide."

"I know," she said sadly. "Inform imperial headquarters of our current situation. They were hooked into our video feed. We're going to need as much help as they can provide. We'll want a decision soon as to the option of blasting the killer to try to kill it.

"Recall Captain Wang. Our ploy didn't work. I want him to head back to the thing's original location and have autopsies done on the dead people in the patrol vessel. I want to determine the cause of their deaths and if the ship is sterile. I want them also to determine if the stricken vessels have any traces of the killer present. We may be able to reclaim the ships. We'll need every one of them we can get, soon.

"In the morning, when we start the evacuations, we'll declare a state of emergency. We'll declare martial law and be able to move more quickly to get things done. In effect, we're in a state of war. We just don't know how to fight the enemy. We've got a lot of work to do. You're dismissed."

The three men left the room to implement the evacuation plan. The admiral sat alone in the room. She glanced over at the side table and noticed the tablet. She leaned over and picked it up. She activated it and saw the transfer request. For ten minutes or so, she just stared at it then raised her head to the now blank screen on the wall placed her thumb on one corner of the tablet, and refused the request.

6

The admiral gasped at the end of the recording she had seen on the wall of the council chamber of imperial headquarters, her four stars gleaming on her lapel. "This is serious, very serious."

A vice admiral responded, "We hoped for the best but I didn't think this would end easily. Rear Admiral Kerchov is doing an excellent job but this cannot remain a sector issue now. This marauder has a great possibility to spread quickly beyond her borders. Thank goodness there is only one of these things at this point."

"As you know, we still have our scientific experts available to guide decision-making. I want to reconvene with them in thirty minutes, so we can show them the latest events. I'll have to take this to the VD and I'll remind him that we have one option to destroy this thing."

The admiral quickly left the room while the vice admiral began setting up the meeting with the scientists.

The admiral did not have to walk far because the imperial headquarters was highly centralised. Long ago, the people of Earth decided to build new cities far to the north, or other non-arable locations, to keep the arable land reserved for farming. This stopped the former process of continually destroying the best farmland to create larger and larger sprawling cities, which ultimately began to increase the price of food and cause famine.

The capital city was one of those cities and the largest complex in it was the imperial headquarters. Built into that complex were the emperor's palace and the facilities to house the central government and military complex. The highest officials in the government lived within it. The highest official was, of course, the emperor who was responsible for peace, security, and good government within the empire.

There were two other important people in the empire, the 'VD' who was traditionally the government's head of the military and the 'Conscience' who was traditionally head of the civil government. These two titles date back to the beginnings of the empire when one of the earliest emperors had two trusted advisors who acted as counsellors to the emperor. The term 'VD' was derived from the name of the first military counsellor, Victor Durocher. The second term is derived from the nickname given to the civilian counsellor, 'Conscience'.

Over time, these posts evolved into very important roles which were crucial to the continuity of the government. They guided the government during an interregnum and ensured general good government. These positions were filled with the best of the best individuals in the empire who were awarded the position for life, or until they resigned.

The civilian side of the government consisted of a governor for each developed and recognised planet but each planet was governed by the choice of the constitution set up by the people on that planet. Most planets chose a form of democratic institution.

The upper echelons of the military consisted of commodores (for fleets), rear admirals (for sectors), four vice admirals (for quadrants) and an admiral. There was no army, as there was no need for one. Each planet had its police force and, if a planet had internal issues, a neighbouring planet was expected to assist, or a special agent under the direction of the emperor would be assigned to intervene.

The admiral arrived at her destination and pressed a button beside the door labelled, 'VD'. About a minute later, a man of about forty opened the door. He was wearing pyjamas and still yawning. His hair was still dishevelled, although it looked as if he had passed a comb quickly through it. He was average in height but had a stately air about him. He had been promoted five years ago after having been an admiral for several years.

"The only reason you'd be here is because of the issue in sector 139, am I correct?"

"Yes, sir."

"Okay, let's go to my office and you can fill me in."

They walked across the hall and entered a rather opulent office of considerable size.

"Let me guess, the 'thing' passed up the cruiser and attacked planet 103-17-4-2 is that correct?"

"Yes."

"How is Rear Admiral Kerchov handling the situation?"

"Extremely well; she has an evacuation plan set up and is implementing it. I'll order the ships we've promised to get there at full speed. I'll also commandeer five hundred more but that will start crippling normal travel and trade within our territory.

"That'll handle the immediate situation but we still have the bigger issue about what to do with the thing itself. As you recall, we discussed this last week with our experts. I've called another meeting with them in a few minutes to review things and see if their recommendations are the same. We also asked special operations for some ideas. We'll meet with their head later this morning."

"Good, I've filled John in on the crisis and I want to include him in future meetings for his thoughts on the civilian side of this situation."

The admiral headed over to the council chamber while the VD walked down a stairway and was soon at John's door with the label 'Conscience'. The VD pressed the button on the side of the door. The door opened to a short, balding man in his sixties. He looked as if he too had had his sleep interrupted and was still in his pyjamas.

"Hi, Mark, I've been expecting you. I've been fielding calls from a couple of governors who've heard a rumour about another attack. I understand the local admiral is keeping things secret for now, so I told them to sit tight and we'll be sending something out when the time is right.

"Come in and sit down. Marjorie's already brewed us some coffee. This looks as if it's going to be a long day."

"I'd like that. We've withheld the story, so people will get some sleep for now. It'll allow us some time to get the ships lined up to begin widespread evacuations.

"We're going to have a meeting shortly with our experts to discuss what's happening and get their opinions. Later, I've set up a meeting with special ops to look at any ideas they may have. I'd like you to be at both meetings, too. I don't think we have to roust the boss just yet, let's get the facts gathered and we can fill him in when he gets up."

John responded, "Okay, I'll be there. I guess you've got the meeting planned for 03:00h?"

"Yes."

"I'll invite the head of communications. That office will have a key role to play from now on. I'll just make the call, slip on a shirt and pants, and be right down."

The VD took a few deep gulps of coffee and put the cup on a table. He left, went back up one floor, ran into his suite, grabbed a shirt, and put it on. The scientists would not notice his pyjama bottoms under the table. Things were very casual when there were round-the-clock issues to manage. He then went into a large conference room down the hall opposite his suite. He entered and sat down.

The room was already half full and five of the seven screens on the wall were lit up with the faces of the scientific experts. Two minutes later, the conscience entered with his coffee in hand and sat down. The head of communications wearing a bathrobe ran into the room, huffing, and puffing as he sat down. Almost immediately, the meeting started.

The VD, as chair, opened. "Sorry I got everyone up so early in the morning but we just got news that our favourite issue has raised its ugly head again. Planet 139-103-17-4-2 has been attacked with 100 per cent mortality. Rather than describe it, I'll let you see it first-hand."

He ran the recording for everyone. There was silence in the room when he was done. He ran it again in slow motion.

The VD broke the silence. "As you can see, it travels very quickly. It didn't make much difference how far apart the mines were or how deep in the ground they were, the people all died."

One of the scientist's lights lit up on the screen indicating he wanted to speak.

"I did some calculations. The populated sites were far enough apart to give us a sense of how it travelled. This thing appeared to pass through the planet as if it was slicing through it. It didn't seem to travel to the surface and go underground. This indicates that this thing can pass through mass and change its shape to make itself cover a very large area."

The rest of the scientists were silent in their thoughts of the situation.

The VD cut in. "At our last meeting, we discussed what this thing might be and considered options for killing it. Two theories were raised that seemed the most plausible; one was that it was a race of people who had developed a cloaking device that made them virtually invisible to us. The second idea was that this was some type of dimensional phenomenon where it was either in another dimension or in-between dimensions, so it would be invisible to us.

"How do the conjectures line up with the current facts?"

One scientist suggested, "I don't think a cloaked vehicle could slice through a planet like that, although they could have used some type of ray that shot out of the vehicle."

"Any other ideas?" the VD asked.

Another scientist chimed in, "This thing apparently can think and make decisions, so it's something intelligent."

"Good point. Whatever it is though, are there any ideas as to if it can be killed, or even redirected, or disabled?"

It was quiet for a few minutes.

Then one scientist posed, "The base thought it was unlikely many of our weapons would work against it but an antimatter bomb may do it. The heat and concussion, if large enough, may shake its connectivity with our universe or if it was a cloaked device could deactivate the cloaking mechanism. We had mentioned this in our last discussion."

Another scientist reminded the group, "But it may break the thing into pieces, particularly if we don't hit it directly and it would be hard to know where it was, as we can't detect it. There may be a chance that the break-up would create more of those horrid things."

Another scientist conjectured, "Yes, and, instead of having one to cope with, we'd have several of them. If we have one, we can try to come up with another solution. Maybe it'll stay just one but maybe these things divide. Perhaps what it's doing is sucking some kind of life energy that'll allow it to grow and divide. If it does, we'll have to move quickly."

The VD cut in. "Even one of these things will create havoc with people in the empire. Please give me your vote on your opinions.

"First, what are your thoughts that an antimatter blast is a good option?"

All of them responded that it was likely to disrupt it in some way, especially with a direct hit, and there was likely a way to increase their chances of doing that. It was suggested that a nuclear bomb would also be an option.

"Second, what is the probability that the blast may create more of these things?"

One scientist abstained but the rest gave a fifty percent probability.

The VD looked disappointed. "We couldn't take a risk with odds like that. What you are implying is that blasting it is too risky and we are stuck with the status quo for now."

Everyone nodded. There was no solution. There was no hope. For now, they would have to wait until they could learn more about the killer and could come up with a more viable solution. An aura of doom descended on the group. Here were the top echelon and top minds of the empire unable to discover a viable solution.

The VD thanked everyone for making themselves available. He also suggested that, if anyone came up with some promising ideas, they inform him immediately.

The scientists blinked off the screens and everyone filed out of the room except the VD and Conscience, who now sat alone.

"Well, so much for that," John said.

"Yeah . . . at 04:00h we have a meeting with the head of special operations. We'll see if she can help us out."

"Let's see if Marjorie still has some coffee available," John suggested and the two of them trooped over to his apartment.

7

At 04:00h John and Mark were sitting in Mark's office. There was a light tap on the door and it opened. In walked an elderly lady who looked as if she should have retired several years ago.

Mark began, "Good morning, Joanne, I'm sorry for disturbing you at this ungodly hour but . . ."

"I got the report. I'm used to this. Remember, I'm twenty-nine, I just look old. I should upgrade my glasses to the latest styles and I haven't put on my beauty cream yet."

The two men smiled.

She bowed to her superiors, walked to a chair, and sat down.

"We should be bowing to you," Mark said jovially.

"I know you should but I just want you to feel bad. This killer is probably the biggest challenge you've tossed my way. There's no magic bullet here. How can there be one? This is not a crime, political event, or anything like that, so we're grasping at straws.

"I've consulted with my top managers, went to our database, picked out our best agents and selected the top three. We did a computer analysis and decided on one. He's one of our oldest active agents but we're not looking for someone fast or powerful. We thought our best bet was someone who has a lot of experience, is one of our most intelligent, and has an extremely strong psychological profile. This person is afraid of nothing. He's overcome brainwashing techniques, torture, and anything else anyone has tossed at him. He's cunning and has never failed a mission – at least not yet.

"He's battle-worn though; there's probably not a square centimetre of flesh on him without a scar. He's on reduced duty but we give him the tougher missions most newcomers couldn't handle. The main problem is, he's at the opposite side of the empire right now."

"So, you think he's the best person for the job?"

"It's hard to determine but we're putting him forward as our best option. If he can't find a solution, I wouldn't be able to suggest anyone else. Here's his file." She held out a memory block to him.

Mark took it and placed it near his pad. The two men quickly scanned the information.

John exclaimed, "My God, I know this guy! He's a legend. I thought he'd retired."

"He's only fifty-two, and if he wants, has many more years to work for us, either out in the field or at headquarters. You might think that way because he's been on so many important missions.

"He's using his last alias which he has kept for the last fifteen years or so. At first, we thought it was a bad idea and even encouraged him to modify his appearance but it turns out, it's to his advantage. In many cases, as soon as he steps on a troubled planet, the bad guys turn themselves in, and I'm not kidding. That's what I call class.

"I'm putting him at the forefront with mixed feelings. To me, this is a fruitless mission and, if I send him, I'll be sending him to his doom. I'm wasting the life of the best agent I have."

Mark responded, "Well, I support your decision and agree with your synopsis and, now, we don't have many options. We'll get the best pilot in that sector in the fastest craft we have, to do whatever it takes to get him to where he needs to be as quickly as possible."

The head of special operations added, "Right now, he's off duty, and I'll have to get his coordinates to the pilot and assemble his assignment package and authorisation, so please pass me that information when you have it." She paused. "For this job, may I have imperial authorisation just in case he baulks at the task, although he has never before turned down a mission? I'll send the local manager out to give him the assignment personally. In most cases, we wait until he has completed his leave before a new job is assigned. Rarely is a mission urgent, as this one is."

"Sounds like a good plan, I'll get everything you need sent to you as soon as possible."

She got up, gave a light bow to her superiors, turned, and left the room. She was horrified at the enormity of what she was doing. With all the terror this monster had inflicted, she was sending this agent to tackle it. How could anyone pin their hopes on one single person? What a waste of life. He did not deserve that. She pulled herself together and hurried off to make the necessary arrangements.

When she left, the VD said, "She's quite a person. I don't know what we'd do without her. It seems as though she's been here forever."

John said, "She probably has." He paused. "I'm going to head back home, finish my coffee, get a shower, and set up meetings with the boss for 05:00h, the head of communications for 06:00h and the governors for 07:00h. Do you want to attend any of them? We'll be worn out before the sun gets high in the sky.

"Only the first one, I'd better get to work on getting our agent collected and on his way. I'll be in discussions with the admiralty around 06:00h. I'll see you at five. I'll come over to your place and pick you up," Mark responded.

It was almost 05:00h and the VD and conscience stood outside the large door of the official residence of the emperor. The door slid open and the two men entered. A sleekly dressed butler greeted them.

"Welcome, gentlemen. The emperor got up about twenty minutes ago. He'll be having breakfast in a few minutes. You're invited to attend. He has briefed up on the current situation."

The conscience responded, "We'd love to have breakfast. We have some things to talk about."

The butler answered, "I'll notify the cook."

The two men were guided into the dining room, even though they had been there many times before.

They sat down in their designated chairs. A young girl about six walked into the room. "Oh, hi Uncle, Mark and Uncle, John."

"Hi, Dorothy," they said in unison.

"I love when you do that," she said. "You sound like Tweddle Dum and Tweddle Dee."

They both smiled.

"How is school going?" Mark asked.

"Oh great, I'm learning about all kinds of things," she responded.

Gillian, a boy about ten, walked in next. "You're always saying silly things, Dory. I guess, since you guys are here, we'll be having eggs – bacon and eggs."

"Why are you two up so early in the morning?" John asked.

"There's a lot of noise around. Dad's been up for about half an hour. He's been doing a lot of research and he's got the kitchen crew in. He's been expecting you," Gillian responded.

"Yes, I guess it's going to be a busy day today."

"Do you want to hear a joke?" Dorothy asked.

The two men nodded.

"What do you hear just before Dad leaves the bathroom?"

They shrugged their shoulders.

"A royal flush!" she said while giggling.

They smiled with a little giggle themselves.

"And what does Mom get when she's annoyed with Dad?"

They smiled with no response.

"A royal pain in the neck." She giggled again.

They snickered.

Mark asked jovially, "Who told you those jokes?"

"Mom," she replied with a big grin.

They smiled, as they knew the princess consort had quite a sense of humour.

The door suddenly opened and the butler stepped in. Mark and John stood up as the emperor walked into the room.

"Hey, what are you two doing in here?" the emperor asked when he spotted the children. "I know, you just want to see the fun but today is not a good day. You'll have to eat in the kitchen today, so off you go."

He hugged each one as they scurried beside him on the way through the door to the kitchen with the butler following. The door closed. The three men sat near each other. The VD filled him in on everything that had occurred overnight. He watched the video.

Soon after that, the food arrived and they ate as they continued their conversation.

"Okay, so I have the update for everything," the emperor said. "Now let's look at what we're planning.

"I like the actions taken by Rear Admiral Kerchov. When do you plan to put out a bulletin on what happened?"

"Around 08:00h," Mark said.

"And I've planned to call all the governors in conference sixty minutes before to prepare them for the onslaught of questions they'll get, especially around the danger zone," John added.

"The timing should allow us to get the spaceships in place to evacuate the most vulnerable planets. It will take a few more days to evacuate the planets farther away. Our five hundred extra ships will help that when they arrive," Mark piped up.

The emperor seemed concerned. "Five hundred passenger vessels are not going to be enough, even a thousand won't do soon. I'll order another five hundred, with five hundred put on reserve. I want you to develop a plan for even more when that appears inevitable."

"We'll start to cripple internal transportation," John said.

"At this stage, a few thousand vacations will be postponed. One sector is in need and soon others will be. People will understand. We'll have to be together on this. As you have no use for military vehicles, let's use them too," the emperor advised.

Mark stated, "Our experts are stymied as to what to do with this thing. They feel we may be able to kill it with an antimatter bomb but there may be considerable risk that, instead of killing it, it may blow it into many pieces and make our situation worse. There is even some speculation that ultimately it may divide anyway. Any order to attack it is a considerable risk no matter what happens. If we kill it, it would be wonderful but if it doesn't, and the matter gets worse, there will be a lot of criticism."

"So, you want my name on the order?" the emperor asked.

"You're a wise man," Mark responded.

The emperor considered it for a minute then said, "It's the only thing to do. It also means there's no appeal and we don't want any waffling about our decisions. If it's my name on it there's no questioning. I agree we can't take a chance that we produce more of these horrid things and I just hope there are no more of these things around to attack us later."

"I'll send the order out," the VD said.

"Good, I also agree with the plan to prioritise the people we evacuate, if we can't get enough ships to do the job. It's going to be horrible and that's why I'm ordering more ships to be available. It won't take long before we're looking at billions of affected people and how far do we move them back?"

The emperor sat with a paleness they had never seen before. Usually, he was the life of the party; his youth and vigour were contagious but now he looked drained.

Mark shot back with a request. "Special ops have an agent in mind to see what he can do with this thing and we would like to have an imperial assignment."

"You've got it but I don't see how this is going to help us. From what I see, this thing just seems to suck the life out of hundreds of people at a time, so how is one person going to survive that? Special ops are for human-to-human problems." He looked at the file on the agent and said, "I'm just sending him off on a suicide mission. I've read his bio. He's a good man but we should be retiring him to a life of luxury rather than doing this to him."

"Do you want me to scrap the mission?"

"No, of course not; I trust all of you to do the right thing. If you think this is worth a try, then it's worth a try. Nobody has any other ideas right now."

John joined the conversation. "I'll be talking soon with communications.

I'll send over what they're suggesting as our message. Later, I'm talking with the governors. I think we've got everything covered.

"Well, I guess we'll be off to get these things done. We'll continue to keep you informed as things progress."

The two men then got up and backed out of the room.

The two children saw them exit the room but could see they seemed to be in a hurry, so Gillian quickly called to them, "Bye Uncle, Mark, bye Uncle, John."

Dorothy yelled out, "Bye Tweddle Dee, bye Tweddle Dum." She giggled, as her brother gave her a frown.

"Bye kids, see you later," they said as they left.

Mark headed off to his meeting with the admirals in the council chamber while John headed to his office to meet the head of communications.

When Mark entered the room, the admiral and the four vice admirals were already seated but stood up when he entered. They all sat down.

Mark opened, "Good morning, as you know, John and I were at the meeting this morning with our experts and I have just come back from a meeting first with the head of special operations and with the emperor. The emperor will put out an edict denying the use of any type of weapon on the marauder for the time being. There are just too many risks involved with doing it. We have decided to try something with a special agent first."

The admiral could see the surprised looks on the others' faces. "What is a special agent going to do? We don't even know what the thing is! Are we going to try to negotiate with it or something?"

Mark responded, "We don't know yet, we'll have to play it one card at a time. If we can negotiate, then that's what it'll be. We'll try this. We have nothing to lose except one of our best agents. What can the military do at this point? We can't risk using military force in a circumstance like this. What I have also come to tell you is that the military will help evacuate the people out of harm's way. We are calling in as many commercial ships as we can and will increase them if necessary but every possible military vessel will engage in evacuations and we expect other quadrants will help in the effort. We don't have any other conflicts going on now, so the best use of military help is on this effort."

Mark looked into the eyes of each of the admirals.

The admiral looked at the vice admirals and ordered, "Thirty minutes after this meeting is over, I want a plan of action drawn up to help in this effort."

"One more thing, admiral, we'll need one of your best pilots, and I understand the Cheetah is your fastest ship, to get our special agent from somewhere in sector 617 to the battlefield."

"That's clear across opposite ends of the empire!"

"Yes, unfortunately, but this guy's our best agent on the job. I should be getting the coordinates and particulars for you shortly. It's imperative to get him there soonest, so use any means possible."

"Yes, sir. I sure hope this works."

"I hope so too. Goodbye, good people."

The admirals could see he was going to get up, so everyone rose, and Mark left the room.

John was now meeting with the head of communications who had brought in two other managers.

He opened the meeting. "By now you guys know everything, so what did you come up with? We want to get the message out by 08:00h."

The head responded, "We'll start by briefly reporting what happened. Our focus will be on what we are going to do about it, to try to make it as positive as possible. We'll not go into too much detail on our decision not to use military measures, by just saying we are not sure it will be a solution at this point. We'll focus on the fact we already have evacuation ships lined up to get people who want to get out of the way of this thing a chance to leave. We'll also focus on the need to help everyone in the danger area and people in other areas who may be inconvenienced to help in this effort, so we can introduce the need to use ships from other areas and the military vessels. People in other areas may be disadvantaged but it's necessary to help the people in the stricken area. We'll emphasise the temporariness of the situation because headquarters is trying several initiatives to resolve this issue using the best minds in the empire and all sections of government, especially the military and special operations. With everyone's help and cooperation, we can beat this thing.

"I've uploaded the presentation for you to see. Let me know if it's good to go."

"Okay, thanks."

The three communications specialists left.

John tapped his computer pad, looked at the presentation and thought it was quite good. He said, "Computer, send this message to the emperor and include the presentation. Send a copy to the VD."

The VD read the presentation and was quite impressed with it. He approved it and sent it on to the head of communications. He tapped on another file on his pad and said, "Computer, send this file to the head of special operations with the following message: 'Here are your imperial approvals'. Please send the coordinates of your special agent to the admiral."

John set up his conference with the governors of the planets and said, "Good morning, everyone. I see everyone is here, good. We've got some important matters to discuss this morning. A few of you probably have heard rumours, and I'm not sure of the message you got but at about 02:00h the marauder attacked the GEM mining facilities on planet 139-103-17-4-2. All people that remained on the planet are now lifeless.

"Within minutes of the attack, we put into place our evacuation plan and by now, spaceships should be in place to evacuate the most likely planets for the next attack. We've widened the danger area now. I've sent you our plan for the next few days. We've decided to use military vessels as well as commercial ships to implement the evacuation plan. We'll be sending in more vessels of both sources from other areas of the empire. The use of commercial vehicles should affect travel inside our territory. Hopefully, this will be a temporary solution but we anticipate everyone will do their best to help our fellow citizens who are now in danger.

"We have also prepared a communiqué that will be broadcast at 08:00h. I have just sent it out to you. Please let me know within ten minutes if you would like any changes made to it. We expect total cooperation from everyone to help us get through this crisis. Also, we would like everyone to be as positive as possible to try to prevent panic in the populace.

"Does anyone have any questions?"

There was silence. Several governors indicated their agreement with the plan and would lend any help necessary to aid the governors affected and the people under their charge.

The conscience took charge again. "Okay, thanks, everyone. Keep us informed of any issues that arise at your end. It's going to be a tough few days or weeks but we've got our best scientists on this and we are looking at all our options. We've decided not to take any military action at this point until we learn more about this marauder. We don't want to make matters worse. With everyone's help, we can get through this. Over and out."

John sat back in his chair and put his hands behind his neck. Now the rollercoaster ride was about to begin.

8

The silence screamed out at her.

Mrs. Crosby opened her eyes and got out of bed. She stared at the view from the window of their condominium. The sun was just peeking above the horizon. In the long shadows, she could see the vibrant verdure. They had only lived on this planet for about six months now but it took time to get used to the silence. They had moved here to find a nice pleasant place to live out the last days of their lives. The brochures had written so eloquently about this place. Peace, they had said and they were right. The other thing people had to get used to was the twenty-nine-hour days. On a dark planet, or one that was way out of synchrony with the twenty-four-hour clock, people just followed the imperial time of twenty-four hours but for planets not too far off a twenty-four-hour day, people kept the planetary time. Scientists have discovered that people could adjust to days containing eighteen to thirty hours.

She looked back at her husband of over forty years still sleeping on the bed. She smiled. They had had a good life together. Their son and daughter had their own families and lives, so Mrs. Crosby and her husband were mostly on their own now. Each child had moved to different planets to live. With existing technology, such as holo-vision and trans-dimensional transmission, they could communicate almost instantly from one planet to another. That gave elderly couples the freedom to move away from their children and start a new life.

She initially had hoped to import some plants from another planet to brighten things up around the condo but it was not allowed for fear of contaminating the planet's ecology. Without surface animals, there was no need for the plants to attract them with colours for pollination, so they were only different shades of green. She also missed the chirps of birds, the croaks of frogs, or the rasping of insects. She turned to look out the window, again.

She heard the rustling of her husband behind her and she glanced back at him. This time she saw his eyes open.

"Come over here beautiful woman and give me a nice good morning kiss."

"Good morning, sweetheart." She sauntered beside him, bent down, and locked her lips to his.

He unlocked himself and said, "Have I still got it?"

She smiled. "You sure do . . . The sun's coming up."

"Yes, isn't it beautiful?" He got up and followed her to the window and wrapped one arm around her waist. "I love the beauty of the sunsets and sunrises."

"You always have."

". . . and you know the best part? There are no bugs to bother us. We can keep the windows open with no screens."

"It's quiet, though."

"I love it. I know you like a little more noise but, in life, people get too much or not enough; it's never just right. Anyway, I'm sure you get enough noise with my snoring."

"You got me there." She smiled.

"Not only that, soon more people will be moving in, and with all the building, it won't be long before people will be making a lot of noise. Better enjoy it while you can."

He was right. Then she remembered and raised her eyes to the sky.

He caught on and looked at the sky too. "You know you won't see it."

"That's what we were told."

"You also know it might not come here."

"It would have to change its direction to do that."

"Well, let's not think about that now. Let's get dressed and have breakfast."

When they were all prim and proper, they went downstairs to the dining room.

"Ah, Lillian and Robert, great to see you this morning, what would you two like for breakfast on this beautiful sun-shiny morning?" greeted the head waiter at the door to the dining room. He led them to a table and seated them. A waiter soon appeared to take their orders.

Bob looked at his wife. "What do you want today, Hun?"

"I'll have waffles with coffee thanks."

"And I'll have bacon and two eggs, over easy, with coffee."

The waiter thanked them and left.

They spotted one of their new friends being led to a table. Bob called,

"Hey, Warren, join us for breakfast."

Warren nodded and the head waiter brought him over. "Good morning, boy, did I sleep like a log last night. The silence sure helps a person sleep well." The waiter appeared and Warren ordered his breakfast.

"Once they build this place up, it won't be so quiet," Bob retorted.

Warren replied, "That won't be for twenty years or so and maybe I won't be around then. That's why I came here, so I can get away from it all and spend the rest of my years in peace."

"I find the quiet unnerving," Lil said contrarily. "It's so unnatural. I'll be glad when this residence gets filled up and we have a few more people."

"Well, other residences are being developed, so there will be more and more people all the time. We'll change from thousands of people to millions, then billions. This planet will be like all the other developed planets – overrun and overcrowded." Warren sighed.

Their meals came and they ate quietly.

Bob turned on the news tablet on the table and read the headlines. "Looks as if the main news this morning is our nearby interloper again."

"I don't bother with the news much. I came here to have peace. I don't like to hear all the problems in the empire. They should have good news but news people seem to dig up the bad stuff. This planet still hasn't had its first killing or suicide and that's fine with me," Warren commented.

"Aren't you rather nervous about being so close to the killer thing?" Lil queried.

"So far, it hasn't moved from the spaceship. Maybe it can't take on a planet," Warren replied.

"You haven't heard the news? A mining planet was attacked a while ago."

"It doesn't mean it'll come here."

"I sure hope not. We spent a lot of money to move here. This was our last move. This is halfway between our children and we were hoping it might encourage them to visit us more often. We can pay the bills with our pensions," Lil continued.

"My last spot is here, too." Warren ended his conversation.

"We're going for our morning walk, want to come along?" Bob asked.

"No, thanks; maybe tomorrow."

Lil and Bob got up from the table, went back to their rooms, washed themselves, and put on their walking shoes. They returned downstairs and walked out the door to the crisp fresh day.

It was a beautiful walk on the trail through the dense forest growth. With no animals to blaze trails through it, the only way people could travel was on well-marked and regularly groomed trails made by the gardeners. They decided to take the short trail and held hands as they walked along. The only scent of the forest was the musty smell of dampness. There were no smells of pollen. This was the thing about these plants Lil liked the least. She loved the smell of flowers.

They stopped briefly at a bench by the path beside a small creek. They could hear the water rippling over some stones. Lil was especially fond of this place, as there was a sound.

Bob nuzzled close beside her and began nibbling her ear.

"You're supposed to be an old man." She giggled.

He stopped nibbling to say, "Only when it suits my purpose. When there's work to do, I'm old but when there's playing to do, I'm young."

"Well, you can't play it both ways, old man."

"Is that a complaint?"

"Of course not, we might be getting old but the day we can't enjoy one another will be a bleak day."

"You're right about getting old, Lil. I don't like what the doctor said on your last visit."

"Diabetes is not the end of the world, Bob."

"No, but with all the other little things . . . the little aches and pains, forgetfulness, I don't know, Lil. If we separated all the good in one pile and the bad in another pile, we'd have one perfectly healthy person and one corpse."

"Even more reason to stick together."

He laughed heartily. "Yes, you've got something there."

I heard from somewhere that little boys don't grow up, they just grow old and I never want you to change. You keep me young."

"And you keep me young, too." With that, he gave her a warm kiss. "Well, we'd better get back."

When they arrived home, Bob checked his watch. It was ten o'clock, approximately 07:50h imperial time.

"Let's get showers and have a snack. I hear there is a shuffleboard game this afternoon," Bob said cheerily as he gathered the things he needed for his shower.

Bob was in the middle of his shower when Lil burst into the bathroom shouting, "It's here. It's here!"

He poked his head out of the shower door and asked, "What's here?"

"The government has offered to evacuate the residents of this planet."

He responded with shock, "So, I guess they think it might come here!"

"The military has announced a general evacuation. They have ships at

54

the spaceport and are ready to take anyone who wants to go."

"Where?"

"I don't know, just away from here."

"You don't know any more details?"

"They're announcing it repetitively right now. They're taking everyone as far away as they can but they have to come back and pick up more people from the other planets because they've expanded the evacuation zone."

Bob had finished his shower, so he left it and dried himself off. He dressed and sat for several minutes watching the video.

"I didn't think it would do this," he said, discouraged.

"When are we going to leave?"

"But where will we be going? We moved here to be fairly close to our kids."

"Shouldn't we be packing our things?"

"Where are we supposed to hide from this thing?" Bob lamented. "We've spent almost our last dollar buying the condo. It won't be worth anything now."

"Well, we've got to go."

"I'm tired, Lil," he said, exasperated. "This is where I was going to rest for the remainder of my days. I don't want to move anymore."

"Well, I can't go without you. I've spent the best years of my life with you. I can't do it alone. Are you saying you want to stay here, even though that monster is out there?"

"Well, where can we go, Lil? If it doesn't get us here, it'll get us somewhere else but it'll get us."

"Maybe the government will compensate us for our losses?"

"Let's see what others are doing."

"But we're losing time, shouldn't we pack or something?"

"They're giving us lots of time to make up our minds. Let's go to the dining room and see what's going on. We could use a bite to eat whether we stay or leave."

They got up and went down to the dining room. They found people there, some seated; some milling around. It looked as if many people had that same idea. They had not been on this planet long enough to know everyone and there had been people moving in regularly since they had arrived. They finally picked out a couple they knew and went over to their table.

"Hi, Bob. Hi, Lil. I guess you two have heard the news?" The elderly woman welcomed them to their table.

Bob replied, "Yes, we've been discussing it since we heard about it."

"We have, too."

"What are you guys doing?" Bob asked, "Lil and I have different opinions; Lil seems as though she wants to get away but I am leaning on taking my chances here."

"We both don't know what to do."

"Well, I'm tired of running. I owned my own company; I was always volunteering my time around the community. I came here to rest and get away from all that; just to give some time for Lil and me to enjoy each other and get some peace. Now, this thing comes along and takes it all away from us.

"Where will we go anyway? We'll be refugees running away from something; just hopping from one planet to another trying to stay one step ahead of it. Maybe I've run too hard all my life and now I'm tuckered out. Oh, I'm not in bad health, although the doctor adds more things to the not-quite-right list each year when I visit him. It's been downhill for me the past few years. From what I've heard, that thing takes you away without pain.

"I've thought about the end and I'm not afraid of death. What I dread is the possibility of having years of ill health, of ending my days on the second floor of the home needing round-the-clock attention; that dreaded second floor."

There was a shudder from the three others.

Bob continued. "It seems as if you share my sentiment. I've also thought of my lovely Lil; the love of my life. The only thing I dread more than being on the second floor is seeing Lil there. I couldn't bear to see her that way.

"As I talk, I convince myself more and more that maybe I've been presented with an opportunity to have a quick and painless death while I can. I hate the thought of suicide, like ingesting something but this is like having a natural death. You just don't wake up. The thing might not strike the planet but if it does, you're gone and you go with dignity; as if you're going to war."

The other man perked up. "Rather profound statements but I don't know if I want to go now. I might have ten, or twenty reasonably good years left . . ."

". . . or not," cut in Bob.

"Ever the pessimist," the other man posited.

"More like pragmatic."

"I know what you mean but I need to think more about it. The will to live is strong and has kept our species going for tens of thousands of years." He paused. "I guess we'd better get back to our room, dear. We don't have a lot more time to make our decision . . . bye Bob." He stood up.

The woman added, "Bye Lil, if we don't see you again, may your life be as you would want it to be."

"Same for you two," Lil responded.

The two others left the room.

Lil and Bob lingered quietly for a few minutes more then went to their room. They watched the latest news. After a few hours, there were less than three hundred people left on the planet. The final ship was leaving within an hour.

"Well, Lil, this is it," Bob said sadly. "We have to make our decision. I've poured my heart out earlier. I can't bear to see either one of us living out our last years here having our diapers changed and sitting like zombies in a wheelchair."

"I know, sweetheart but do you want to die now?"

"It's not a matter of wanting to die. No one has the decision of whether they go or not. It's inevitable. Sometimes, people get afforded the decision of when. Some choose a natural death, others an assisted death, or other choices; and we have the option here for a quiet death together. Like a game of Russian roulette – we leave it up to the killer as to whether we live or die. It can choose to pass up this planet, or not.

"Neither of us is in the best of health right now. Sure, we may live a lot longer but with what quality of life? If we escape, we'll be starting over. Is the thing going to follow us, so we move again? Can we take all this additional stress? I came here to get away from stress and it's found us again.

"What do you want?" he asked quietly.

Lil said softly, "I want what you want. I've been with you all these years and I want to stay with you. If one of us dies, the other will be alone and I know I won't like that. We married to stay together to the end. If you want to stay here, I'll be with you."

"I asked you what you think of staying here. I want to consider what you think."

"I don't welcome death. I wish it would stay away forever, however, that's silly, because it's impossible. I know we'll deteriorate and, like you, that's what I fear the most; how will it end? I just want to go with you, so I won't ever be alone."

"Then, are you saying you want to stay here?"

"I guess so. At least, we'll be together."

"Where do you want to wait?"

She thought awhile then said, "By the babbling brook."

"So, it will be. Let's notify the authorities of our decision, and notify our children to say a possible goodbye. We have no idea when it will happen, so let's make several lunches to take with us as it might be a long time."

The two of them embraced warmly, kissed, and began to make ready.

9

Space cruiser 3849-3731 approached its destination and slowed to 1,000,000 kilometres per hour outside of a 1,000,000 kilometre distance from the stricken "P" class vessel. The crew of the cruiser already had computer communications with it and had now turned on their scanning devices.

Captain Wang spoke to his crew over the communications unit. "We're now nearing our destination. Everyone hold your stations. We've been through the drill. We anticipate that we won't encounter anything but we must remain vigilant. Our mission is now a scientific investigation, so carry out our plan as of now."

The ship moved closer and continued to decelerate. As expected, the stricken vessel was still fully functional but devoid of life. For two hours, they continued their journey. The tension of his twenty-five-person crew was intense. They had all kept abreast of the news and were aware the entity had moved from the ships to the mining planet. Their only hope was that the killer was a single entity and had not left any part of it in either ship to attack them.

As they pulled up beside it, their attitude grew more confident and relaxed. From the history of this thing to this point, if it was going to attack them, it likely would have done it by then.

The chosen five-man crew, in their spacesuits, entered the shuttle which already had been loaded with the instrumentation required for their tests. Everything, including the exterior of the spacesuits, had been sterilised. When they were all aboard, everyone assisting the process left the airlock, the interior door was sealed, the air was evacuated, and another sterilisation process was carried out.

Once finished, the shuttle accelerated from the airlock toward the passenger ship. The shuttle locked onto one of the hatches of the other ship and the five crew members went inside. They looked at the air quality figures in the vessel and confirmed what they already knew. They scanned with their instrumentation and confirmed it again. They wiped the surfaces within the vessel, including some of the dead, with sterile swabs, rolled them onto sterile agar inside Petri dishes, and locked the dishes within a case, so they could later be incubated.

When they had finished their work, they loaded some food, equipment, and other supplies from the passenger ship into the shuttle, and returned to the cruiser.

The ship's captain sent the results of their investigations to the base and, after twenty minutes, received a message to proceed with the same process with the patrol ship. The crew decided to load some waste material into the shuttle. The cruiser travelled to the patrol ship, let out the shuttle and carried out the same investigations as before. After dropping off the waste material and collecting whatever supplies the vessel had, the crew returned to the shuttle and flew to the cruiser. Their mission was completed.

Again, a message of the results was sent to the base. This time the response took forty minutes and it was personal. Captain Wang went into his cabin to receive it. When he sat down at his pad it recognised him and the admiral's face appeared on the screen.

"Admiral, it's a pleasure to speak to you."

"I thought it would be best to talk to you personally. I'd like to thank you for the effort and bravery exhibited by you and your crew for having volunteered to do these last missions. Nobody will forget this.

"Continue to keep me informed of anything you find, especially the agar results, although we already know them. If there is any bacterial life at all, it should grow on the agar. The interior of the ships is, indeed, sterile according to our instrumentation, which confirmed this thing sucked the life out of all living entities.

"We've been discussing your results with our experts here, as well as headquarters, and feel sure the killer hasn't left anything harmful behind, so it appears it is one thing we are dealing with. This could be false and a part of it resides inside the ships but is not attacking, however, we feel confident that isn't the case. We don't think this is a Trojan horse. Although the vessels are small and not much use to us, in this crisis, we need every ship we can get, so we want you to re-commission them and send them by autopilot to Merlin 3 where we can bury the dead and get the ships back into service."

Merlin 3 was an icy planet mined for water for the more arid planets and had a significant population. It was a suitable location for a military base. It was also not in the current trajectory of the marauder.

The admiral added, "To continue your mission, we want you to go to the coordinates I'm sending you and wait for orders. It's close to GEM's mines but should be far enough to avoid the killer moving toward you. We suspect it will continue its current path to more populated planets. Again, this is a voluntary mission."

"I'm sure my crew will continue to provide service to you, Admiral. If not, I'll let you know immediately. Are there any further instructions?"

"Not right now. Congratulate your crew on their work. We'll continue to feed you with any, and all, the information we have associated with this marauder. You'll have the control to tap into any source of information you want. In other words, you're able to have as much information as you can gather. Even the emperor cannot get any more information than you."

"Thank you, Admiral, we appreciate that."

"Is there anything we can do for you?"

"No, Admiral. We still have sufficient supplies; in fact, we took some supplies from the two stricken vessels as there was no need for them there."

"Excellent idea; I'm signing off now. Again, Captain, thank you for your excellent work."

"It's our pleasure, Admiral. Thank you for this opportunity to serve the empire."

The screen went black.

Captain Wang sat quietly for several minutes. He sighed then got up and stared into space through the viewport. He realised their work was important but this was no glorious battle. How can you battle something you cannot see? How can you fight, when you cannot attack? How can you beat something that can wipe out a planet in a matter of seconds? Except for his ship, the military was now being relegated to evacuating planets. Certainly, it was necessary in situations like this but this was not a war, it was a rout.

He turned, left his cabin, and called his crew to the bridge. When everyone was accounted for, he said, "I've had the honour again of talking to Rear Admiral Kerchov. She sends her best regards to all of you. You've done a great service to the security of the empire at great risk to your lives and she appreciates our efforts to study the nature of the entity that killed everyone aboard these two vessels. We are now being asked to move to a position not too far away from the GEM's mining planet but far enough so as not to be a temptation to it. We will wait there for further instructions.

"Again, I must confirm your acceptance of this mission and remind you that there is no shame in turning down a potential suicide mission. As we'll be sending the two vessels to Merlin 3, it will be an excellent opportunity to get off this ship and head for safety."

Nobody moved.

"Okay then, we're heading for our next coordinates in five minutes. Number one, get those other vessels on their way and get us to our next waiting spot."

"Aye, aye, Captain."

Captain Wang continued. "Communications, tie into the next high-risk planet, so we can monitor what's going on there. I want to know exactly when the killer strikes, then we can move onto GEM's planet and explore."

About fifteen minutes passed. "I found something, sir," the communications officer said. "There are just under two hundred people left on the planet and most of them are in their rooms or somewhere else beyond the surveillance cameras. This elderly couple sitting near a creek may be as good as anyone to monitor activity on the planet."

The captain glanced at the image on the screen. "Yes, that will be fine. It's a little incongruent with what may happen and is a beautifully, peaceful setting. They look very content where they are and they're holding hands."

"I feel as if I'm snooping," the communications officer confided.

The first mate cut in. "Well, there are not too many other targets. I like this one because it's such a tranquil spot. When you listen, you can hear the water flowing down the stream."

The captain added, "Remember, our marauder doesn't appear to deliver a violent death."

After almost twenty-four hours of travel, they reached their destination and slowed to a stop.

The elderly couple had gotten up several times to return briefly to their residence. One person had come by and talked with them for a couple of hours then left to continue along a longer portion of the walking trails. Before night fell, they returned to the residence and had not returned. Other cameras had determined they had returned to their room, probably to sleep. The crew saw other people from time to time wandering the premises and other areas in the town under construction.

The captain could tell his crew was nervous. They all knew they were relatively close to GEM's planet and its marauding killer. The thing could always change direction and come after them. The only things on their side were that they were slightly farther away than the next planet and the cruiser's much lower number of people may be less of a temptation for it.

Now, it was a waiting game.

The communications personnel were monitoring the images on the planet around the clock. Often other personnel joined them. Two members of the crew were present when the elderly couple, who had returned to their bench by the creek and were reading pads, slumped. The man slid off the side of the bench while the woman continued sitting as she had, with her chin on her chest.

There was a brief ruckus as the crew realised what they had seen and alerted the others. For the next thirty minutes, more and more crew members watched the repeats of the image. Other cameras in the town had shown nobody else visible at the time.

Captain Wang watched sadly. So, another two hundred people had met death but the saddest thing as he looked around the environment was the apparent effect on the planet. The light breeze was causing many of the leaves to detach from the trees and flutter to the ground. The planet was now filled with massive stands of lifeless wood.

The communications officer came quietly over to the captain and whispered, "Captain, there's a message from the admiral."

He acknowledged and quietly went into his cabin.

He sat at his pad, the computer recognised him and the screen brightened. There was a pause then the admiral's face appeared. "Sorry for the delay, Admiral, I was on the bridge."

"No problem, Captain. I can guess what you were preoccupied with. You must have seen what we saw?"

"Yes, Admiral. The marauder has moved and attacked its next planet."

"Now that we know it has moved, I want you to examine GEM's planet and pass on your results. We know what you'll find. We're sure now the killer will continue to move to more planets. We've intensified our evacuation efforts and are trying to guess, as best we can, the direction this thing is going to take. We want you to continue following it and determining anything else you can glean about it. Also, particularly look for survivors, which I'd be surprised if you ever find. We'll inform you when we want you to change your mission. These are sad days for the empire and we appreciate the risks you're taking. I wish this was an easier task."

"We appreciate your comments, Admiral. This is our responsibility. We're here to serve. We'll continue our mission."

Captain Wang was carefully examining the admiral's face. She looked older than she had a few days earlier. He could see the strain this was having on her. She held the safety of everyone in her sector in her hands. He knew how helpless she must be feeling, and there was much more to come.

He now knew he was on his own. The base would be too busy with evacuating planets to be concerned with one small space cruiser. He would have to make decisions on his course of action on his own.

She probably sensed his perceptions. "I'm signing off for now, Captain. Best of luck to you," she said as cheerily as she could under the circumstances, trying to hide what was really within her.

The screen faded to black.

The captain sat helplessly in his chair. The admiral wielded all the power of the empire and could do nothing. He could do no more. The look on the admiral's face told it all.

The captain left his cabin and went to the bridge. Most of the crew was waiting for him. He took his seat and switched on the central communications system, so everyone on the ship could hear him.

"I've had another message from the admiral. Things are going to be very hectic from now on. The push is on to get everyone who wants to leave onto a ship and away from the at-risk planets. With the marauder of GEM's planet gone now, we're going to move there and see what we can find. I think too, it may be good for us to give people a decent burial then we can follow the thing and continue to provide those services for the dead.

"Remember too, that you are free to leave anytime."

The first mate stood up. "Captain, I speak for the crew," he spoke slowly and deliberately. "We'll continue to back you on this mission to the end. You'll have our full support and loyalty. Some of us have families that have already been affected by this thing and soon others will, too. The temptation is there to join our families to help them but we know they are doing well and are cared for. Our best position to help in this crisis is here on this ship, and here we stay. Our families support our decisions."

The captain responded, "Thank you, ladies and gentlemen. I appreciate this. One thing I want us to do is maintain strict adherence to sterility rules, so, every time we leave this ship to travel anywhere, to an uninhabitable planet, habitable planet, or another spaceship, we do not contaminate it. Until our superiors decide what to do, I don't want to limit their options by contaminating sites with our bacteria, viruses, or human tissue. This would permit our masters to have options like using the DNA present on some planets to re-create what was there before, if possible. Life is no longer present but the DNA may be viable and there is nothing to decompose it except for normal oxidation. Undisturbed, the planets should maintain viable DNA for quite some time.

"With that stipulation, let's move onto our next planet, shall we?" he added cheerily in an apparent mimic of the admiral in the last call.

It took them several days to get there, thoroughly scan the planet, and then stop at each mine site to bury the dead. The planet did not have much soil to bury anything but the spaceship blasted holes in the planet's surface, the crew placed the bodies in them and covered the holes with the rocks from the blasting and the existing thin soil. They thought it was unnecessary to bury the people inside the sealed mineshaft as they had effectively sealed themselves into their graves.

Near the end of their task, the ship's crew witnessed the thing attack a cruise ship holding a full load of evacuees. There was much criticism about that. The ship was not supposed to be in that area. The lieutenant commanding the ship was trying to take a shortcut.

When the crew was finished on GEM's mines, they moved on to the next planet. There, it was much quicker to bury the dead. There were fewer sites with much fewer people and this planet had soil, so it was also quicker to dig and fill in the tombs.

Two crew members went to pick up the elderly couple they had watched not so many hours before. It seemed strange to see them there, almost life-like. The woman was still sitting on the bench, while the man was still bunched up on the pathway. Their surroundings had changed drastically. All the leaves were off the trees and most of them were, by then, crunchy, and dry. The stream was carrying many of them with the flow of water. Like the bodies of the couple, the leaves were fresh with no fungus, bacteria, or fish bites on them.

It had taken billions of years of evolution for nature to create this beautiful garden and in a matter of seconds, the planet had become a sterile lifeless globe. The crew did soundings in the oceans; they looked at whatever nook and cranny they could detect. Everywhere was the same. Left undisturbed, these leaves, and naked tree skeletons, would rest un-decomposed for millions or billions of years. It would take billions of years more to regenerate life, even if the planet could do that again. Certainly, scientists of the empire could rekindle most of the original life using the existing DNA but it would still take thousands or tens of thousands of years to get back to its former grandeur.

One of the crew members was interrupted in thought by the shrill call of the communicator.

"Well, we'd better get back to work; we've got lots to do while we're here."

The two crew members picked up the elderly couple and started to carry them over to the residence but changed their minds. They found a dry spot next to the creek, blasted an appropriately sized hole, placed the bodies in it, and covered them up with soil. They placed a marker at the site and took one more look around. They could see the beauty of the site and why it had attracted them. It was only fitting to set them near the spot they had chosen to die.

Now, the crew was almost ready to go back to the cruiser and travel to the afflicted cruise ship then on to the next attacked planet to continue their work.

10

The air was crisp and cold. The sky was a deep blue with the slightest wisps of clouds. Some clouds were high above him and others hovering just above the peaks of the other lower mountains below. Far in the distance, he could make out the form of a pterodactyl-like bird hovering in the air and riding the updrafts of the winds to drive itself ever higher into the sky. He was breathing heavily at this altitude but the higher oxygen level in the air of this planet was allowing him to breathe unassisted. From here, it seemed as if he could see forever. He took a panned shot with his camera to get the image recorded for posterity.

He was very likely the first person ever to stand atop this mountain and he liked that. His life was full of firsts. He sat down on a crag on the peak, had lunch, and a long swig of water.

He soaked up what he saw. Each peak he had conquered in his life was unique; each had its peculiarities, both in the climb and in the scene at the top. Each day of life was like that, too. He opened his eyes in the morning and never knew what was going to befall him; a new day of exhilaration, of decision, or doubt. What was his favourite mountain? Was it the last one, this one, the next one? Did it matter?

He had been a solitary man, unfettered and free. He loved it. He could lead his life as he had to and it was necessary. Then, one day he met love, not intended but like a rush, then lost it and the pain was more than he had borne with all the injuries of life. There was no other, it would never be again; it could never be again but it was a stubborn foe. And strange as it was and is, like the mountain, each step must be strong and sure and quick. One mistake and life would be shorn and one makes the decision in an instant but love is not like that. It is filled with uncertainty and doubt. For him, life and love were anathemas. How many men before him had searched high places for truth and came back empty?

Now, again, he was at a crossroads. He closed his eyes and concentrated.

She finally emerged from the fog wearing what was going to be her wedding gown of so long ago, like an angel appearing from a mist. Her hair was black as night, her complexion of the palest cream, her lips the reddest red. She looked at him sternly then with a smile and he knew what he had to do. He resisted but could see the joy in her eyes. Then, like the mist, she left and he felt alone again like love sucked, drained, and empty.

After about an hour of enjoying the sights, deep in thought, at this elevation of just a little less than twelve thousand metres, he began his journey down. He did not want to be caught too high on the mountain when it got dark. With all the pitons in this section still affixed, the first part of the journey was quite quick then the slow part of the descent began. After the first sheer cliff was done, he followed the little trail he had discovered on the way up until it turned into another sheer cliff again.

Halfway down the cliff, a piton dislodged and he fell three metres before his rope caught the secondary pin and it held. He cursed and struggled to regain control of his situation. He set another piton into the cliff face, then another. He was secure again. He rested for a few minutes to regain his composure and let his adrenaline level stabilise.

Never climb a mountain alone, he thought but that offered no great challenge. How can you be the only person to have been on a peak, when you have a partner? He probably had the record for the number of mountains climbed and the number of peaks conquered for the first time on different planets. He was also probably the only person who had never used supplemental oxygen, although he always carried it with him, just in case.

He picked up his pace a bit, as he had planned to be at a certain location before nightfall and it was fast approaching. Soon, he was at the base of the cliff and on a path again but it was extremely narrow. He slowed down for the trickier places but sped up when he had a clear path. He finally hit a part where he was almost running. He was glad that two of this planet's three moons were out tonight, so he could continue to make out the trail until he neared his destination which was a broad shelf on the side of the mountain. He had stopped there on the way up. It gave a beautiful view and afforded a safe, level spot to spread out and pitch a tent.

He finally arrived at the site, removed his backpack, quickly opened it, and set up the campsite. He securely fastened his tent to the ground. He lit his small burner and boiled some water. He placed his pouch of food into the pot and left it to heat up. He pulled the pouch out of the water and used the water to make some tea. He opened the pouch, ate the food, and downed the tea. He could not take too long as it got cold quickly at this elevation. It had been very chilly at the peak, just below zero but even this much lower from the top it was already minus ten because the sun was dipping below the horizon. He crawled into the tent, rolled out his sleeping bag and, exhausted, fell asleep almost instantly.

He was awakened before sunrise by the howl of the wind. He knew the winds here were fierce enough to blow a tent off the side of a mountain and it was probably not wise to leave it but the winds would not remain for long. All he could do was to wait it out, so he read a book with his lamp.

It was three hours into the day when the wind velocity dropped enough so he could leave the tent and start the morning. He cooked breakfast and ate then disappeared into the tent to warm up and get another two hours sleep.

When he finally got up, the temperature, although cold, was more tolerable. It was too soon after breakfast to eat again, so he had a snack and a swig of water, which by now had started to freeze even though the container was insulated. He rolled up his bedding, took down the tent, and packed his backpack.

He stood and gazed one last time at the scene before him. His altitude was still above all but two other peaks on this side of the mountain. There were more clouds today and he predicted rain would come, probably during the night. He hoped it did not last long, as he was anxious to get down. He pulled out his camera and took pictures again. He put the camera back and took a drink of water but did not get much this time, as by now, the water was almost frozen. In case the temperature did not rise much, he placed the bottle into the pocket closest to his body to help melt the ice.

The first hour of the trail was along a ledge then he had a short cliff to descend. He skipped a circuitous route around the mountain for another steeper descent by using his ropes to get him down faster but it was riskier. He finally finished that and stopped for a cold lunch where he had some tea to help warm him up.

He continued following a trail where he jogged for quite some time until he came to another ledge to have supper and pack it in for the night.

In the morning, he found his prediction had come true with a chilly rain falling but he realised it was not just rain, there was some sleet mixed with it and, in some cases, the water was freezing to the ground. He was thankful he had made valuable time descending, as it was now noticeably warmer but at this time was hovering around zero. If he had been higher up, he would have been in a much trickier position; he would have been frozen in for a day or two.

He waited in his tent for two hours past sunrise and exited to have breakfast and tea. It was still raining but he decided to fold up his gear anyway and continue his trek. It had warmed up from the heat of the star but there would still be ice around. He had to descend soon, or he would not make his next planned stop.

There was a short trail to follow but he was slowed by the icy areas where it was shaded from the star. He descended another sheer wall. This would be his last one. After this, it would be an almost clear way to the bottom but it turned out not to be as easy as it was coming up. Often, he found that descending was more dangerous than climbing. It was the ice that foiled him this time and, perhaps, his added haste. At one point, he lost his footing, smacked up against the rock face, and then scraped on it until the rope grew taut but the pinion popped because of the hard jerk of his weight suddenly jolting it. He thought this was the end. He was able to slow his fall somewhat until he felt the rope grow tight again but this time, the next pinion held tight.

He breathed a sigh of relief. He quickly reassured his position then rested briefly and had a swig of water. The rest of the descent was uneventful.

On the last day, he travelled through the night with the glow of three moons. When he arrived at his spacecraft, he was exhausted and hungry. For the first time in days, he could cook up a real meal. He did not even unpack his backpack. Soon, he was frying up bacon and eggs, or at least its space equivalent, and he wolfed them down. His head dropped to the table and he fell asleep.

He was jolted awake by the sensation of movement in the kitchen.

"Oh, you're awake. I'm sorry I woke you up," a female voice broke the silence.

His eyes focused and he smiled. "That's what you get when you fall asleep in a kitchen in the morning." He looked at Elizabeth. He had met her five years before and had fallen in love with her. She was short, had long auburn hair, which he particularly liked, natural ruby red lips, and blue eyes.

"Did you always used to do that?"

"Yes, of course, every day; me, Tarzan."

She had introduced him to this series of stories because he reminded her so much of Tarzan. He read the series and adopted the quips she had introduced to him.

"Yes, and I'm Jane." She leaned over and kissed him on his head. "I see you've already eaten."

"I meant to cook something for you too but, as you can see, I fell asleep."

"That's what all men say."

"Oh, so you know all men?"

"Of course; me Jane." She giggled. "Are you still hungry?"

"Yes."

"Okay, so go wash up, or, take a shower. You smell like you need one."

"Oh, sorry," he said, embarrassed, "the last stretch I was kind of racing to get back."

"For food, I suppose?"

"One does get tired of pouched food."

"You're made of pouched food."

He looked at her intensely.

"Go on and get your shower, maybe make it a cold one and stop staring," she smiled. "You should eat before dessert."

He smiled lustfully, went into his bedroom, and pulled out clean clothes. He entered the bathroom, showered, dressed, and sat on the side of the bed to put on his shoes.

11

Elizabeth cooked some food for her and a little more for John. She wanted it to be special because she was anxious about what would happen after. She sighed. When it was ready, she went over to the bedroom door and opened it. She glanced at the bed and saw him slumped on it fast asleep. She went over to him and covered him with the blankets as best she could.

She returned to the kitchen and sat at the table, staring at his empty plate. He had been away for what seemed like forever, even if it had been only a week or so but his exhaustion had taken him away from her. That was not much of a welcome. She would rather have had him take more time to get back, so she could spend time with him.

She got up, put the food in the refrigerator, and wandered out of the spaceship to the side of the lake. How peaceful it was there. The time he was away had given her a lot of time to think. She sat down on what had now become her favourite rock; her thinking rock.

Her thoughts were interrupted by movement behind her. She turned around.

"Hi, Mom."

"Good morning, David."

David was her only child. He was thirteen and, like any boy his age, likely wanted her to cook up three eggs and bacon, or perhaps a stack of pancakes.

She smiled at him. "You're hungry?"

"Famished," he replied. "Did you already eat?"

"Actually, no."

"I saw the plate on the table and smelled food, so . . . oh . . . is John back?"

"Yes, he is. He got back early in the morning. He had breakfast but was so tired he went to bed. My breakfast is in the fridge."

"Did he have a good climb?"

"We didn't get any time to talk."

"Oh . . ."

"Well, let's get inside and get you some food. What would you like this morning?"

"Pancakes and sausage. Is it going to be another lesson on cooking?"

"No, not this time but you need to learn to look after yourself. In a few years, you'll be out on your own."

"But, when do I have to cook? I can just pop the food into the micro and zap it, or use the food generator. No one cooks, mom."

"It doesn't taste the same."

"I don't care. It's just to eat."

"Maybe you'd like to go somewhere else where there is no spaceship or hotel around then you'd have to do everything yourself."

"Unlikely, mom."

She sighed. "It's like learning math, or history, huh, when you will rarely have to use what you learned?"

"Exactly."

She shook her head, got up, and went back to the spaceship, with him right behind her.

She cooked pancakes and sausage and reheated her breakfast. They settled down to eat. He helped her put the dishes into the vapocleaner – a waterless dishwasher using a laser. When they were done and the kitchen was clean, she went back to her rock, while he went to clean up and get dressed.

In about half an hour, she heard him behind her. She turned her head and noticed he was bringing out a chair.

"Joining me for a while? I sure like John's idea of restricting the amount of time you play your holo-games. We haven't talked so much since you were a little tyke. We've been canoeing, hiking, and just hanging around when you're not doing your school work."

"Well, there's nothing else to do."

"Haven't you liked being out in the wilderness and exploring a new planet?"

"I guess so, although, I didn't like the sterilisation process and now have the runs all the time."

"That's it, show some enthusiasm," she said sarcastically.

"Show me some sarcasm," he quipped back.

She smiled. "Oh, how I love teenage years."

"So, John didn't say anything when he got back?"

"He said he was still hungry."

"That's all?"

"Pretty much; he went in to take a shower and the next thing I knew he was asleep on the bed."

"It must have been quite a trek."

"I think he was pushing too hard to return here."

David stared at his mother.

She glanced back at him. "So, what's with the big stare?"

"You and John have been going out a lot in the past year, and he has taken us out to so many exotic places. Are you guys getting serious?"

"We've been going out for almost six years."

"Yes, but it's not the same."

"What do you mean?"

"Just what I said before. You just occasionally went out but now you're together almost all the time. I can see your reaction to him. I can see there's something more, sort of a glow or something. I'm not dumb."

"You know what happened with your dad? I knew I was not the best-looking woman on the planet and when your dad said he loved me, I fell for him. He was not a nice man and couldn't settle down. I knew there were warning signs at the beginning and I thought he'd change but he didn't. When he walked out on me, I swore I'd never get serious with a guy again. I kept that promise. It didn't mean I never dated but I never let it get serious, always just friends."

"Yes, you told me that before but I think you've broken your promise; and, Mom . . . you're a good-looking woman, what are you talking about?"

"You're a little biased, aren't you?"

"Mom, I wish you'd stop saying that. John loves you, doesn't he?"

She blushed. "I'll never believe that again. He can't commit himself. I just accept him as a friend. I hardly know him; he's away so much. How can anyone get to know another person, if they're hardly with you? I don't even know what he does when he's away. He could have another woman friend or more. He says he doesn't but he's so mysterious. For all I know, he could be a criminal, a killer, or a gang member with all the scars he has everywhere."

"Yeah, I always wondered about that, too. At first, I was even afraid of him."

"I noticed that. It took me a long time before I brought him home and introduced him to you. I sensed your fear but you never told me about it."

"I thought I'd spoil things for you."

"He told me a little about his past but when I'd asked him what he did for a living, he'd say he couldn't tell me. He did tell me other parts of his life. He filled me in a bit. For example, he said that his mother was still alive but I've never met her. He also told me something in his life that explains why I know he'll never make our relationship serious. Just like I'll never get married, he'll never settle down with anyone either. We're both locked in our pasts."

There was a long silence.

"Aren't you going to tell me why?" David finally broke the quiet.

"He's a very private person. I'm surprised he even told me."

"Well, now that you've got my curiosity up, you've got to tell me."

"No, son, someday, maybe when you're older."

"I'm older now, mom. I'm not a baby. I can see the sparks between you two."

She blushed. "There are no sparks."

"Yeah, sure," he said assertively, "I see the way you look at him. I can notice it in him too. Do you think I'm blind? Even now, when I mentioned it, you blushed."

His mother had a very serious look on her face. "He is a very private person. I don't think he wants me to talk about him."

He knew he could not pursue that topic with her anymore. "You must like him a lot."

"Let's just leave it at that. He's one of the most interesting men I've ever known. He's been to so many places. He knows so much. I can never get bored with him. I've gotten over his rough edges. He's kind of a man's-man as you've noticed. Maybe he's a millionaire playboy."

"In your dreams."

"Why, what do you think he is?"

"I don't know but a playboy wouldn't be all marked up like that. He may even be a fighter, like boxing or wrestling but that's illegal, so we may not know of him in that profession but nothing can explain how he can come here. Individuals may discover other planets but only the imperial authorities can authorise occupation of a planet. I looked up this planet before we got here and it's in quarantine. That means he's here illegally, or he's a very high imperial official."

"Like a prince or something?" her eyes lit up.

"No, I would doubt that. Not too many princes would let someone beat them up, so I'm stumped again. I don't want to guess any further than that."

There was more silence for a few minutes, as the two of them looked across the lake which nested in a valley among the local mountains. It was rain and spring-fed, so it was extremely pure.

"The water looks so clear, you almost see the bottom and the lake's deep," David finally said.

"Yes, isn't it wonderful?"

"This planet hasn't evolved any large animals except for a few types of bird-like creatures. It doesn't have any mammal-like creatures yet either."

"Well, it does have now . . . What do you think of John?"

The sudden switch in topics again caught him in a confused look. "As I said before, I wondered who you were going out with. When I first saw him, I was initially afraid of him but after meeting him and talking to him several times, I found that he was cool but still a little scary, as I knew if I didn't fall in line, he'd give me his dead-man look."

She laughed. "What do mean his 'dead-man look'?"

"He gave this glare that would bore down into my soul. I even, at times, thought he could read my mind."

"Maybe you could relate to him, being a male?"

"I don't know, I think it was more than that."

"Do you like him?"

"Yes, I guess I do. As I said, he's cool. It's hard to explain – he knows so much, and the best thing is, he treats me like an adult . . ."

"So, I don't?" His mother cut him off.

He blushed with embarrassment and added, ". . . Well, you're my mom and you've had me my whole life as a baby. Sometimes you should realise I'm older now."

She thought he was exaggerating but she also realised it was difficult for parents to keep up with their maturing youth, especially when they often acted very immaturely. She was doing her best to adjust to his growth but it was harder to do as a single parent.

In the silence that followed his comment, she grew to realise the benefit of David having a father figure around and John was a particularly good one. She had not been an outdoorsy person but she could see the good influence of the outdoor activities on David. She smiled a little. He likely would not have said what he did, if John had not been in his life. He was becoming a man, and he had matured significantly over the last few months.

David interrupted her thoughts. "Sorry, Mom, I didn't mean to say it quite that way."

"You said it just fine, David."

"You're a great mom . . . an awesome mom."

She reached over and squeezed his arm; he had grown out of getting a hug.

"I'm really happy you met John, Mom. I think you two get along nicely together. I've never seen you so happy. Even when he disappears as he does, you seem happy; and to tell you the truth, I miss him too."

She peered into his deep blue eyes. The one good thing her former husband had given to her was David. Sure, he was a constant reminder of that jerk but David was also his person and he was an intimate part of her life. She could never live without him. In a way, she was a little too protective. Maybe she loved him a little too much. She hated the thought that one day he would leave and start his own life but that was the beauty of life. She sighed.

"I'll go fishing for a while; maybe I'll catch some fish, or whatever else you could call those creatures in the water. If they weren't so tasty, I would never think of eating something so ugly. I guess ugly is in the mind."

She smiled. "Off you go then. Be careful on the boat."

"Mom . . ." he retorted as he wandered down to the water's edge, grabbed the tackle box and rod, pushed the boat into the water, jumped into it, put on his lifejacket, and paddled onto the lake.

She watched him for a while and went into the spaceship in case John got up. She peeked into the bedroom but he was still sound asleep.

A couple of hours later, David ran in with four fair-sized fish strung out to show her.

"Are you going to prepare them for lunch?" she asked.

"I hate that part, Mom. You know I do."

"But isn't that part of fishing?"

"Not when you have a mom around." He snickered.

She gave him first a scowl, then a resigned look, as she took the fish from him and began lunch.

"Save some for John, too, Mom."

"Sure, he'd like that."

When lunch finished and they washed up, David asked, "Do you want to go on a hike, Mom?"

"Maybe I should stay around in case John wakes up."

"Oh, he'll be all right. It's so nice out there; it's a shame to stay in here."

"What about schoolwork?"

"I'm ahead right now, so a little hike isn't going to hurt."

She packed a snack and some water and they were off.

Hiking was her time for contemplation. Between the rock and hiking, she had done a lot of thinking. Walking single file was not conducive to conversation anyway.

As they headed up the trail, she thought of John back in the spaceship. She was at a defining point in her relationship with him. She had struggled in the last few months with the oath she had taken never to cross a line of friendship with a man, and never to get involved again but he was so unlike any other man she had ever met before. He was an enigma. He was so rugged but so gentle and thoughtful. He was intelligent but did not overpower you with it. He could be very serious and at other times so playful. She could see his influence on David and that was the strongest pull on her. She knew John was good for David and could see the strong bond forming between the two of them. She knew John loved children and David was filling that void in his life.

David had never done very well at school and had spent a lot of time in the hands of neighbourhood bullies; that age-old scourge that, over the millennia, had never been eradicated. The last four years exposed to John had changed all that. When John found out about the abuse, he taught David to defend himself and within six months, and a few fights, his problems disappeared. She had been opposed to that at first, as she considered any type of fighting was not right in any situation but David's self-confidence soared and his marks improved, and she realised it was the best thing to do in this case.

It was almost too good to be true both for David and her. John was filling a void in her life too. She kept feeling, however, that the universe would soon be crashing in on her but why did she feel that way? She was so torn within. She never wanted to feel the pain she felt with her breakup again but she felt so drawn to this man and she knew he could never let her into his heart.

He was a man, too, who had been in love; and had loved a woman so deeply, so intensely, that he could never love any other; a man who hurt so badly and with pain so intense, that he had shut out any other love and lived his own mechanical life of cold and death; a man who had left her for but a fleeting moment and had her taken away from him so violently and cruelly; a man who had seen her so broken up, bloody, and torn. The rage had forged an impenetrable wall to his heart.

She could understand and respect that, and she had her shield, so she felt safe. The contact with John was good for David but she was a woman and to such a man and the pain and suffering he had endured, she now so wanted to comfort and so wanted to soothe and take him into her heart to replace what he had lost. He was a magnet and her shield no longer could hold him out but she had to break from him. The pain was too much with him and would be too much without him. How could she let John go and ultimately hurt David, too? She was so torn inside. Why did she have to meet him? Why did her friend set her up at the party? Why did she not ignore her initial reaction to him, when she saw his scars? Was it pitying?

Why had she not considered their fifteen-year age difference?

But, that red hair of his; it was rare to see anyone with red hair and she felt drawn to it. He had told her he liked her almost-white blonde hair. He even joked that, if they were ever to have children, they would end up with pink hair.

But something had to happen. She could not live like this. She wanted to spend her life with him, whether it was a formal marriage or not. If she could not get his heart then he could at least give her his time, any spare time he had when he was not 'away' and, if his away periods were with someone else, she wanted to know and wanted it to stop. She might lose everything but while she still had whatever shield that remained, she had to stop moving forward to where she lost control.

She almost ran into David, who had stopped suddenly and turned around but halted her forward movement in time.

He stared at her briefly then asked, puzzled, "Mom, why are you crying?"

She had not realised she was; she was in so much angst and turmoil. She had not cried since she had gotten over her marriage. This must have been a sight for her son, as he would not have remembered anything about his father and what happened.

"What's the matter?" he asked in earnest.

She caught herself and lied. "Oh nothing, I was thinking about a lot of things, like how fast you're growing and stuff."

"You must be upset. I've never seen you cry before."

"I guess I'm tired and have too many things going on at the same time."

"Like what? John's back and we've had a nice relaxing day today talking about stuff, and now this hike. Is the hike too long? Is that why you're tired?"

"No, no, everything is fine. Women don't need a reason to cry."

"You're sure? You can talk if you want."

"No, David, it's fine. I'm enjoying the hike, so don't change your plans. You know how I like hiking with you."

He gave a quizzical look for a few more seconds then turned around and continued following the path John had previously cut through the forest.

They arrived back at the ship late in the afternoon. They had a quick supper and then watched a movie. Several times she got up to check on John then they retired to bed.

79

12

John woke up warm and rested among a pile of blankets. It so contrasted with the time he had spent in the days travelling up and down the mountain. He had slept extremely soundly. He could vaguely remember going to the washroom once or twice, or was it more? He looked over at the clock. It was two o'clock, so he had slept for eight hours. No, he checked closer, it must have been over twenty hours! He had wasted almost an entire day.

He rose quickly and stiffly then felt the pang of his injury. He stopped to stretch it a little to loosen it up. He had not thought it was so badly injured. He went to the washroom, turned on the light, opened his shirt, and looked at his chest in the mirror. His heavy clothing had protected his chest for the most part but it was badly bruised. He must have hit the cliff quite hard. He felt the tenderness but it did not appear that any ribs were broken.

He closed and buttoned his shirt, and wandered into the kitchen but no one was there. He expected that. He did not think they would wait up for him until this hour of the morning. As quietly as he could, he grabbed a bowl, poured out some dried cereal, poured in some milk, and sat down to eat. He was almost finished, when David walked into the room.

"Oh, you're up!" David said almost in a whisper.

"Just got up. What are you doing awake? Did I wake you?" John asked softly.

"No, I just came out for a snack."

"Good, I was trying to be as quiet as I could."

"How was your climb?"

"Shh, let's not wake your mother. We can talk about it outside later if you'd like."

They finished their meals and wandered out of the ship. They went over to the boulder by the lake and sat down.

"So, did you get to the top?" David opened the conversation.

"Yes."

"What did it look like?"

"I'll show you later with your mom."

"Was it a rough climb?"

"Not the roughest I've ever climbed. I had more problems coming down than climbing. I hit my chest hard against one of the cliffs."

"You, okay?"

"It didn't hurt much at the time but it sure hurts, now."

"Someday can I climb with you?"

"You'll need a lot of training first, and conditioning. You'll need to be very fit. Computer games aren't going to do that. I know you have simulations of climbing but the real thing is not the same. One mistake and you could end up dead. You can't instantly regenerate like in a game."

"I know, and it seems so cool."

"It's a wonderful experience. It's a challenge and, when you get to the top and look around, it's exhilarating; a most delightful experience and such a sense of accomplishment."

"Wow."

"But don't ever do it alone."

"You do."

"Yes, but I'm taking chances and am very experienced. I'm a little stupid, too; kind of a bad habit I have. Just, don't take any unnecessary chances. Think of your mom. You're her only child and you'd hurt her terribly if you ever injured yourself. She'd also kill me for getting you into climbing . . . I think this was my last climb."

"Oh, yeah?"

"I'm getting too old for that. I think I should settle down."

"You're not that old."

"Most people at fifty either have slowed down their pace considerably or are going to do it soon.

"How about I pull out the telescope and test you on what you've learned? Look how clear and crisp the night is. It's not often all three moons are absent from the sky."

John ran into the ship for a few minutes then came out with the telescope in his hands. He set it up in an almost flat spot not too far from the rock. He levelled the instrument by adjusting its legs.

"Okay, find Sol," he called out to David. It was a human tradition to keep a link to mankind's home star in this way.

David had done this search two other times on this planet but never this time in the morning. He had to adjust to the star's situation in the sky, which was not much different from finding the North Star on Earth. To the ancients of Earth, their planet was the centre of the universe. For people of the stars, you come to know that even Earth's star was not any more special than any of the other millions visible. To find it, all one had to go on was the pattern of the stars in the sky where Sol was. After several minutes, David finally remembered part of the pattern and pointed to a star.

"Hey, excellent job; you have a good memory." John rubbed his hand in David's hair.

They spent more time locating stars in the sky, as well as some nebulae and galaxies. One of the galaxies he identified was Andromeda.

John said, "You already know Andromeda is the closest galaxy to us. One thing you may not know is it is racing toward us and will eventually collide with us."

"Wow, I didn't know that. Will it destroy us?"

"It won't be here for billions of years, so mankind might not be around when it does. Remember that space is exactly that – stars with lots of distance between them. There will be a lot of gravitational effects but the effects on most individual star systems might be minimal.

"Well, you should get to bed again and finish your sleep."

"What about you?"

"I'll lie down and read for a while. If I sleep again, okay, if I stay awake, I'll just keep reading." He paused. "How about after breakfast, we'll catch some fish for lunch."

"You know I like eating the fish but they're the ugliest animals I've ever seen."

"I agree but what a thing looks like doesn't mean it isn't good to eat."

They took down the telescope and carried it back to the ship. David disappeared into his bedroom, while John settled onto his bed to read. He half thought of catching up on the news in the empire but he had long ago made it a rule never to mix his vacation and the realities of the empire. He finally drifted off to sleep.

John was startled awake by the door opening.

Elizabeth peeked her head inside. "Oops, sorry, I didn't mean to wake you up. I was checking up on you. You've slept so long I keep thinking you've died or something."

"You'll never get that pleasure. I was up earlier to get something to eat then spent some time with David looking at the stars."

"Oh, that's why he's not up yet." She closed the door and walked beside the bed. "Mind if I join you?"

"You need to ask?"

Doom

She slid into the bed. "I missed you."
Their lips met.

13

David's stomach growled. He looked at the clock. "Heck, it's after eight. I slept in," he mumbled. Of course, hours during holidays meant nothing. One slept and lived when you wanted. John had taught him that. The darkness might slow you down but you missed a great part of your life if you did not experience life at night. A whole other side of life existed there; the stars and a full set of new animals.

But he was hungry now and John had promised him they would go fishing which would lead to even more learning, as it was their own private time to talk and to hear the stories John could tell.

He whipped himself out of bed and went into the corridor. He spoke softly at his mother's door. If she was not up, he did not want to wake her. There was no answer. He walked farther up the corridor to the kitchen.

"Good morning, John," he opened.

"Good morning, David. I figured it's only been a few hours and you'd wake up famished. I've already cooked you some pancakes. You probably smelled them."

"No, this ship is so big you really can't hear or smell anything from one cabin to another. Why do you always vacation with such a big ship? Heck, it holds about thirty people, doesn't it?"

"Yes, about that. When I'm on vacation with you guys, I want you two to be comfortable." John filled a plate with food and placed it on the table.

"It must be costing you a fortune."

"Not really; anyway, just sit down and eat."

John watched him.

David noticed. "Why are you staring at me?"

"I must have looked like you when I was a kid. I don't remember too much. I wonder if I ate as much as you do. You're so skinny and eat so much."

"I can't help it. I get hungry. I eat. I get hungry. I eat again. It's easy."

"Yes, I guess it is," he said with a knowing smile.

The door to John's room opened and out came his mother, in her pyjamas, rubbing the sleep from her eyes.

David smiled. "Good morning, mom. Did you get lost and wander into the wrong room?" he teased.

"I was just making his bed," she replied matter-of-factly.

"Yeah, making his bed again, or is it 'making it in bed'."

She ignored him and sat down to eat.

John began cleaning up while she ate. David finished his meal, left, and went to the canoe beside the water.

When she was done, he pulled her dishes off the table, put them in the cleaner, and turned them on.

"I promised to go fishing with David this morning. We can have fresh fish for lunch."

"That'd be nice. I'll go get my clothes and we can get showered up for the day – together."

"Oh? You must have missed me."

She smiled. "More than you'll ever know."

After their rather lengthy shower, they dressed. She left to make the beds. He left to join David on the shore.

When David saw him, he began to push the canoe into the water. John was soon behind him and they paddled to their favourite fishing spot.

David quickly caught a fish.

"That was a great fish you caught. We'll be able to have some for tomorrow," John said. He turned his head away from the fish toward the boy and stared for a few minutes.

David was feeling a little uncomfortable but said nothing.

"You and I are getting along quite well, do you agree?"

"Yes," David responded.

He continued to stare. "You like me quite a lot and missed me while I was gone."

"Why are you asking me?" David asked, quite puzzled.

John ignored the question. "Your mother is a little harder to read. Her actions inform me that she is very interested in me but her mind is still undecided and maybe a little confused. Has she said anything about me?"

"You mean does she like you, or not?"

John smiled at his prescience. "Yes."

"Have you asked her?"

"She doesn't answer directly."

David sat quietly for some seconds. "Can you read people's minds?"

"Why do you ask that?"

"You didn't ask me if I liked you. You told me I did."

"Oh, I didn't realise I did that . . . No, not exactly; I've been told I have an extremely sensitive mind."

"So, you pick up vibes or something like that?"

"I have no idea. It's hard to explain. Now my question . . ."

"My dad hurt her a lot and turned her off men. You can understand that she's not going to just open up to a man again."

"She told me about that."

"More importantly, do you love her?"

"I've been too busy with my life to be interested in women but about thirteen years ago I met a wonderful woman who saved my life in many ways. I had fallen out of a building and she picked me up off the street and nursed me back to health. She was a very loving person and it was easy to fall in love. I was going to retire and marry her but she was murdered, and I have never been able to forgive the whole empire for that. She is still with me and I can never say goodbye. She was my only true love."

"So, the two of you are alike, where neither one can give love to the other or is afraid to."

"We seem to be locked in that loop, yes. I may sound crazy but I've been thinking about my old girlfriend a lot lately. A good time is on a mountain top. That allows me to feel so much closer to her."

"She's dead, John," David said matter-of-factly.

John ignored him. "I didn't do as much mountaineering before she died but I picked it up after. Do you want to know what she's saying?"

"You can talk to dead people?" David asked, surprised.

"Not exactly."

"Then how can you say this dead woman is saying something to you?" David questioned incredulously.

"Her name is Emily."

"Maybe you are crazy!"

"On the mountain top, we connected and, crazy or not, she wants me to find love again, or at least wants me to share my love. When she was alive, I told Emily I would never give my love to anyone else but her. I like your mother but I want to know how she feels about me. If she's ready to accept a new man in her life, I'm willing to accept a new woman in mine."

"This sounds like a business deal."

"For people who've been hurt as much as we have, we have to be sure. We need to know our feelings are real. I think each of us is also afraid to hurt the other. If I tell her I love her and get rejected, then I get hurt and vice versa."

"I don't know what to say. As far as I know, my mom is crazy about you. I've never seen her as happy as I've seen her with you. I want the two of you together. I think you'd make an awesome dad and a wonderful pair. If you tell her that you love her, and you don't tell her that crazy part, I think she'll say, yes."

"You think so?"

"Well, with women you can never be sure but I think so." David grinned.

"And I'd make an awesome dad, huh?" John smiled back.

"I just put that in, from me."

The two of them paddled back to shore, pulled the canoe near the rock, entered the spaceship, and looked around.

"Um, your mom is nowhere on the ship," John said puzzled. "She doesn't usually wander off near lunch."

"Let's cook lunch with the expectation she'll be back."

"Sounds good to me."

John cleaned and filleted the fish, while David got the frying pan and spices ready. He also set the table for three.

When she had not arrived and the food was served there was tension in the air, until they heard a thump at the entrance to the ship.

"Hi boys, wow, look at the lunch we're going to have." She was carrying a huge bundle of flowers in her arms. "I saw you two pulling in the fish and decided to collect some of the flowers I noticed growing along the path of our last hike. I thought I'd contribute, too."

David said with a big smile, "Wow, they smell nice."

John just smiled.

In minutes, she had placed the flowers in a vase and everyone was ready to eat.

In the afternoon, John showed them the pictures he had taken on the climb up and down the mountain. His guests were both fascinated. In some cases, they questioned how he had taken some of them, particularly the ones he had taken from the side of a cliff.

They had a wonderful supper together, followed by a huge bonfire. From its glow, John knelt in front of Elizabeth and produced a small box.

She sat there staring at it for several minutes, stunned. She took it from his hand and slowly opened it. "Oh, my gosh. It's beautiful. It's a pink diamond from Sirico. If I remember correctly, it's the only planet in the empire where you can find them and it's huge. This must have cost you a fortune."

"Well, it wasn't cheap. To top it off, I'll be retiring, so I won't have to travel anymore. It's about time I retired for good. I almost did it for Emily. Once she was gone, there was no point in retiring anymore, as work kept my mind off her."

"You mean, you'll be staying with us full time? This is too good to be true. This can't be happening. Too much has happened in my past to believe this is true. I'm with you forever?"

"Yes, I'll always be with you from now on, I promise."

She just stared at him incredulously. "How about Emily?"

John glanced over at David and then back at her. "You're my number one girl, now . . . so, will you marry me, Elizabeth?"

"Well, David comes along with me. David, what do you think?"

"Come on, Mom, just say, yes."

"Okay! Yes, yes, yes." She handed the box with the ring over to David, so he could see it then John took it from the box and slid it onto her finger.

She held it out to John, so he could see it on her finger and he raised her hand to his lips and kissed the ring. She felt like a princess. They hugged each other for a while then held hands until the fire died down. David stayed back to extinguish the fire, while John and Elizabeth returned to the spaceship for an early night.

14

It had been a glorious two days. Their time on this planet was nearing an end but John was going to request an extension of vacation time for another few weeks then they would head off to an inhabited planet where they could get married and start their life together. It was as if they were having their honeymoon before their marriage. Elizabeth was happier than she had ever been in her life and John had accepted someone else into his life. David was enjoying himself too. He was pleased his mother was so happy and relished the day when he could call John, Dad.

She got up early to get breakfast started for the men who were going to head out for some heavy fishing in the morning. In the afternoon, all three of them would boat over to a small island for swimming along a beautiful sandy beach. How different it was from her life at home where everything was so automated and robots did most of the work. Despite the fact they had some comfort in using the spaceship as a base, this was so primitive but she had come to enjoy it. She could see why John was so attracted to this way of life.

John and David finally dragged themselves out of their beds, ate quickly, and scurried away to bring home food for the lunch table. They paddled over to their favourite fishing spot and David dozed off from the peacefulness, while John manned both lines.

About an hour after they had settled in and caught five fish, John suddenly noticed Elizabeth waving excitedly on the shore. He was too far away to hear anything she might have been saying but she appeared to be waving him back to shore. He was puzzled but he reeled in the lines, picked up the paddle and got into position to begin the journey. John's action woke up David who grabbed the second paddle and began to help.

David looked at his watch and asked, "What's the matter, John? Why are we going back to shore so soon?"

"I don't know. Mom has called us back to camp."

"She's not there now."

"I think she went back into the ship."

"Are you sure she called us back?"

"She looked anxious about something."

Soon, they were back on shore. They pulled the boat onto the sand bank and went into the ship carrying the fish. John froze in his tracks.

In front of him was Elizabeth with a perplexed look on her face, a young space lieutenant, and an older man who looked as if he was in his sixties.

The older man spoke first. "Hi, John, I'm sorry to disturb you during your leave. I would never have done this if it wasn't for a good reason."

"You know there's nothing that important that can't wait," John responded gruffly. "I'm with friends, too. When I disable the ship's beacon, it means I don't want you to disturb me," he said firmly.

"Yes, I'm aware of that. It took us a while to find you. It was only your registration to visit this planet that finally led us here."

The older man reached into a pouch he had in his hand and pulled an envelope from it. He handed it to John.

At first, John resisted taking it but curiosity got the better of him. He reached out, grabbed it, pulled it to him, lifted the flap, and peered inside. He could immediately see it bore the imperial seal. He raised his eyes to the older man's. "What's with this?"

"You'll have to see it."

John looked over at Elizabeth then at David, and then back at the older man. "Joseph Engelmann, I'd like you to meet my fiancée, Elizabeth Johansson and her son, David. This young man is Lieutenant . . ." He squinted to look at the officer's name strip. ". . . Bagwana. From his insignia, he's a flying ace. Joe is one of my superiors I report to, depending on where I am in the empire."

He turned to Elizabeth, slid out the contents of the envelope and handed it to her. "You'll likely never see anything like this in your lifetime again. It's an imperial commission. I've never seen one before either."

He turned back to Joe and the lieutenant and asked, "Would the two of you please leave us for a couple of minutes."

The two men understood immediately, walked toward the door of the craft, and left.

John looked at Elizabeth deeply and said softly. "I guess Joe has blown my cover. Sweetheart, you've constantly asked me what I do for a living . . . I'm an imperial special agent." He waited for what he said to sink in.

The first reaction came from David. "Whoa . . . that explains it!"

John responded, "Explains what?"

"Why you're away a lot of time and why you have those scars . . ." He blushed with embarrassment. "Sorry, I don't think I said that right."

John smiled and David relaxed.

"Why they're likely here is to give me another mission. I can turn this down and I will. This is straight from the emperor, so it must be particularly important. I've cut us off from the news, so I have no clue what the mission is. I'll let Joe know I'm not interested."

David responded, "Aren't you going to find out what it is?"

"I'd rather not."

John turned to Elizabeth. "I told you I was retiring and I am. At fifty-two, I'm done negotiating, fighting, killing, arresting . . . I can either take a desk job like Joe, or quit completely and the latter is my preference. I have a lifetime expense, right? You may not know it but I don't get a salary, instead, I have the right to spend what I want, hence the expense of using the ship we have now and the cost of the ring on your finger. We're expected not to abuse that right but I've spent my whole life scrimping and I think this will not cause a stir at headquarters. Agents are well respected there.

"You're silent and in shock, yes but you should say what's on your mind."

The shock held her spellbound. She did not know what to say. What were the odds of anyone running into an agent?

David spoke for her. "Do you know most people have never heard about imperial agents? There are only about 100 of them in the whole empire. That means meeting one has the same odds or less than winning a lottery." His face was beaming proudly. "Whoa, I met an imperial special agent."

"I'll call in our visitors and give them a nice meal of fresh fish then send them on their way." He leaned over and gave Elizabeth a gentle kiss on her cheek. He gazed at her for a few seconds.

John continued. "I couldn't tell you I was an agent. Our identities are secret. I would have told you when I officially retired. I was going to retire, marry you, and say what I wanted. You have quite a mix of emotions right now but it doesn't matter what I was."

"You can read minds, can't you? I can feel you," she muttered quietly.

He turned away, walked to the door and called out, "You're welcome to stay for lunch. I must walk away from this mission if indeed that's what you're bringing. We're planning to stay a few days more on this planet, then I'm retiring and we're marrying."

He called the two men who entered the ship and sat down while David and Elizabeth set the table. John prepared and cooked the fish within minutes and served.

Once everyone was seated and lunch began, Joe opened the conversation. "John, I think it's important that you look at this one."

"I'm not interested."

"Maybe it can be a family decision."

"I don't think so. We aren't even a family yet. Let us at least get that far. They aren't even past the stage of getting over my being an agent. I didn't tell them about that yet. You've introduced it prematurely."

"Sorry about that but we had to contact you. You were specifically chosen for this mission. Since you've turned off your beacon, I'm guessing you've cut yourselves off from what is going on in the news lately."

"That's right; I'm tired of hearing about robberies, killings, and other bad news stories. I don't need to hear about them when I'm on vacation."

"The latest news is not the normal news. The empire is in peril. These are black days."

There were several seconds of quiet.

"Isn't something like that the job of the military?" John said condescendingly.

"I wish it was. May we bring you up-to-date?"

John's head dropped toward his chest. He raised it again and looked at Elizabeth, with sad, exhausted eyes. "It's up to you, sweetheart." He sighed. "If I'm not taking this job, I'd rather not hear about it. I know it's been thirty-three years since an agent turned down a mission. I've never turned one down myself but if you want me to hear about it, I'll do it for you."

A surge of panic overcame her. She had hesitated in making the final decision to take him into her heart. Something had gnawed at her; was it intuition, or some premonition? She was hoping this would be some routine mission. How could she make him turn down a direct request of the emperor, especially because this was the only one, he had received?

She took a deep breath and said, "You should at least see what the problem is. After all, it may be that the emperor is in trouble with a coupe or some danger like that. We would find out eventually when we returned to civilisation and we just might regret not being involved."

John sighed deeply then gave his assent, "Okay, at least I should see what I'm turning down."

Joe took the emperor's mission pad gently from Elizabeth and turned it on. He handed it over to John who placed it on the table, so everyone could see the screen. John's thumbprint and image activated it.

They first saw the face of the emperor followed by recordings, with commentary, of everything that had happened with the thing that had attacked their empire; from the attack on the "P" Class vessel to the current almost chaos in that sector of the empire. Following that were scenes of discussions of scientists and specialists on possible courses of action, leading to a personal plea from the emperor for John's help.

When it was over, he looked at Elizabeth who was rocking gently back and forth in a state of shock. David just sat there pale and blank.

"This is a job for the military, what the hell can I do?" John finally asked coarsely.

Joe responded earnestly, "You heard the discussions on that. An attack by the military may aggravate the situation, not correct it."

"Well, again, what the hell can an agent do and why are they asking for me? I'm old. They should use someone with more energy, or am I expendable?"

"You heard that, too. That's probably why they picked you, because of your experience. They know you are the only hope they have. If you can't find a way to solve this, then nobody can."

John got up and left the ship.

Elizabeth sat for a few minutes then followed. When she got outside, she spotted him immediately. He was sitting on her thinking rock. She walked down to join him.

She had tears flowing down her cheeks. "I knew this was going to happen," she sobbed. "This was a fairy-tale dream that couldn't have a happy ending. I guess I am fated to be alone."

"It doesn't have to happen that way."

"You know you can't walk away from this," she said forcefully.

"Yes, I can, and will. Surely others can take care of it, or maybe nobody can and I throw my life away for nothing. When I get a task, I can quickly size up the situation and come up with one or two approaches to deal with it. This time, I'm blank. I don't want to do this anymore. I want to settle down with you. I just want to live the rest of my life in peace. You are my shining star, the Good Earth, my Jane, and that's all I want. Why can't I just have that? I lost Emily, must I lose you too?"

"Why did we have to meet anyway?" she cried out in anguish. "I've thought of this so much over the last three years. The first three we didn't see each other much but I never wanted to get involved with you. Somehow, I knew you were like poison, that somehow you were too good to be true. We were never meant to be, you were part of some other great plan."

He could feel her angst and it swallowed him up. He stood up and embraced her tightly as if they were fusing. In a moment, their minds joined. They shared thoughts. They probed their emotions that had fused into one. To Elizabeth, it was as if she was in a vast ocean and the two of them were swimming. Suddenly, a huge wave hit her. All her fears and uncertainties were engulfed and she felt complete peace. Somehow, she knew she would see him again. Somehow, she knew they would be together forever. Somehow, she saw Emily and how beautiful she had been; no, how beautiful she was. She was real. She knew how intense the bond between them had been, and she shared that. She understood how Emily had affected him and had affected her now, too. To John, he knew it was okay. He knew Elizabeth accepted, his father approved, and Emily just loved.

He broke the mind-bond and Elizabeth began to slump to the ground, drained but John swept her up in his arms and carried her back to the ship. He nodded to the two men as he passed and entered her room to place her on her bed.

He went into his room to pack. David joined him, asking. "Need any help?"

He paused then said, "Thanks anyway."

"You're going, aren't you?"

"It's one of the hardest things I've had to do. I love you two. You're a great young man. You have a wonderful life ahead of you and you have a great mom. I don't know how I'm going to beat that thing but I'm going to try my best. Despite the dismal-looking odds, I'm going to come back. I'll be with you again, okay? I promise you I'll come back."

"That would be nice. Mom needs you; you know. She has never been so happy before and it would be sad to see her sink into her old self again. What did she say when you told her you were going to do it."

"She understood. I didn't talk to her but she understood this was meant to be. I had to have this one last mission then I could retire. Each person has some great mission to accomplish while in this universe. Everything else you did before, prepares you for this one role, like school. Now, I'm ready for my final exam. I'm not sure what to do but in the next few days that it takes to cross to the other side of the empire, I'll be as ready as I can to meet my nemesis."

"I guess I can't go with you?"

"Climb your first mountain, live a full life. You'll know when you're ready. My father was a hero you know; a great hero who saved many lives. I always wanted to be like him but knew I never could. I only hoped I could be even a quarter of the man my father was. I guess that kept me going and striving for more. I hope that, at the end of my life, someone could say I was a good man."

"I can't say that about my dad," David responded.

"Everyone has at least one hero, mine just happened to be my father."

"If someone were to ask me who my hero was, I would have to say it was you, especially now. Not too many people would drop out of their own lives and try to save millions of lives. Even if you fail, at least you tried."

"I haven't thought of it that way. I saw all my missions as a duty, my job . . . well, whether I can do anything or not, I have to get to the other side of our empire quickly."

Soon, John was done. He did not take much with him; only the essentials.

He left his room with a small backpack and David behind him. Elizabeth had returned to the kitchen. He stopped just outside the door, gazing at her.

"So, you're all ready to go?" she asked. She stood tall and proud.

"Yes, I don't take much stuff . . . Say the word and I'll put this down and ask these gentlemen to leave."

She looked long and hard at him. "Do you think you can beat this thing?"

"No, but I'll do my best. This thing seems to kill instantly and nobody knows much about it, so I have no information about what I can do to stop it but some people and a computer program can say I can."

"That sounds promising," she said sardonically. "Can you hug it and drown it in the ocean?"

He laughed. "I'll certainly try," he quieted to whisper, "Me, Tarzan."

"I'll be waiting for you." Then she lowered her voice. "Me, Jane."

He walked over to her and wrapped his arms around her. "I promise to see you again. I've never lost a mission, and, although it looks bleak, I don't intend to lose this one either. There must be a way of beating this killer."

She whispered into his ear, "If anyone can, it'll be you. I can't hold you back, as you may be the only one in the entire empire who can save it. You'll save trillions of lives; somehow, you're special. I don't know what you did a few minutes ago but maybe your special gift may be what'll save you. The emperor has singled you out to do this."

He said quietly, "Yes, me, Tarzan and I have you rooting for me."

Their lips met for several seconds then they parted.

John walked over to David. "Well, young man, another trip. I hope I won't be long." He held out his hand.

"Let's, not mince words, you're not coming back," he said with certainty.

"I wouldn't be so sure, young fellow."

"I'm really glad to have met you. I had hoped to learn so much more from you. I think you're awesome and cool." His eyes were glassing over. He united his right hand with John's and gave it a shake.

John reached over with his other hand and grabbed David's shaking arm. "Best of the best to you. You're a fine young man. Look after your mom for me while I'm gone."

"I will."

He glanced once more toward Elizabeth and blew her a kiss.

She blew one back and said softly, "Bye, Tarzan."

He gave her a wink and then turned toward Joe. "What's the plan?"

"You're heading out with the lieutenant because you've got to get out to the target as quickly as you can. I'll get your family home."

"Take good care of them."

"You've got my word. They'll get home safely."

He turned and waved to the two of them. Elizabeth was fighting back tears. She was trying not to let them show.

John and the lieutenant walked for a while up the shoreline and, before leaving sight of the campsite, John took a quick look to see David helping Joe carry the canoe back to the ship. It was another ten minutes to the speeder. They had landed it far enough away not to disturb the family and effectively do it undetected.

They were soon there. He halted to look at the speeder. John had never seen one of these sleek versatile vessels before. It seated only two people and was not built for comfort but for speed in space and the atmosphere of a planet.

John turned to the lieutenant. "So, what are your orders?" he asked with a sigh.

"Make sure I keep you alive and get you to the other end of the empire, yesterday, if I can. Besides, we have the fastest ship in the empire, and we've equipped it with everything you need to keep informed of what's happened and what's happening. It would normally take about two weeks or more to cross that distance but I'm going to try to do it in a week. That means crossing through at least one wormhole, although they're risky. Sometimes you can end up taking longer that way, too."

"Two weeks? I thought it would take more than five or more weeks."

"Yes, you're right but these speeders are made for speed. They're very small with very light mass and a super-size propulsion system. It's ninety per cent propulsion.

"It's a long way from the ancient rocket propulsion systems of early technology Earth. That technology would have required thousands of years to do that. Even travelling at the speed of light, would have taken centuries. Those people would never have left that solar system without the invention of the inter-stellar drive, which can, in effect, travel faster than light. Of course, it doesn't do that, because one can't break a law of physics but this drive uses a property of the universe to cut across it through interstitial space. Neat, huh?"

John was familiar with the subject. Physics always fascinated him. "Yes, humanity has learned so much from those early days but I love the more primitive life as you can see."

"If you need anything, let me know. Your job is simply to prepare yourself for your task. The military has been given orders to supply you with everything you need. You want ten battleships, they're yours. Right now, you have the commanding authority of the VD himself."

They entered the ship and fastened themselves down. When they took off and flew over the campsite, Elizabeth looked up, waved at the ship, and could no longer hold in her anguish as she gave a loud piercing scream that reverberated throughout the mountains. David ran over to console her.

Then the speeder was gone.

15

John immediately went to work reviewing everything that had happened over the past few weeks. He considered the advice of the experts; and listened to the opinions of the military brass and governors. He watched the videos of the attacks, from the first one in the "P" Class vessel, slightly smaller than the one he had used at his campsite, to what was happening now. Still, he was stumped. He could not determine how he could counteract anything like that. The option to use an antimatter blast on the thing that had been rejected by the experts looked like the best option in his view. If it made things worse, so be it, they were not much better off as it was but if it ended the thing, then it would be done. The lieutenant had said he had the power to order the military to do anything, as he had the authority of the VD behind him. He had one problem though; a higher authority had signed an order that no attack was to be made against the thing – the emperor himself. That option was not open to him.

He was not happy he was not allowed to contact anyone but agency members while he was on duty but he communicated with Joe about Elizabeth and David. Joe told him they had arrived at their destination safely and they wished him luck and missed him. He asked Joe to let them know he was on his way, he loved them and would be back as soon as he could. He also requested that, for the record, he inform the agency that Elizabeth be considered his wife, so she and David would be entitled to a very generous death benefit and pension should anything happen to him.

On the third day of their voyage, Lieutenant Bagwana woke up John to prepare him for the wormhole jump.

"Sorry to get you up but you really should be awake for the event; first, because you may get jostled, and second because it's a sight to see. You haven't made a jump before, have you?"

"Nope. I'm looking forward to this though. I like doing things at least once. If I achieve anything on this mission, I'll have at least done this."

"Well, I beg to differ. Performing this mission will be a lot more worthwhile than going through a wormhole.

"I'm almost ready to go. I must warn you these jumps are risky. Almost all the known holes have been tested and most are too tenuous to use for anything. Although, we find they don't put people in the past or future as some early scientists predicted they do allow for what seems like instantaneous jumps in space, as if you were popping out of our universe and returning somewhere else in our universe, however, they are very unstable. Some last for seconds some for years, and others can move you to unexpected locations. We test them by sending un-peopled probes which respond with what happened to them. They also only work one way. The other end seems not to exist.

"The one we'll be going through is one of the more stable ones but it can still be quirky, so let's hope it behaves for us.

"Here we go."

The ship shuddered as it passed the event line. There was a tremendous light flash then a kaleidoscope of colours contorting around the ship as the space contorted in front of them. Then, in another flash, it was over with another shudder of the ship.

"I'm giving the ship a chance to determine where we are. As you can see, we seemed to have made it safely through but this ship is specially built for travel through the wormholes. The most important property is that the ship is small but also buffered and shielded properly to withstand the event horizon. Commercial or large military vessels would not be able to get through one. The holes can be quite tiny in size or occasionally large enough to take a small ship, as this one is."

The lieutenant looked down at his control panel and said, "Shit . . . pardon my language, sir. We didn't make up as much time as I had hoped. We moved but it was not in the right direction. There is another wormhole we can try not too far away which might be able to make up some time from that location. I'll try that one. We'll get there in about a day and a half."

"What's our target?" John asked.

"We're trying to guess the trajectory of the thing and get us somewhere not too far in front of it. So far, I'm guessing here," and he showed John the location on the three-dimensional holographic map in front of them.

John examined the chart. "It looks as if almost all the ships are tied up with evacuations. This cruiser, number 3899-3731, over here seems to be doing other work. I want everyone off the ship and have it ready for me at our arrival spot."

"You can use this one if you want."

"Yes, I can but I want to present something tempting to that thing. It may not register a small ship. To help, I want the cruiser loaded with cattle or other large animals. We should not kill anyone else needlessly."

"So, you're luring it to you."

"It doesn't make sense to run away from it. I may only get one shot. If I die, it doesn't make any difference when. I've been told time is of the essence."

"You're right. That's why we're using the wormholes."

"Tell them I also want a spacesuit my size on board; in case."

"Will do, sir. I've done some calculations and the cruiser will have time to meet us at our target."

"Excellent."

"So, do you have a plan?"

"I know as much as I did when I started and that was nothing, so I have as good a plan as I had, which is nothing. I won't have been the first person to be sent off on a suicide mission."

The next day, he received word from the cruiser that the captain wanted to remain on board with him to manage the ship for him. John did not think it was necessary but he honoured the captain's tradition of remaining with his ship to the end.

Late that day, they neared the next wormhole.

"We're fifteen minutes away now. This hole's trickier than the last one. To fulfil my obligation to keep you safe, I want you to get into the emergency pod," the lieutenant implored.

"What do you mean by tricky?"

"It's fairly good, like ninety per cent, or more, to get us to where I want us to go but about thirty per cent of the time it can give us a rough time. You might be shaken up a lot."

"Can we just avoid it?"

"Yes, but this jump should wipe out a week of travel time and that's my other obligation; to get you to your destination as quickly as possible."

"What about you?"

"I'll be well strapped in. I want to be able to be by the controls if needed. Please get into the pod, now."

He was familiar with the use of pods. It was mandatory training for space travellers. It was a life raft for space. It was well padded to protect a person from shock and provided an occupant with basic survival necessities, like water and food. It also had a basic propulsion system and a beacon for retrieval.

John pressed the button to open the pod and its lid snapped open. He got into it and told the pod to seal him in. The lid shut, he heard the sound of rushing air and felt the weight of material pressing around his body.

For several minutes, he just lay there and waited then he felt it; the pod seemed as if it was going in several directions at once. He became extremely disoriented then vomited and blacked out.

16

The marauder had picked up its pace and was now moving more quickly from planet to planet. It might have been because it was trying to compensate for the constant evacuation of planets ahead of it to get more food. As well, the lives it was taking could have been energising it. So far, over thirty occupied planets have been attacked. The new military base, which had been built near the edge of the frontiers of the empire, was now in the updated evacuation zone and some planets with significant populations were also now in this zone.

So far, everyone who wanted to leave a planet was able to but that would change soon. Most of those who stayed were choosing to commit suicide rather than be killed by the silent attacker. Problems were also developing on where to move the evacuees; how far they should be moved away and where these people were going to be housed. Facilities were quickly becoming scarce and it would get worse.

Adjacent solar systems to the afflicted area were now refusing to send more ships to help with the evacuation, as they knew some of them would soon begin to evacuate their people. The emperor had commandeered many passenger ships from the interior of the empire to assist in the evacuation and they were on the way to help with even more military craft but more would be needed. Within weeks, the entire system would break down as the millions of people who needed help would become billions, then trillions.

There was unease in three sectors and many people were emigrating from those sectors, further taxing the transportation system.

In the imperial headquarters, the mood was gloomy. There were briefings hourly now and the upper echelon of the government was rotating their schedules so someone was available at all hours of the day.

The door opened and John, the imperial conscience, walked into the council chamber. Mark, the VD, was the only person there at the time.

"Good morning, Mark."

"Good morning, John. Anything new?"

"Another planet was attacked around three in the morning. We estimate another one will be attacked later in the week. It's continuing to be aggressive but we're still managing to stay ahead of the monster. We've received more ships from the centre and more are on the way. We should continue to receive ships in waves from now on but this is unsustainable.

"As you know, our agent went through Wentworth's Hole but did not make much headway. Lieutenant Bagwana decided to take advantage of Borowski's Hole to gain more time. He'll be in a position in a few hours."

John said, "Each day that passes without our agent in action will result in thousands and thousands of people being killed by that monster. Going through the hole is a risky move but if it works out, they'll gain a lot of time."

In frustration, Mark countered, "Does it make much difference? It's just one more life lost. We've had maybe a hundred thousand people or more killed at this point and the numbers are going to grow exponentially as our inability to get people out in time increases. This thing still has a 100 per cent kill rate. We're asking this agent to engage it, to survive, and do something about this thing – kind of a tall order."

"I know. I've had the profiles of virtually everyone in the empire run through our computer and I keep getting the same results. We have no plan B. This agent is our best and only viable option. I hate having no options. We have all our eggs in one basket. We try this idea then we're done. We raise the white flag."

"We still have the antimatter bomb."

"And a fifty-fifty chance of making our problem worse . . . How's the emperor?"

"Still in a slump. Here we are talking rather casually about what's going on in the empire and he's so shaken by what's going on."

"That's the best part of our system. We, the bureaucrats, coldly do what we need to do, while the emperor, the heart of the empire, keeps us focused on why we're here – the people. We provide the options and he, in the end, must make the toughest decisions. I love our system. The empire is so large that a democracy wouldn't work, the representatives would dissolve into indecision and worry about getting re-elected."

Maybe your first job today should be to console the emperor. Our special agent is still on his way, so that should be some consolation. Have you eaten yet?"

"No."

"Join him for breakfast."

"I might just do that."

"I'd better head off to bed. We've had a long night . . . See you later." Mark left for home to spend time with his family and then get some sleep.

John checked over the updates from the previous eight hours and made a few notes on his pad. The door slid open and the admiral entered. She bowed to the conscience and said hello.

John looked up at her sadly and responded, "Good morning, I'm glad you're here. The rest of the team should be here soon. I'll pop in to see the emperor. I'll be back later."

She acknowledged with a nod.

He got up, left the room, walked to the emperor's office, and tapped on the door.

The emperor looked in the corner of his pad and saw who was at the door. He allowed entry.

"Good morning, sir." John bowed briefly.

"Good morning, John. Did you have a good rest?"

"Yes, I did. Did you get any rest?"

"Not much."

"A good sleep will do you good, sir. Everything is under control."

"Yes, I know it is. You guys are all doing an excellent job. We're doing everything we can. I see our agent is on his way. It'll be some time before he can engage the thing. I'm a bit concerned about choosing to use Borowski's Hole, though. It's known for its instability."

"We want him to get there quickly, sir. It's the lieutenant's choice. He's experienced in using wormholes."

"We might save time using it but we can't risk losing our agent."

"I agree with you but it's a trade-off. I'm sure he'll be safe. Mark has ordered three other speeders to be at the other end of the wormhole just in case something goes wrong. They'll be ready to pick them up and complete the journey; that way we won't waste any time. The thing we're up against is moving much more quickly and you need to deal with it soon.

"In the evacuation process, I've looked at all the current reports and it appears everything is on schedule. I see that personnel have managed to pick up the pace of the evacuations and we've ramped up production of personnel carriers. That'll help to relieve stress on our transportation system, in time."

The emperor dropped his gaze to his desk. "But at what cost? The people, for the most part, are holding together well. We've had a few cases of looting. The stress is getting to a lot of people but when they start losing faith in the system, we're going to start seeing a breakdown in discipline. It'll start near the affected location and spread farther out. As more people become uprooted it'll get worse, then we run the risk of rioting. Authority will diminish and the empire, now affected by the crises and unable to do anything about it, will fall into chaos."

"Don't forget we're not done yet. We still have options."

"Yes, we have our agent and we have the last desperate action with nuclear or antimatter weapons," the emperor responded.

"And any of those might work."

"Might . . ."

"Let's see what our agent can do. Remember, I met him about fifteen years ago. He's got an extremely quick mind. He beat me in chess every game I played him, except for one game. He was the agent who beat the smugglers off Tarlan. They used every trick in the book to try to get him to tell them what he knew about their operations and he didn't break. The computer rates him with a very strong psychological profile."

"Is the computer considering this entity we're up against to be a thinking being, otherwise why would it propose him as an option?"

"What we asked the computer to do was to provide the most likely agent to deal with this thing, although we then extended the search to the total population in case it could come up with someone else better. He still came up on top. We never asked who the second top individual was but I wouldn't be surprised if it was me." John smiled smugly.

"You're trying to cheer me up with humour, are you?"

"Well, the agent and I got along so well that he chose my name as one of his aliases and he's still using it. It may also be that I was the only person who ever beat him in a chess match. That proves he's brilliant." John smiled with the grin of a Cheshire cat and noticed the emperor had smiled slightly.

"The computer must have used some valid criteria to select him," the emperor said more seriously.

"Sure, but remember, it doesn't have much to go on. We just ask the question and it makes some assumptions on the problem and the characteristics of the people being evaluated. It would likely decide this object is not physical, so the best qualities a person would have against it are their non-physical attributes. So, it would look for a person with the strongest non-physical attributes, ergo, a person with extremely high psychological traits. John has one almost unique additional ability. He is suspected to be a telepath."

"He can read minds?"

"Likely, and maybe that is why he was singled out. If the marauder is a living entity, he may be able to at least find out who it is."

"That's interesting. I asked the computer what his chances were of success and all it told me was it didn't have enough information."

"Of course, it would do that because, if it has no information, it can't calculate a probability. I took the liberty to have it tell me what the chances were anyway and it gave me zero per cent or a number so small it may as well have been zero. A computer always does that. You ask it to calculate something when it doesn't have enough information and gives you some ridiculously small odds."

"In this case, maybe it's not so ridiculous," the emperor stated matter-of-factly. He added, "Have you eaten yet?"

"No, I wanted to find out what was going on first."

"What would you like to eat?" he said as he opened an outside communicator to the kitchen.

"Just two eggs with toast are fine for me."

The emperor added that he would like cream cheese on a bagel with black coffee.

John added, "I'll have my usual coffee, too . . . How are your kids?"

"Okay, I think they miss me. I spend a lot of time in here now."

"You should get out more and split your time between the people in the council chamber and your kids."

"It's too noisy in the council chamber. I can hear them in here if I want to."

"Have they come up with selection criteria for evacuation yet?"

"I hate that part. We no longer have the luxury of taking everybody. Soon, we're going to have to select people. Sure, maybe everyone can be collected in some circumstances but in others, we're going to have a problem."

"I know, it's going to be tough."

"I've got it now. I'll have the computer read it to us."

The voice of the computer filled the room, "The order of priority for evacuating people will be: families or people with children under eighteen; orphan children under eighteen; people under thirty in good health; women under forty in good health; men under forty in good health than healthy people over forty by birth date. Health will be determined by the severity of chronic illness then the severity of acute illness."

As they listened to the listing, the butler entered with their food and they ate.

For about thirty minutes they discussed the options then the emperor approved them without change. John left to stay with his family for a while before returning to work in the council chamber.

It was on Mark's night shift when the news came that they had lost contact with the speeder after entry into the wormhole. There was panic in the council chamber.

Within thirty minutes though, things calmed down, when one of the three speeders placed strategically in an area where they expected the vessel carrying the agent to arrive, picked up the pod's beacon. Within another thirty minutes, they had confirmed that the agent survived the passage through the wormhole but Lieutenant Bagwana did not. The hole had cracked the spine of the craft, leaking the air from the cabin into the vacuum of space. The pod was picked up shortly after that and the agent was on his way again. The tragedy had cost the life of the lieutenant but had gained six days in travel time. The agent would be at his rendezvous with the cruiser in less than three days.

The increased evacuation area was creating a difficult logistical challenge, as three of the planets in the zone had populations of over one billion people. Taurus, with a population of over nine billion, was of particular concern. The military was assisting in building the ramps necessary for docking the ships as they arrived. Many ships did not require ramps but the larger ones did. It would take many days to evacuate all the people. The military set up the schedule so the planet would begin the process before some of those closer to the marauder. The governor of one of those closer planets complained about the schedule, to no avail, and she had begun to interfere in the process by trying to purchase help from private firms who were already involved in the centrally controlled process, in effect, offering the firms a higher price to evacuate their planet first.

Other problems started on Taurus. When the ships started to land, there were long line-ups at the bussing points as many people were not following the designated schedules and were trying to jump the queue. The first day ran rather smoothly, despite this. By the second day, fighting began at some of the bussing points and one of the loading docks. By the end of the day, one city had riots in the streets. Planetary police were able to deal with the situation but there would be no recourse to get police help from surrounding planets in case of further problems. The military help was restricted to assist people in loading the ships.

In the evening, the VD, conscience, and emperor sat together in the emperor's office listening in on the pandemonium in the council chamber while keeping their conversation private.

The emperor asserted, "We can replace the governor."

John countered, "Yes but it would be a tough time to replace her. She knows the planet and its people and the Taurans may be upset with that action, which would make things worse."

"It's important during times like this for planets to have a united front. The governor may not be happy that her people must wait awhile before they get evacuated but she must be aware there is a big picture. We'll evacuate them in time, it's just going to take quite some time to evacuate Taurus, so we must get going on it. At least, we'll have to reiterate our plan to her and the justification for it."

"We'll get a formal message drafted and sign your name on it. I don't think she'd dare to defy you. You were the one who put her there."

Mark changed the subject. "I'm following the situation on Taurus closely. That's going to be the biggest problem to tackle. I feel so helpless. It'll be difficult to get more police in there to help control the situation. We've got no local planets that can help, as their police are assisting in the evacuations of their planets. We could pull police from elsewhere but it'll take more time to get them there. Also, do we want to send more police onto a planet we're going to evacuate? Are other planets reasonably close by going to want to send their police on a task somewhere else, when they might soon have the same problem on their planet? It might already be getting beyond where we have a simple solution. Now, even the tough approach is not feasible as our space forces are occupied with the evacuations."

The emperor suggested, "We could muster a fairly large contingent of space officers and crew to help with the policing. The ships can operate autonomously."

John countered, "Yes but what's or who's going to police the overcrowded ships? We're in the process of producing more specialised androids to help and we will be sending them there soon."

The emperor responded that there could be a compromise solution by sending at least some forces there to help for now, although they were not trained for that purpose. People generally held the space forces in high esteem, so just the fact they were there would be a good thing.

The emperor continued. "We can't blame the Taurans. They all want to get off as soon as they can, unfortunately, 9,000,000,000 people can't be first. It's getting to the point where some who know they're lower on the evacuation list are considering that, if they can't get off early then maybe nobody gets off at all. We talked about that earlier; first the panic, then the riots, finally chaos, where it's every person and planet on their own."

Mark added, "I think we should continue to do what we're doing and keep a news block. That may reduce the spread of chaos to other planets but we can't do that forever and it'll happen somewhere else independently. We'll just keep appealing to the people of Taurus that everything is okay and we'll get them off the planet if everyone cooperates. I think that's working to some extent. The governor is beginning to hire more police to help with crowd control. That may be okay until people realise that we can't get them all off."

"Good." The emperor smiled. "An internal solution is the best."

They spent some time going over some statistics related to the movement of people and the capability of accommodating them. It was evident that, in a matter of months or even weeks, they, in many cases, would run into a situation where they would begin to move already evacuated people. This was already occurring on the sector's base. People had been moved there early in the crisis as a haven. Now they had to move again.

Mark announced, "In a few weeks, we should be able to move people behind the thing. It's unlikely the killer will reverse direction. Why would it not continue to move to greater population areas?"

John responded, "Yes, it's a good idea, the crew of one of the cruisers has buried the dead on most of the planets before it was directed to assist our agent. It's feasible. One thing about it is that we have completely undamaged facilities."

"There are several negative points. First, the existing facilities are not built for high-density populations. There's no life on the stricken planets. We would have to repopulate the habitable ones with plants and animals, etc. I also don't think people will want to move to them. The stigma of this thing is there. It would be like living in a haunted house. I think the psychology is not going to be there."

They sat back quietly for a few minutes and soon noticed the noise level in the council chamber had increased. The emperor changed his view on his screen to match what was visible in the council chamber. As no news was being reported from the planet, what they were seeing was from on-planet security cameras. Several scenes were visible on the screen; two showed mobs overturning buses and setting them on fire, one was a fight near one of the loading ships, where the people had damaged it and it would not be able to take off now without repairs. Other people were trying to stop the fighting and get the evacuation reorganised. There were sirens in the background where police were trying to get to trouble spots.

The emperor turned to John. "It's begun."

17

When the alert went out to the citizenry about the marauding killer, many people first evacuated to the base, as it was considered the ultimate haven and it quickly filled beyond capacity. The base was now within the danger zone and those people had to be moved farther away. Ten large ships had already evacuated the bulk of the people and another had just arrived. This would be the last one, as no other ships could be spared because many inhabited planets were also within range of the killer.

The admiral had been waiting for the ship and could see on her monitor how many people could be crammed into it. There would not be enough space for everyone. She had the computer give her a list of people still on the base prioritised according to the newly established criteria and transferred it electronically to her first officer, a commodore of the fleet, who was organising the loading process.

Captain Weyburn sauntered into the room. He looked at the screen, scanned the list and said, "Admirals are important people and will be needed in this dire time to organise the military to deal with the crises. You can leave you know. You don't have to stay here. Many military personnel will escape and I'm sure all of them would line up to volunteer to stay back in your stead. They adore you."

She stood up, began staring out at the stars through the observation window, and responded, "You can do that too, there are junior officers who would give you, their seat."

"Probably but that's not for me."

The first officer called in from the loading area. "Some of the people have committed suicide and a few have decided to stay here. They said they were tired of running. That means there is a seat for you, Admiral."

"There are still others on the list that can use the space," she responded.

"Does that mean you are not going?" he asked, surprised.

"That's right," she said firmly.

"What about you, Captain? That means you can go now."

"Afraid not . . . I'll stay behind, too. Just get everyone else eligible onto the ship and get going, or there won't be any point in leaving."

The first officer hesitated for a few seconds, as if he was hoping she would change her mind then ended the call.

Captain Weyburn joined the admiral at the window and stared at the stars.

"When I was a boy, I used to spend a lot of time looking at the stars dreaming I could, like my father, join the military and travel to other planets. I did, and it turned out I was good at it and I loved it. It's my passion. My father died among the stars and it now looks as if I may end up in the same predicament. The only thing I never did was to settle down and have a family as he did, although, he was rarely around and I was his only child. Now, I kind of regret that part of my life.

"When I was young, my first thoughts were not of having a family, although, I loved playing with kids. It's only been the last few years that I began to realise what I had done – or rather didn't do. I think my father would have liked me to carry on the family line – most parents do, I think; whether it's a boy or girl. Now, I'll never be a parent or grandparent."

"So, with all your alpha-male exploits you never fathered a child?" she queried, rather harshly.

"Not that I know of."

"What is this; some type of confession time?"

"I'm just talking. The last couple of nights, I've been thinking of many things. I thought of the possibility of not making it out of there. For the first time in my life, I became afraid of something. This thing we're up against isn't something I can fight. When you're young, death seems so far off. You never know when your day will come and that gives you comfort because life seems eternal and you're invincible. Now, I know the end will come. I don't know exactly when it's going to happen but I know it's soon. Oh, yes, the killer may pass us by but it hasn't let anyone off the hook so far as we know.

"To me, I've left some unfinished business . . ."

"I don't think anyone is ever really ready to die," she responded. "We almost all leave unfinished business. Perhaps only the old people get into a state where they are prepared for the end." She sighed. "Why are you telling me all this stuff?"

She was now eager for him to stop. For the past few months, she had maintained an impenetrable wall up against him and she wanted nothing to weaken her resolve. She was happy to keep him on staff because he was an exceedingly good manager and officer but she wanted nothing to do with him, even as a friend. To her, he had spent his life mistreating and taking advantage of women, and she could have no respect for that part of him. She willed herself to hate him.

She turned away from the window saying, "Want to join me in the mess for some tea? It would be more comfortable there."

"Will there be other people there?"

"No, I don't think so . . . well maybe."

"Maybe your cabin would be more private."

"You, in my cabin?" she said with a shocked look on her face.

"Or, what's the matter with staying here, then?" he replied apologetically.

She thought for a while then led the way to her place. After a short walk, she approached a very familiar door which opened for her. He followed her in. She heated some water and poured it into a teapot. Within minutes, she poured some of the hot liquid into two teacups.

He spent his time looking around her cabin. As far as he knew, only the service personnel had ever been inside it. He stopped by her dresser and watched as pictures of her at various stages of her life flipped one after the other in an electronic frame. He saw her days as a girl with her mother and her early days in the military as she progressed through the ranks. She was beautiful even then. He scanned through the knick-knacks of her four military medals and of the medals and trophies she received in sports, mostly in basketball and volleyball. Her height would have given her quite an advantage in the girls' leagues for those sports. He ended up staring out of a massive port window with a tremendous view of the stars.

She brought him a cup. "I believe you drink yours black."

He took the cup and saucer into his hands and answered, "You're correct . . . You have a beautiful place here."

"Perks of the job," she responded proudly.

"Its beauty comes from the way you've decorated it," he complimented her again.

She stood at the window again staring out at the stars while she sipped her tea. He stood back a little watching her. She looked so regal, standing tall and proud; her jet-black hair, as usual, in its tight bun which acted in its way like a crown on top of her head making her appear taller and even more imposing. Her uniform, despite all the crises of the past few weeks, was clean and crisp but on her face, she now wore only a facade of cool and calm, behind it he knew was worry, confusion, frustration, and fear.

He continued the conversation. "Funny thing is I've never wanted to be an admiral; it's too far away from the action."

After a few minutes, she picked up her teapot and sat down on a settee that faced toward the view of the stars. She refilled her cup and placed the teapot on the small coffee table in front of her. She sipped her tea as the queen she was.

He stayed standing in front of the window for a few minutes then finally sat beside her. His presence seemed to calm her somewhat and they sat staring at the stars until their exhaustion took hold and they fell asleep.

When he awoke, he went over to where she sat catching up on the news on her pad.

Overnight, not far from the base, an evacuation ship had been attacked with the total loss of its passengers and crew.

"I've set the base's computer to sound an alarm if there is any power surge," she said.

"That's a good idea. We may not even get to hear it, though."

"You could be right . . . Do you want anything to eat?" she asked.

"No, thank you for the thought."

"I don't feel hungry myself." She got up and sat down on the settee.

After a few minutes of staring at the stars, he walked over and sat beside her. He turned his head toward her and asked, "Why didn't you want to leave?"

"There were other lives to save. I'm not any more deserving than anyone else."

"But you finally got your seat legitimately," he said.

"My response is the same. I must save lives. Even when we're at war, I must protect, as much as I can, the lives of the people under my command. If I decided to take the seat, then someone else wouldn't be able to have one."

She shot back to him, "Why did you stay here?"

"Well, nothing so altruistic . . ."

"Well?" she responded with interest.

"You might think I'm being much too bold."

"What do you mean?" she asked.

"Well . . . I'm here to be with you."

She looked at him, puzzled. "What?"

"To be with you . . . I know it seems strange." He shrugged his shoulders. "My life was spent wooing women but I never loved any one of them. I knew nothing of love. It was just a game but I never forced myself on them. I would never have done that. I had a knack for figuring out what they liked and played to that. It was a bit uncanny.

"I arrived on this base about four years ago but about two years ago I became very interested in you. I read everything about you. About eighteen months ago, I started to follow you places when I could, at first a little furtively, and then a little more boldly. I didn't know what was going on. The more I studied you the more I wanted to know more about you.

"I think I've finally figured it out . . ."

"You wanted to hit the jackpot and make it with an admiral," she added mockingly.

He responded calmly, "No, nothing like that, surprisingly. I guess I had just grown up. I realised I had fallen in love for the first time in my life."

She spun her head toward him and looked deeply into his eyes. She sensed he was telling her the truth. Her face turned red and she said, almost angrily, "I guess you're referring to me?"

"Yes."

"You know nothing about me," she said gruffly, "You're enamoured about the story of a person you've read about; like in a magazine or book. You can't love an imaginary person."

"Remember, I told you I have this uncanny sense. When I got to know you more personally it went beyond the enamoured. You are deeper and more complex than most people. You hide pain and sadness, and dark secrets but you have an intensity of thought and emotion that is overpowering and has drawn me into you like gravity, or even a black hole."

She kept staring at him still trying to determine if all this was real. She knew his history. She was trying desperately to be sceptical and not being taken in. Either he was telling her the truth, or this was the best act she had ever seen. She did not want to receive love or give it, especially with him. She wanted to reject everything he was saying.

He continued. "You told me you suspected that I was tailing you and staring at you. Well, I was taking a huge risk with my attention on you. I know your history. At least two men were banished to working in the nether regions when you thought they were paying attention to you."

She snickered.

"Why didn't you ship me out? You knew about my attention before this incident happened. It might have been even more obvious lately but you nailed guys a lot earlier before."

"Well, we've been busy lately, haven't we? And, I wasn't sure if it was my imagination. I tried to ignore you . . . or maybe I'm getting old and don't want to fight anymore." She sighed.

"No, I think it was more profound than that but let's just leave that for now. As you can see, I've made no pass at you. I have a lot of respect for you. I'm not after the physical stuff at all . . . I want your heart." he said sincerely.

There were a few seconds of silence while she gaped in awe at what he had said. "Remember when you asked me why I joined the forces?" she sliced into the silence.

"It seems like ages ago. So much has happened since then," he responded.

She stood up, turned, took two steps, and stared at herself in a nearby full-length mirror.

He could see both the back of her body and the reflection of the front in the mirror. He realised how fit she kept herself. He could see how beautiful she was but she had tried to hide it every way she could. He had never seen her wear makeup or jewellery, not even lipstick.

"You've had your confession time . . . I'm not such a good person. I don't deserve anyone's love nor am I willing to give it." She half snarled. "You wasted your time on me and probably wasted your life," she said acidly. "You could have gone your own way and gotten off this base."

She reached back to her hair and began pulling pins out of it.

Captain Weyburn watched as pitch-black hair began flowing down her shoulders and onto her back.

"You were right when you said that I was a country bumpkin. I grew up on a little farm that hardly gave our family enough to eat. The worst part of it was my father drank most of the money we could scrape up. I don't know why he drank, maybe he was angry at being so poor, or maybe he was just a bad person. He sometimes took out his anger on my mother and sometimes on me. One day, he got so drunk he beat my mother until she bled. She was crying so hard, I thought she would never stop. After that, he stomped out of the house and we never saw him again. He had jumped into our hover car and drove it into the side of a cliff in his drunken stupor."

She reached into a drawer, pulled out a brush, and began to brush her hair.

"When I got older, I met what I thought was a wonderful boy and fell in love with him. We got married and it was wonderful for a few weeks, but then it got bad. He started bad-mouthing me, then hitting me. I could picture my dad all over again. I got pregnant, and I think he couldn't take the thought of being a father. In any case, he walked out on me and went with another woman. I had such wonderful thoughts of us. I loved kids and wanted to have a family and live a normal life. Why couldn't I have a normal life? Is there something wrong with me? Those men had ruined my life. They had ruined my dreams."

Captain Weyburn got up, approached her, gently pulled the brush from her hand, and took over her brushing task. He loved the feel of her softly flowing hair which glimmered in the soft light of the room. He picked up a handful of it, raised it to his nose then closed his eyes and took a deep sniff. She could see him do it in the mirror. He was not sure what it smelled like but it was a wonderful mixture of scents. He could not understand why any man could mistreat anyone as alluring as this beautiful queen. He did not answer her. How could he? He returned to brushing her hair.

She continued. "I hated my father. I hated my husband. I hated all men. I vowed never to have anything to do with men again," she raged angrily.

She closed her eyes for a few minutes, as she focussed on the brush's gentle tug on her tresses. Her head was pulled back a bit as the captain hit a snag.

She began to cry softly. He thought he had hurt her, so he apologised. She said nothing, so he resumed his brushing.

She continued but was choking on her words. "As I said, I was pregnant and when the doctor told me it was a boy, I was so angry. I was just so, so angry, I had an abortion." She choked more and her words were becoming almost unintelligible but she forced herself to go on. "I didn't want to have a child with that man. It would always have reminded me of him, and being a boy was just too much."

She stopped to catch her breath and used the gentle tugs on her hair to gain some composure, some sanity. "But now, I'm over forty. I know I'll never have kids, and I killed the only one I ever had. I killed my only child and I can never get him back. I can never forgive myself for that.

"I joined the military to protect myself. I would survive in the world of men protected by military discipline. And I did better than that, I thrived. So, you think I like having men stand up for me when I enter a room or leave, damn right," she added assertively, "but killing my child I can never forgive."

He stopped brushing her hair, put the brush on the table, wrapped his hands around her waist, hugged her gently, and gave her a little kiss on the back of her neck. He whispered, "You're forgiven, so now forgive yourself. We all make mistakes. We must look ahead and not backward."

She said softly, "But, there's no future now. Here I am together with a man who loves me."

He corrected her. ". . . Who does love you . . ."

"But what good is it, now? Where were you ten or twenty years ago?"

"We were not ready then. Both of us had too much baggage from our past. It would not have worked out then," he said.

"Then it's too late, isn't it?"

"It's never too late. We missed love before but it's good to experience it, even if for a moment."

She slid to the floor on her knees, covered her face in her hands, and burst into uncontrollable tears. He dropped beside her, held her warmly in his arms, and cried with her.

Through her tears, she said softly, "You're right you know, something prevented me from booting you off the base. I didn't know what it was at the time but I kept you here while a battle raged within me, and now I know why . . . I love you. I got caught up in all my raging hatred and could not let it through. Somehow, I knew you were different. Boy, it's hard to say that."

"I know, I've come to know you so well but it's nice to hear it. You finally realised it yourself."

They heard the first note of a horn blast.

18

John was falling. When was he going to feel the bottom? For how many minutes more did he have to fall?

But he did not hit the bottom. He found himself in a packed bar where he had been many years before with Tom, an old high school friend. They were pushing their way through the barroom into the games room. They touched their hands for the first time to the golden pad of the game, their DNA scan activated it and they each sat down on its golden chair. For what seemed endless years, they had awaited the moment. They were sixteen and could not understand why they could not have done it earlier. They were of age now and a whole new level of pleasure awaited them.

People since before recorded history had learned of artificial pleasures, from the discovery of fermented beverages to the wonders of smoking tobacco or poppies. Since that time, other humans have fought the damage caused by using these substances, both the chemical dependence and the horrible physical and psychological damage caused by them. In that fight, black markets formed, as humans' cravings for excess seemed forever a curse.

Come the modern age and the realisation, especially after prohibition, that the war could never be won, the governments, in their wisdom, licensed alcohol, tobacco, gambling, marijuana, then more. With the advance of technology, they substituted the chemicals for direct stimulation of the pleasure centres of the brain. The game most favoured by people was life simulation. Hook yourself up to the game and the old bars, cinemas and drugs paled in comparison to its pleasurable effect, for your experience was visual, aural, and sensual, and one could immerse entirely into whatever you were experiencing. You were part of the event, whatever event you could imagine.

Eventually, the empire, in its benevolence, provided low-cost pleasure service to replace the chemical one. This technology wiped out the black, and government-regulated, markets in chemical substances and avoided past health disasters. It even replaced other types of dangerous activities like parachuting, bungee jumping, horseracing, car racing, etc. You could get that, and more, if you plugged yourself into the system at almost no cost, so there was no exploitation and no risk of dying an early death.

Researchers found that the game had to be started early enough to avoid youth getting into something else before the legalised system came into play.

Sure, there was a very small portion of society that gave up their real lives to that undertaking but gone were the ruined families living in poverty and people who had destroyed their lives physically. A huge portion of the people would get their 'fix' of wanton pleasure and could join society. Built into the system was an education system to reorient the users and, at sixteen, John was now involved in a race for his life on a track against a hundred other people.

Slowly his world began to fade . . .

He felt pain and was trying to open his eyes but their heavy lids would not part. He was confused and was taking time to collect his thoughts. He began to recall basic information about where he was and who he was. Finally, he pried his eyes open.

John's first sensation was the smell of vomit which helped to refresh his memory. He could vaguely remember entering the pod and feeling as if his body was being torn apart. He soon remembered where he was going and why. He looked around the small cabin he occupied.

It looked as if the lieutenant had taken him out of the pod and they were still in the speeder zipping along in space. The kaleidoscope of the wormhole was gone and he could see stars in the view screen, although it was a computer-generated one, as they were travelling too fast to see anything but black.

He did not feel too well. The event horizon had shaken him up a lot. He still felt stiff and a little nauseous. He tried to move but all he felt were aching muscles. His groan must have been heard by the lieutenant, because he spun around and their eyes met but they were not familiar eyes.

John blearily looked around the cabin again; nothing had changed there.

With a raspy voice, he asked, "What happened to Lieutenant Bagwana? Are you taking over for him?"

"Not exactly, sir."

"What do you mean, not exactly? I got into the pod, went through the wormhole, woke up in here, and found someone else driving the ship."

"Lieutenant Bagwana is dead, sir."

"What do you mean, dead?"

"He died in the jump, sir."

"So, you took over the ship?"

"No, sir."

There was silence.

John was getting frustrated. "What's your name?"

"Um, Lieutenant Ruskin, sir."

"So, I went from African to Russian surnames." After hundreds of years of interbreeding, the different races of humans had, for the most part, become very similar in appearance, especially for those off of Earth. People might be slightly darker or lighter; with slightly rounder or more slanted eyes but gross differences had, for the most part, disappeared.

"Yes, sir."

"Okay, let's get something straight here. You don't have to talk to me as if I don't want you to talk to me, okay; like speaking only when spoken to. We'll end up taking hours for a five-minute conversation. I know you've probably been told I'm a miracle worker or something but cut the crap – мозги мне не парь."

"Oh, you know how to speak Russian?"

"I know it a bit – enough to say, 'cut the crap'."

"Well, we're even, that's about as much I know, too."

The two of them laughed for a few seconds.

The lieutenant continued. "It's hard to keep the minority languages these days, especially off Earth, although most languages of Earth have become extinct."

"I guess there are only six or seven major ones that remain and only on Earth, with maybe another five or six hanging on by a thread. It's almost the end of Babel."

"The lieutenant was puzzled for several seconds until it came to him. "Ah, you mean the Tower of Babel. I've heard of that; the ancient explanation for all the languages of the Earth."

"Exactly."

"An old wives' tale."

"But an interesting story that was believed for many thousands of years. Inquisitive people were always searching for an explanation for things, just as they are now. When we don't understand something, we search and try to understand, and if we don't, we'll make up something. You don't understand thunder, so you say it's a war god doing that.

"Look at this new situation. We've come up against something we've never known before and it won't be long until someone comes up with some idea that will attempt to explain it but it might bear no reality to what it is."

"Yes, maybe a new god and we'll make sacrifices to it."

"Who knows . . . So, to go back to where we were, without the 'yes sirs' and 'no sirs', would you tell me what happened from the end of when the other lieutenant entered the hole, to now?"

"Okay, sorry. You guys entered the hole and the turbulence destroyed the ship. Lieutenant Bagwana was killed but the pod saved your life. I had been ordered to come to a certain spot on the other side of the wormhole in case you needed me to pick you up and here we are. You've been sleeping for about eleven hours. We're about three days from your destination."

"Wow, we did gain some time but it was a high price to pay."

"The life of one officer, and a junior one at that, for thousands and maybe millions of civilians; if this works, if you can somehow stop this thing, it would be well worth it. This is our job."

"Yes, I guess it is. I'm not the only one putting my life on the line to protect people."

"My dad told me about you guys, even though he had never met an agent, and I've never seen one either. I can't say I'm impressed."

"What do you mean?"

"My father spoke of agents as if you were mythical creatures. I had pictured you as someone who could blow fire out your ass and you don't look like anything special."

"Well, if I had my fill of beans, sat close enough to a campfire, and let loose with a large enough passage of air, I might be able to put on a good show," John said with a smile.

The lieutenant turned his head to spot John's smile and laughed out loud. "Well, I guess that you are mythical creatures after all."

"Fathers are always right," John added with a grin.

The lieutenant changed the subject. "They're not letting very much information out about that thing out there. It sounds kind of dangerous to me. What the hell are you going to do about it? What's your plan?"

"My fiancé suggested that I drown it in an imaginary ocean. You gave me another idea of blasting it with a methane flame. I have no idea."

"You have no plan! Why are you going?"

"Like you, I'm told to . . . Headquarters told Lieutenant Bagwana to possibly give his life to get me to where that thing is, right? Well, I was told to go there to do whatever I could. I guess the managers of the empire are not much better than your dad. They believe in mythical creatures too . . . Do you know I'm doing this instead of getting married and retiring?"

The lieutenant swung around again and stared at John for several seconds. Because the ship was small and not made for conversation, he was cursing the fact the seats only faced forward. "My God . . . my dad was right. What a choice. Bagwana gave his life for a dream. I guess I'm also willing to do the same but now I realise this is a farce. There's nothing we can do. This is a show for the public."

"It's not a show, as they haven't hyped this up as the ultimate solution. They haven't said much. They've only said they've called for the assistance of an agent, not that I could do anything. They're very political. It's the media and public that have built it up to what it is. If I somehow succeed then good, the matter goes away and everybody's happy. If I don't succeed then they'll say they never said anything specific, and they'd be right. There's nothing they can promise anyway. They have no sure way of solving this problem. This is just a shot in the dark. They have no way of knowing if this initiative will be successful.

"There are about a hundred agents and they could have packed us all into a ship and threw us at the thing with the same result. From what I know, they asked the computer who was the best agent for this job and I won the lottery, so here I am.

"There's not much difference between our service and yours. We pride ourselves in our loyalty and task acceptance. In other words, we rarely say no, no matter what the odds. We have great trust in our managers and they have faith in us. They try to select the person to fit the job and they have an excellent success rate. So, if they tell me I'm the best person to do this job, then they're putting their faith in me, so I fight to the death. Now, I must reconcile that with the promise I made to my fiancé. I told her I'd see her again."

"Well, I hope we have an uneventful rest of the trip. I want to drop you off and get out of there as quickly as I can. I've got a wife and three kids at home."

"I'd love to do that, too. I must attract the thing, so it will come to me. It has sometimes ignored small ships like this in its vicinity and sometimes ignored larger ones, like a cruiser. I secretly hope I fail, although I know I'll end up trying something else."

"I'm glad you're doing it and not me."

The rest of the trip to the meeting point was uneventful.

The speeder reached its rendezvous point but the cruiser was not there.

The lieutenant double-checked his coordinates. "We're at the right spot."

"I'm looking at the traffic map. Look over here, the cruiser is almost a day away."

"Should we contact its captain?"

"No, he knows where I am. I'd prefer to keep silent. I don't know what that thing can do and what kind of sensing it can do. If we communicate, it might give us some information that might bring attention to ourselves. It might make it wonder what we're doing and dissuade it from attacking us.

"Here is the trajectory of the thing so far." John pointed to one part of the holographic map. "It's just beyond the sector's base. Our predictions have been pretty good, so far. The last thing it hit was here." He pointed to another location. ". . . Which is not far from us but I think we should move ourselves over here . . ." Again, his finger moved. ". . . To account for the slight deviation from our predictions and the fact the cruiser is late."

"Do you want me to fly there now?"

"Umm . . . no." John thought for a few seconds. "How about if we get there at the same time as the cruiser, and with a parallel velocity, so I can get into it without having to change our course? We can then link up, get me inside and you can get away from there. The other ship's captain should realise what we're doing and act appropriately."

"Sounds like a plan to me," the lieutenant said with a nervous grin. "The sooner I get away from that thing the better."

The lieutenant then set a slow trajectory that would coincide with that of the cruiser.

As they slowly moved in front of the killer, John noticed Lieutenant Ruskin got more and more nervous.

After a few hours, John finally reminded the lieutenant it had not been demonstrated, in several accidental incidences, that the killer had attacked any vehicles which had only two or three people in them.

"I don't want to be the first case . . . Don't you feel nervous?"

"We're not that close. I figure we're a day or two ahead of it."

"That's too close for me."

A few hours more passed and the ships were moving into position. John ate a hearty meal but the lieutenant did not feel hungry.

The two ships were visually near now. John said, "Well, there she is, finally. Now, move in on her and get docked. When we're done, I don't want you to zoom out of here. I want you to keep your present velocity for a few hours then you can slowly accelerate and arc away. It's been nice knowing you these past few days."

"Likewise, for me, it was nice to get to meet an agent. It's been an honour and you have lived up to my expectations. My father was right; you guys are a special breed of people."

"I began my career in the forces and met thousands of its members throughout my life, so I have a lot of respect for you guys, too."

The ships needed no guidance in the docking process but the lieutenant kept an eye on what was going on. When the two ships were locked together, John gave the lieutenant a final handshake. He heard the door between the two ships open. The speeder's door was opened and John entered the small airlock of the cruiser. The speeder's door was closed, the door between the ships closed, and he could hear the ships uncoupling.

A few seconds later, the inner door slid open and he was greeted with the most putrid smell imaginable. Besides mooing, bleating, and grunting sounds, a strange man welcomed him with a military salute. He was dressed in a long, flowing, colourful robe.

John gasped. "Captain Wang?"

"At your service, sir."

"What's with that outfit?"

"It's clothing like some of the greatest fighters of one line of my people, sir."

"I didn't think they changed the military uniform recently."

"I thought, since we're going off to battle, I would don this honourable garb of my ancestors. This is my first battle, sir. This may be a strange kind of battle but it may be one of the great battles of history."

"Well, I am awed but it also may be one of the shortest in history. I don't think we've ever measured battles in microseconds before."

The ship's captain smiled. "I like you, you're funny."

"And you look kind of ridiculous."

John looked around the control room. "You seemed to take this animal thing to heart."

"Yes, sir, you said to fill the ship," he emphasised.

"There's hardly enough room for us . . . and I said cows. What's with the sheep and pigs?"

"There weren't enough cows where I was, so I grabbed what I could get."

"Well, we're in for a lot of fragrance in here."

"You'll get used to it, sir."

"Did you leave a cabin or two free of animals?"

"No, you said fill, sir. That's what delayed me. Have you ever tried to pack a cruiser with animals? They didn't cooperate, especially with the pigs. My crew got quite a kick out of the event, particularly when they pictured me inside with them."

"I guess I did say that, and no; I've never done anything this bizarre before. This looks like a university frosh prank."

"I did leave the airlocks clear, sir; regulations."

"Aren't there any regulations about animals on board a ship?"

"No, they're silent on that. They just say all locks are to be free and clear of obstructions."

John smiled at the humour of everything becoming a three-ring circus.

The captain continued. "How about we sit down, sir? Would you like something to eat or drink?"

The two of them pushed their way through the animals.

"It's good you kept silent on your trip here," John said. "Thanks."

"You didn't contact me, so I didn't contact you."

"And you matched my plan exactly when I moved the rendezvous point."

"I knew you had to move the point because of my delay. From your trajectory and velocity, I extrapolated your end-point."

They finally reached the mess where they picked out what they wanted to eat and drink. They sat down.

"Well, sir, what's your plan?" the captain asked as he began to eat. One of the cows had nuzzled up to him eyeing a piece of lettuce hanging from his sandwich.

"Soon, I want to slow us down, so we'll be overtaken by our friend out there. Before then, I want to get into the spacesuit and hooked up to the ship, as I have no idea how long I will be in there."

"Hooked up completely?"

"Yes."

"Do you think the spacesuit will protect you?"

"No, it's been proven that it doesn't. If I survive, I want to make sure I can be better maintained, like going to the bathroom, eating, and drinking."

"Sounds like a good plan but how do you think you're going to survive when no one has done it before."

"That's the flaw in my plan."

"That's a pretty big flaw, isn't it?"

"Yes, but what options do I have?"

"I got it. Now I know what you meant when you said you'll measure this event in microseconds. Some battle! I guess I got dressed up for nothing. I should have worn a black suit."

"Sorry for the big disappointment. Was part of your delay caused by looking for those clothes?"

"No, I always had them in my kit, just in case."

They finished their meals. After about three hours spent chatting, preparing the spacesuit, and hooking it up to the ship, John stripped and slid into it. The captain fastened on the intravenous lines, the monitors, and the faceplate. John was ready.

The first thing John did was to check if he could eat food and drink water then he checked his oral link to the communication system in the ship.

"Computer," he called out. "Acknowledge."

There was a pause then the computer responded, "Confirm authority."

John put his thumb on a small pad which recorded his thumbprint and took a DNA scan. The computer finished with a retinal scan. There was a slight pause for the vessel to communicate with the sector's central computer. The computer said, "Authority acknowledged, you are in control of the ship."

Now, the big test – could he control the ship silently? Inside his helmet were electrodes close to his skull used to monitor brain activity. He was going to attempt, through his thoughts, to link into the ship's brain centre. He was not always able to do this with computers as the electrodes were not made for two-way communication and was unaware of any other person who could do it.

John concentrated and thought, "Computer, acknowledge authority."

There was no response. More often the flaw in this was on the part of the ship's system. The electrodes had to be extremely fine-tuned and they could be quite individualistic. John was counting on this method of communication if the circumstance warranted it. He needed to give himself the greatest possible probability of success. He had to be ready for the flood of direct energy when he did connect.

John thought again, this time with more force and, in turn, the force returned with a flourish. He had to instantaneously re-modulate the connection's current in case his brain was damaged in the process. Both his brain and that of the computer, adjusted to a comfortable communication level. He was now intimately linked to the computer's 'brain'.

He thought, "Agent 37-3877393871 connect code SHQ-ISS1 acknowledge."

"John, is that you?" John had successfully connected to the head of special services.

"Yes, ma'am."

"So, you've installed yourself into the cruiser's system, wonderful. We're now fully monitoring everything that happens on the ship, as well as its contents. We can see that Captain Wang didn't leave you much space to lie anywhere unless you use the airlocks."

"He meant well. The more mass of life we have on the ship, the greater the probability of being attacked. He had the right idea.

"Send a note off to Joe to notify my family that everything is going well and I love them. He was supposed to have notified HQ about that."

"He has and they will be looked after. Is there anything else?" she responded.

"No, I don't have any specific plan in mind. I intend to wing it as I go along."

"Best of luck to you. You're the best we have against this menace. Other options are few. We're counting on you. We're all behind you. The emperor has taken great interest in your mission and sends you his best wishes, also. We're confident of your success."

"Thanks, I can only do what I can do. If it's impossible for me, it can't be done but I am here for you, the emperor, and the empire. Long live the emperor."

He cut the connection. After three hours of catching up on the latest news through this link, John fell asleep to replenish himself.

While John lay in the spacesuit, Captain Wang sat at the helm and began to read. After three hours, he noticed John had drifted off to sleep. He went to the mess to eat then returned to the helm to read some more. Three more hours later, he got up and stood before the view screen to look at the stars. After several minutes, he turned to return to his chair to read. Before he even got back, he slumped to the floor.

19

John jolted awake and found himself walking among the stars, or was it, bright light, or was he even walking? He seemed to drift endlessly, or was he stationary? He was dreaming, or was he awake?

Had he ever had a dream like this? He could not recall but a person has several types of dreams: those you never remember; those you remember for a brief time after you wake and drift away forever; and those you remember forever but John would soon be awake and would only know the category of this dream shortly after it was over.

But he did not wake up, or was this the way it would be? He had no sense of time. Was this one second or was it an eternity?

He tried to focus. Right now, he was in 'nothing'. He had to make sense of this. This 'nothing' must be something. He was something. He remembered from Descartes; "I think, therefore I am". If he existed, did something else exist? Did he create his existence? Should he create his existence? Must he create his existence, or did his existence find him?

In this nothingness, he searched with his mind furtively at first, and then more assertively, and sensed something. He did not know what but it was something, and he latched onto it. He felt a tremendous repulsion but he fought to hold onto it. Instead of acceptance, he felt rejection; he was fighting something. It was pushing him away forcefully but more strongly; he was pulling it to him. What was it? Should he pull it in, or should he let it go? He felt an overpowering sensation to release it but his mind latched on to it like a vice and held fast. He felt pain then felt as if he was in the fires of Hell. Again, he felt an overwhelming sensation to push it away and he almost let it go but decided he could not release it or he would have nothing in this space, so he held it more tenaciously than ever.

Another eternity went by, and a cloud formed around him, then out of the cloud came . . . Emily. At first, he thought it was a dream but then she spoke, "What's the matter, why are you so stunned?"

He raised his hand toward her and took two steps forward, although he felt no sensation of feet. He looked down but saw only fog. He touched her. She was real, or at least he felt she was real but he knew she was . . . dead. He knew she had communicated with him before . . . many times in his dreams and thoughts but this seemed different. She seemed more real, before she had seemed more surreal, even though where he was, was unbelievable. All this did not make sense. He was very confused.

"What's the matter?" Emily asked again.

"Where am I?"

"You are where I am."

"Well, right now, I'm nowhere."

"Then that's where you are."

"So, I'm nowhere?"

"If that's where you are."

"Emily, why are you talking in riddles?"

From behind him came a familiar voice and he whirled around and gasped, "Dad!" Behind his father stood many formless figures, which he could not make out in the mist.

"Hello, John, at least that's what you call yourself now, is it?"

"Yes, Dad."

John could not believe what he saw before him. Two other forms made their way from the figures, and his grandparents stood before him. He went to each one in turn to hug them. Then two more figures came forward, one was an old friend who had died in an accident when he was a teenager, and the other was one of his uncles who had died a few years ago.

His father said, "Everyone is here, son, not just those you see now."

"What do you mean, Dad?"

"Everyone you knew in your life and are no longer there."

He thought for some time, puzzled, while his father just stared at him. He turned around to look at Emily and she was smiling at him.

"If I'm with you now, does this mean . . . I'm dead?"

"If that's your perception."

"Now, you're talking around in circles. I asked a 'yes' or 'no' question."

"Have patience, son. Where you were no longer exists to you. Your perceptions here are beyond terminology to you now. We cannot talk of things as you perceived of existence."

Okay, be patient; I can do that, he thought. Okay, if I am having a dream, this should end at some point. If I am not dreaming this must be the afterlife. There is no fire and brimstone, so this is not Hell. I have not been judged, so I may be in some nether land but then why am I here, unless I went straight to Heaven?

His father laughed a little then said, "You think too much. Just accept what you have. Indeed, all is possible."

John said aloud, "So you can read my mind!"

"Yes," his father thought back at him.

John just stared at his father for several minutes then glanced at Emily again. She was still smiling at him as if she was soaking in what was going on. He looked at the rest of the people in this group and they, too, were looking on in interest. He looked farther but the rest of the others were indistinct and farther away.

He looked around again and thought, "Are there others I know here?"

"Oh, yes, hundreds but most of them you probably don't want to meet again," his father thought back.

Several other people stepped out of the mist. His father was correct; he did not want to see them again as they were some of the people he had killed in his line of work.

Throughout his life, John had met two people who were weakly telepathic, a man and a woman. One of the men who had stepped forward was one of them. He had met him in his adventures on the planet Tarlan combating an interplanetary smuggling ring. During torture sessions at the hands of this man, he discovered he had two levels of thought; his open thoughts and his closed thoughts. Through caching his memories and thoughts in the closed section of his mind, he had learned how he could block this smuggler from tapping into his mind and extracting information from it. Before this experience, he had never known he had that capability and he could now use that knowledge with these suspect beings.

Using his shielded thoughts, he was wondering if, if this was Heaven, should he have to use this capability. He was not certain his shielding even worked here and on these beings. He could try a test on them but they could deceive him by not responding to his questions.

With his shielded thoughts, John asked in a whisper, "Dad, Emily what is this place?"

There was silence and nothing in their demeanour to indicate they read his request. He repeated the process with a little more force, "Dad; Emily what is this place?"

His thought screamed out, "You bastards, what is this place? It's urgent that you answer me!"

They did not respond again and still did not show any indication on their faces or other physical signs that they read him.

He was confused by what he had experienced so far. If this was Heaven, why would some of the people, like the smuggler, be standing before him? Maybe this was not Heaven but merely a neutral nether land where all dead people went, good or bad. Or maybe all people went to Heaven regardless of the merits of their life activities. He decided he would use his shielded thoughts only when he thought it appropriate, so they would not suspect he had that capability if he really could shield his thoughts from them.

He said in his unshielded thoughts, "Dad, Emily, why don't you show me around," and he gently grabbed Emily's hand.

"There's not much here," she responded, "but we can be alone if you'd like." With that, all the distinct and indistinct forms disappeared and he was alone with just the two of them.

John asked her, "If the others can disappear like that, are they gone and are we alone?"

"If they're gone, we're alone," Emily answered.

"What do you call this place?" John asked.

John's father responded, "We have no name for it. It is here and we are here. It needs no name. Why do you ask so many questions?"

"I'm a curious person, Dad, you know that."

"Well, here you need not be curious."

"Is there nothing else here? I asked for a tour of this place."

"Why?"

"While I'm here, I'd like to have a look at what's here."

Emily and his father looked at each other and shrugged.

"I'm afraid there's nothing else here!" his father responded without emotion.

John looked first at his father then at Emily and released her hand. "What?" he said in surprise. "There's nothing else . . . where did those other people go?" he said as he pointed to where the others once stood.

"They just went away."

"So, they're still here but I can't see them . . . Of course, I didn't see them go anywhere, they just disappeared."

"Well, you just don't see them."

"But I asked earlier if they were gone and you said, yes."

"You didn't see them, so they were gone."

"Then they're listening to us?"

"Yes."

"You implied that we were alone."

"There's no alone here."

"So, you're all together and there's nowhere to go."

"That's your perception."

"The together part, or the nowhere part?"

"We're together, we're one but we're individuals. There is no perception of going anywhere but we have movement."

"You said 'we'. How many are you?"

"Over a million."

"I don't think I saw that many people here a few minutes ago."

"That's your perception."

"Okay . . . another question; how did I get here?"

"We don't know."

John confirmed, "You have no idea how I got here?"

"No one else has come here before."

John stared at his father. He did not want to ask the next question. He dared not even to think of it in his open mind. They lived once, died, and came here, so how could his father say what was just said?

Would they know he could shield thoughts from them? Until he could figure out what this was all about, he wanted to be cautious but why would he hold things from his father? His belief in this place being Heaven diminished with the population number. Surely, Heaven had a larger population than a million or so. There should be more than that in the hundreds of trillions of people who have lived from the dawn of time. God must have more mercy than that. The only explanation for the small number is Heaven consisted of more than one location.

"I haven't seen you in such a long time. I've heard you in my mind from time to time and have seen Emily. Now that I've met you face to face again, I've got so much catching up to do, and reminiscing. It doesn't seem like the best time to talk when everyone can hear us."

"What you say is open to all. There are no private thoughts here. You can be one with us. You are one with us. You must let go and be one with us."

"I want to be with you . . ."

But he went no further. He was blocking thoughts again now. He wanted to ask what he had to let go of. If he was supposed to be here – why wasn't he here? When you die, you were supposed to go somewhere were you not; or was it nowhere? If it was nowhere, then he should be nowhere; but this was somewhere. He was bewildered but being with his father and his former fiancé was comforting. Without them, he would be very lonely here.

Even though he was still very sceptical about what was going on around him, he decided to relax a little. He wanted so much to talk to them. Doing so would serve a triple purpose: it would let him reacquaint himself with the two most important people of his life who were not living; he would learn more about what happened since their deaths; and, if they were genuine, allow him to confirm the veracity of what they were telling him by comparing what they said about what happened when they were alive and his memories of that time.

With his father, he talked about some of his experiences when he was a little boy, how much he admired his father, and how much he missed his father when he was gone. John recounted how anguished he was when his mother told him his father was dead. Then he wrapped himself into his father's arms and wept.

He did the same with Emily's talking about their experiences together and, in the end, his embrace was long and hard. It felt good to unload these feelings of loss and loneliness.

When he was done, he asked them about what happened to them after they died and they resorted again to vagueness.

He decided to try to peer into their minds but gently, to avoid tipping them off but received nothing but what they had been talking about. Either they had no private thoughts, or they were blocking him.

In this place, it was impossible to get any idea of time. It seemed as if he had been there only a brief period but he also had a sense he had been there much longer than that. He was always around the bright constant light. He was growing weary and he could see his father and Emily remained as alert as ever. He wondered how he was going to able to sleep but everything was now beginning to overwhelm him, so much so, he blacked out.

Almost immediately, he was in the middle of a melee and was fighting for his life. A mob was attacking him with axes and pickaxes. They were clawing at him. Others came at him with swords. He had nothing with which to protect himself but his bare hands. Blood was everywhere – his blood. He could see his entrails covering the surfaces of the weapons used in this attack.

He tried to make out his attackers but they were not human faces he saw. They were not animal, nor plant; nothing he had ever seen before. He shouted at the top of his lungs . . . "Nooo," but it just would not end.

20

John woke up lying in a bed, which was startling enough after the previous day if you could stop for the day. Even though he had a sleep, he did not feel refreshed. He still felt very tired. It was a beautiful bed though, with four tall posts, sheer lace around it and a canopy. The sheets looked and felt as if they were made of silk. The quilt, which had a light floral pattern, made him feel warm and comfortable.

He pushed back the lace between the posts surrounding him, glanced around, and realised he was in a room. The nothingness he had felt on the previous day had been replaced by a room about eight by five metres in size with white walls and sparse furniture. He had a night table on each side of the bed and a large dresser and wardrobe along one wall. Along a wall at the other end of the room was a large window with lace over it and large drapes on each end. On the other side of the room were two doors. There were no other adornments in the room.

Suddenly, one of the doors opened and a woman entered. He did not recognise her from anyone he had seen before. She had long flowing blonde hair, and a slightly pale complexion, and was wearing a long billowy white dress. If she had wings, he would have identified her as an angel but maybe, angels did not bear wings, as what would they use them for? As she neared the bed, he could pick up the scent of jasmine and the beam of her smile. She was the most beautiful woman he had ever seen.

"Good morning," she said with her sing-song high-pitched voice as she stood by the side of the bed.

He gasped and cleared his throat and, at first, nothing came out. He tried several times to respond, until he finally stuttered an awkward, "Hello."

"What's the matter, the cat caught your tongue," she responded amusedly.

He said nothing, expecting still to be awestruck and embarrass himself further.

"Did you have a pleasant sleep?"

He opened his mouth and was pleased it responded, even if it was choppy, "Actually . . . no."

"Oh," she half sang. "The bed is not comfortable enough?"

He stared at her for several seconds and thought to himself that it would be better with her in it but he responded, "The bed is fine. I spent the whole night having nightmares."

She had a knowing smile on her face and she raised her hands over her shoulders as if she was going to pull the ties at the back of her dress but stopped herself and dropped them.

Then, he realised his mistake and switched to secured thought. He had let his guard down and had not thought that maybe she could read his unguarded mind and it might not be a good thing. He was still in unfamiliar territory and, until he could find out more about this place, all his private thoughts would best be guarded. He would leak out only the thoughts he wanted the inhabitants if there were any others, to hear until he could gain trust in his surroundings. If he let nothing out, though, they may suspect he did have a capability of blocking them out, if they already did not know that.

He hoped this place was Heaven, finally. This was more as he had pictured it. This appeared to be a different environment from before but could he trust this place as well? For a test, he suddenly blared out a guarded thought, "You are a slimy bitch" but there was no physical reaction from the beautiful guest in front of him. He still could not know if it was because she could not detect his thought, or she was pretending not to hear him.

However, if this was Heaven, could he, and would he, have to hide his thoughts? Did all new entrants have the same suspicions he did until they learned to trust where they were? Did they bring with them their old human baggage until they could slowly shed it? This was all new territory to him and his old agent ways were tough to shed.

"I'm sorry about your nightmares. That must have been horrible. I hate nightmares, too," she agreed.

"Do you get nightmares?"

"No, not here," she answered.

"Oh, how long ago was that?" John asked.

"Time is immeasurable and irrelevant here. The only time we have here is external to us."

"So, you've had nightmares in a place that had time?"

She looked at him and asked, "Yes but why does it matter? You come from a place with time so we must exist in it right now but we preceded and followed that time. Everything here is very hard to explain, and yet quite simple."

"Then explain the simple part."

"Can you explain God? There are many wonderful things you now understand about the nature of things but there are also many things you must learn. Once you learn, then you will see it should have been self-evident."

John was getting frustrated. Was it just him? Was he not supposed to be inquisitive? In this place, had people lost their inquisitiveness? "Well, then, do you have a name?"

"Oh, yes, you have a proclivity to naming things. You may call me, Anna."

"Okay, Anna, may I get out of bed now? I feel a little hungry and would like some refreshment. Do you have anything here to quench that need? I'd appreciate that."

"You certainly may."

He realised he had no clothes on. "First, do you have clothes I can wear?"

"You'll find what you need in the dresser and wardrobe. I'm guessing you'd like me to leave while you dress. Because of your vanity, I'll ensure the others here clothe themselves."

"Are there others here?"

"Certainly, when you've dressed, you'll meet some of them."

"Thanks."

She turned and left the room.

He pulled himself out of bed and went over to the dresser. There were few clothes there. He grabbed underwear and put that on. He looked at what else was there. There were shorts and t-shirts. He went over to the wardrobe and found more casual, and formal attire; two suits and sport coats with a pair each of formal and informal pants. Since the clothes were in the wardrobe and dresser, he assumed any of them were accepted in this place. He decided to go the middle-of-the-road route and put on the casual pants and shirt. At the bottom of the wardrobe were formal and casual shoes, and runners. He put on socks and casual shoes. He had no choice of colour for any of the clothes; everything was white.

He stood in the wardrobe for a few minutes, not knowing exactly what to do next. He looked toward the doors and went to the one that had not been used by the woman. He opened the door and stepped inside. It was a washroom with a shower, toilet, and sink. He wondered if he should take a shower but, as he was already dressed, decided against it. He looked at the toilet but did not feel as if he needed to use it. He noticed the absence of a mirror and that was the only thing he wanted to use. As he had no comb, he straightened his hair with his fingers, guessing at its appearance.

In his guarded thoughts, he realised he had not had to use any of these facilities all this time. If he was dead though, he should not have needed them. Why then were they here, unless they just served to keep him linked to something familiar? If this was Heaven, this room served no purpose.

Then he thought of something else. He felt a little hungry and had asked to eat. If he was dead, should he feel any hunger at all?

He left the washroom and went to the next door but he knew he would find Anna on the other side and he wanted to do more exploring before he saw her again. He glanced at the window at the other end of the room and decided to go there first.

He opened the curtains, the sheers, the sliding glass doors, and walked out onto a balcony. He looked down four floors over a small park with sidewalks running through it. The park had no trees, nor flowers, only grass. People were milling around, others were walking, some hand in hand. They were all dressed in white, in similar styles of clothes. There were other buildings surrounding the park. He saw no sign of any vehicles but if everyone was dead here, why would they need vehicles?

He looked up and there was a sky but he could see no light sources, unless it was behind the building but there were no shadows. If the source was on the other side of the building, this side should be in the shade; another oddity. The building had four floors above him and looking around the park he saw all the buildings were identical in appearance.

He enjoyed the view of the park for a few minutes then re-entered the room, closed the sliding doors, walked to the door through which Anna had left, and opened it.

The door opened into a narrow hallway. Anna was about four metres down the hall waiting for him. The hall had other doors on both sides of the wall, as one would see along a hallway of an apartment building or condominium. He looked up and, just as he had seen in the bedroom, there was no source of light.

Anna greeted him, "Well, you're well dressed. You said you were hungry?"

"I sure am," he replied.

He followed her down the hall to the elevators. She pushed the down button on the wall, and in a few seconds, the door opened. They got in and she pushed a button for the ground floor.

He remarked to her orally, "I see you have old-fashioned elevators here.

Ours are automatic that senses a person's presence at the door and responds to oral commands rather than pushing buttons."

"That's nice," she responded. "This suits us fine."

The door opened to the entrance of the building. Anna led him out onto the park's sidewalk, and onto another sidewalk that led them around to the other side of the building from the park to what looked like a small shopping area, although the shops did not have any signs on them and all looked the same – like little houses. They passed a few other people on the way who smiled as they passed. He searched the sky for its source of light and found nothing, just a uniform white. Farther up the sidewalk, Anna turned to one house and opened the door.

"Here we are," she said with a smile.

He walked by her into the house. She followed. Inside, it was quite stark, just small tables with chairs. The tables did not have tablecloths but they did have plates, utensils, and wine glasses.

John enquired, "These houses look the same and they have no signs. How do you know what they sell?"

She looked puzzled. "Here, we don't need anything. If an individual felt as if they wanted something they'd know where to find it."

"Would you mind telling me where we are?"

"Again, your proclivity for names. You can call this anything you want. You may call this 'Paradise' or 'Heaven' if you'd like. We don't need a name for it. In this specific case, this restaurant has no name; it doesn't have to be identified, as our minds are linked with the occupant."

John thought privately, that yesterday, or what seemed like yesterday, he had been somewhere that appeared to be a form of Heaven. This place seemed different but was it, Heaven? The previous 'day' had made him sceptical of anything. Maybe it was just overactive agent senses. Here he was still getting the vague answers he had gotten before. Where were Emily and his father, or were they not in this area? If he was in Heaven, he thought they would want to be here with him.

Soon, a waiter appeared with a one-page menu. It had only four dishes: pork, beef, chicken, and fish.

"Hum, I'll take the chicken. I've had my fill of fish for a while. Do you have any wine?" John asked.

The waiter responded, "We have a red and white house wine."

"I'll have the white, please."

"What are you ordering, Anna?"

"I understand it would likely be considered impolite not to eat with you," she said matter-of-factly. "Waiter, please bring me a chicken with white wine, too."

The waiter left.

"Okay, another question; you don't seem to be hungry, have you already eaten, or do you never have to eat here?" John asked.

"We don't have to eat. We don't get hungry but if somebody would like to eat, they can."

Within a few minutes, the meals came and they began to eat. It was quite delicious.

John was constantly in thought. He thought openly that this is what he would have expected Heaven to be like, not exactly but how could anyone know without going there to find out? Each person's idea would likely be different. A gambler would expect it to be a giant casino. Was this heaven conforming to his expectations?

She was just listening to his thoughts.

They finished their meals. In his private thoughts he was puzzled that, even after eating a rather substantial meal, he still felt hungry.

"Well, now that we've eaten, I'll show you around. We don't have vehicles here, so I can't show you everything now by walking but, in time, you can see as much as you want to see," Anna said.

"That'd be nice. We can also get to know each other better," he responded with a wink.

They wandered around for hours. The basic structure of where they lived was similar everywhere; apartment buildings between six to ten stories high surrounded by a central park. Surrounding the building squares were smaller houses of various shapes and sizes that she told him were to live in, or for commerce, although there was no monetary system. After a few blocks of these houses was another building square then more houses.

He asked her, if there was no monetary system, then how did people live? To her, there was no need for a system, because people lived where they wanted and could do as they wished. If they had an interest in culinary skills, they would set up a restaurant. They would do it out of love for what they did, not because they wanted to make money. If a person wanted to taste food, they would visit one of the eating establishments to do that.

Another of his questions was, what was beyond the houses and apartments? Her response was some people liked to do things like farming, hunting, or other country-like activities. Beyond that was nothing. Why would anyone go farther?

During their walk, he asked why he did not see any children.

To that, she responded, "We can't have children, because we have no physical form. We're all that's left of our people."

John wondered how far they had walked. He did not know how long he had been walking and felt no concept of time. Without clocks, calendars, or day and night, and no passage of a sun to guide a person, there was no way to determine time. To top it all, even though he had a feeling that he had walked for quite a distance, he did not feel physically tired. Walking was effortless as there was no real surface to walk on, and no friction.

John said, "Well, this was a great walk and I loved our conversation. This place is interesting. How long have we been walking?"

"Remember, there is no time here. There is no day and night, there are neither weeks nor years. There is no getting tired or sleepy. There is neither hunger nor thirst."

"These are all heavenly concepts but you said there were no children here and children die in the mortal world, do they come here as adults or do they go somewhere else?"

"I don't know."

"And where does God fit into this?"

"I don't know. You are the person who tries to fit your concepts to where you are. You want to name this place and put your concepts onto it. The important thing is, do you like it here and do you want to stay?"

"You mean I have a choice?"

"We want you to stay. I want you to."

"What do you mean?"

"I've grown quite fond of you and would like you to stay," she said quite briskly.

With that, she stopped walking and he did too. She faced him and threw herself at him in an embrace. Their lips met.

He soon softly pushed her away and said, "We hardly know each other. I just got here. I want to know more about this place. I find you to be very nice and you're a beautiful woman but let's not move too fast here."

She responded with a blush, "Sorry, I was so forward . . . It was just a spontaneous act . . . Just around the corner is someone I'd like you to meet." They started walking again.

He did not mind her kiss. It was hinting at what she thought about him or felt about him. He found her attractive. He had a fiancé back in the empire but that was irrelevant now, but there was still Emily. Where did she fit into this picture?

Anna guided him to a small house. She knocked on the door and they entered. A man, all dressed in a white suit, approached from another room and joined them at a small table.

"This is Boris," Anna introduced him.

"Hello, I'm John." They shook hands and sat down around the table.

"Where do you fit into this place?" John asked.

"What do you mean?" Boris asked, puzzled.

"Well . . . does this place have some kind of hierarchy?"

"Hierarchy?"

"So, you don't have any kind of organisation in this place."

"Organisation?"

"Like a manager, boss, leader, president, king . . . something like that."

"We're a collective here. Our thoughts are bound together. We don't have any one person we would call a boss."

"Anna says I have a choice to stay here, does someone here decide whether I stay or not?"

"No . . . if she says you can stay, you can stay. It doesn't take anyone else to say you can stay. If you want, I too want you to stay, if that makes you feel more welcome."

"What happens, if I say yes?"

"Then you can join us and we can facilitate the process."

"Facilitate . . . there's something else I have to do?"

"Not really." Boris faltered.

"Okay, what happens if I want to leave?"

"Then all you have to do is go and we can help you to do that too."

All this puzzled John. He guarded his thoughts carefully. He felt some probing of his mind. They probably wanted to find out what he was thinking. He was leaking puzzled thoughts but he was thinking back to when he was groping in the nothingness after he died. Whether this was Heaven, Hell or somewhere else; was this what he pulled in? That could explain the choice they were mentioning but he was dead, so did he have a choice?

Unless, maybe all the choice he had was what place he goes to. If this was Heaven, then is the choice not made by 'God'? If this was Hell, then perhaps they would try to seduce a person into joining them instead but this was not the way it was supposed to work. Your belief and mortal life activities were supposed to decide your fate, not some later seduction in the afterlife. It was beginning to make some sense but it was not matching his view about what happens after death.

He was now resolved to make a good decision. If he was in Hell, then it was the last place he would want to be. If it was Heaven, then its inhabitants would understand his scepticism. He was not joining anything unless he found out more about it but how was he going to do that? If he pushed too hard and they found out his doubts, what would they do? Did they know he could shield their probes? He could read their minds but was he getting everything, or could they shield their minds also? If he probed hard, could they detect it and what would happen if he did? If he did succeed in breaking in, did that open his shield to them too?

One other thing he had to consider. Maybe he was presumptuous in thinking he merited Heaven and this was some further test he was being put through. He had killed many people in the line of duty. He was their judge and executioner but did he deal with them all fairly?

He did not spend a lot of time with his father, who was away from home often and who died when John was ten but one thing, he told him was to deal with everyone honestly and fairly and never lose your cool; because once you have lost your temper, the other side had already won. Whatever John did in life, whatever he merited, he would have to be careful and stealthy, and he wanted more information before he decided on what was happening here.

John ended the meeting by saying, "Well, I have no more questions for now. Anna, will you lead me back to that apartment I was in earlier? I wouldn't mind a little rest. I presume the offer is still available to me."

She was very agreeable. "Surely, you can think about things, and the room is yours while you're here with us, just follow me."

They got up from the table and exchanged goodbyes with Boris. Anna and John left the little house and began their walk back to the apartment.

Anna piped in with a comment, "For a person who says he would like to think about things and asks a lot of questions, you don't do much thinking."

"What do you mean?" he asked, although he was realising that, although he had been pretending to have some thoughts openly, most of his heavy thinking was not open to them. He might have been too obviously indicating that he could hide important thoughts from them. However, he was also feeling the same about them. What he could get openly from them was rather sparse also. They may both be playing the same game.

She responded, "Well, you know we can both communicate mentally and can openly exchange our thoughts but I detect that you're not thinking much."

"Well, I'm getting tired from all my activities of this day. So much is new to me and I need a rest. You don't need to rest but I still appear to need it."

"It's another advantage of being here."

"Will I gain that trait when I join you?"

"Probably."

"Why would I get it only when I join you?"

"I don't know, maybe you won't get it at all," she said, as she shrugged her shoulders.

They both walked the remainder of the way in silence. John shared only superficial thoughts to amuse her.

Before they parted at the apartment door, Anna shared another kiss.

"I hope you decide to stay with us," she said as she left.

He closed his door and lay on the bed to think. Soon, he drifted off to sleep.

John had the same dreams as he had had during his last sleep period; repeatedly. Why was this happening to him? He did not usually get nightmares. It was as if these beings were trying to get something from him but what and why? Each time they attacked him, he felt his resolve getting weaker. If he gave in, would they go away? He felt so exhausted.

21

John woke up soaked with sweat and with one of the most painful headaches he had ever had. He could not guess how long he had slept but the nightmares had seemed interminable through his sleep period.

At first, he just lay there immobile, staring at the incessant light with his mind blank. He was going to think but changed his mind and waited longer. When he finally thought, he used his sealed mind. Much of what was happening did not make sense to him. He could not be in Heaven, at least what he learned of it. He could not conceive of a Heaven with nightmares, headaches, and slight hunger but the endless light, the lack of time, and the equality of people seemed fathomable.

Then there was the previous – could he call it a 'day'? What was that? The people he had met in this place seemed nice enough but could not provide substantive answers to some of his questions. So, where did he go from here? He felt a little uncomfortable about his predicament and why should he feel like that? If he had an eternity, why should he feel hurried?

He turned his head with great difficulty. His neck was stiff and painful, which exacerbated his headache. He then realised he was not in his room anymore. He was sleeping on the 'ground' that did not feel solid. He felt as if he was floating on his first day in this different world. It was all mist and white but no source for the constant light. He turned his head in all directions but saw nobody around. If this was the first place again, then the beings would be here, only invisible.

For a while, nothing happened. John sat up and spent his time exercising his neck until the tightness in it diminished. He finally stood up and started stretching muscles in the rest of his body. After more time passed, he began wondering when he was going to see anybody. He wandered around his environment a bit but found no limit to how far he walked.

He did not sense anything in his mind. Was there nobody out there? He stopped walking. He was not sure if this place went on indefinitely, or if he was walking in circles as there were no landmarks; there was nothing physical here.

He wondered if he should actively probe, because he wanted to know if there was no one there, or if was he being tested. He questioned what he should do. If there were somebody here, should he wait them out, or seek them out? What were they expecting him to do? If nobody were here, then where was he now? Had he been in two other places since he had died, or were these three separate forms of the same place?

He waited. His father had always told him to be patient. If Anna or Boris, or whoever they were, were here, why were they not showing themselves? Three days ago, when he left the confines of the ship and spacesuit and suddenly found himself alone, he had searched his surroundings and latched onto something. Had he lost it? Had he let it go, or had it escaped? Since he latched onto this thing or place, he had constantly felt it tugging back as if it was trying to escape. He felt nothing now and was worried. Was he alone now? He wanted to tug to test the connection but did it want him to fall into some type of trap?

Had he not had anything at all and it was all a dream? Did he have to search for it again? But, to his knowledge, he had not released anything. He should still be attached to something.

He waited longer. If he stayed quiet like this, would he not give himself away that he might have shielded thoughts? Did it matter? If he could not 'see' it, or them, could they 'see' him? He thought of all the times he had gone fishing. Most times when you hook the fish, it will struggle to get free and alert you to the fact it is there. However, sometimes the fish will relax on the hook, so you think nothing is there and it is only when you tug on the line you realise the fish is there. This was not the same thing, as he had no visible hook or fish. So, did he have something and, if he did, what did this 'fish' look like? Was it what he had experienced over the past few days, or something else he had not experienced yet; or then again, was he now stuck in this void alone and for how long? Was this his eternity?

He waited still more. Was this like the cat and mouse games in the ancient Earth wars between submarines and the surface ships, where the enemy submarine hid on the bottom of the sea pretending to be dead and waiting silently until the surface ships gave up and went away but there was no way for the submarine to know for sure whether the surface ships had indeed given up and gone away?

He had no way of knowing how long he had waited until a strange being suddenly appeared before him.

They stood staring at each other for some time until the being began to speak. "Hi, John . . . I'm Anna . . . or Emily."

John did not hide his thoughts as he looked her over. Instead of the tall lithe beautiful woman dressed in white, or his love, Emily, he saw a naked, hairless being, he guessed as female, just over one metre tall, that looked somewhat humanoid, with overly long arms, highly bowed legs and an oversized head with large ears and eyes but an almost non-existent nose.

John stuttered, "Um, hi . . . you're quite different from what you had demonstrated to me before."

"In this place, we can have any form, as we have no corporeal existence. We present ourselves to your mind, so we can appear as any person you have in your mind, either a memory or a dream person. First, I thought I would mimic someone familiar to you, then an ideal person generated by your mind. Now, I present myself as I used to be when I had a corporeal existence. All of us, including you, have no real existence physically; we are linked in thought only. We are all invisible to each other. In a way, this has its advantages. If a person is not good-looking, they can make themselves appear in any form they want. For example, I can be Emily, or an angel, or anything you can imagine." She cocked her head to the side and winked at him coyly. "Imagine what we could do together."

She continued. "We can also, in your mind, create physical locations. At our first encounter and now, we just kept our reality as it is but in the second encounter, we used a mixture of what you would find in your former existence and our former existence to create a setting directly in your mind. In other words, we can be nowhere, a castle, a palace, or anywhere else. I know in a corporeal existence you can imagine things as individuals but with our minds linked, we can make them as real as reality." She winked again.

"Wow, you kept me confused," John responded, still a little in shock. "So, you're essentially thoughts living in nothing."

"That's correct and it wasn't our intent to confuse you. We didn't know what to do when you came on the scene. We struggled initially with what to do with you. We had to ad-lib as we went on, trying to learn more about you."

"So, can you tell me where I am now?"

"We've told you the truth. We have not named this place. It is nowhere but somewhere. Our scientists discovered it during our corporeal existence well before our star went supernova on us. A large group of us escaped here to survive."

"Why didn't you just escape from your planet for another one somewhere else?"

"You mean by spacecraft?"

"Yes."

"We did have spacecraft for travelling around our solar system initially but our other planets were uninhabitable and we never established colonies on them. We never invented an interstellar drive as you did, so we could not fly physically to other stars' planets. We were more centred on other areas of science, like dimensional physics, the occult, and other areas. So, we learned to move ourselves through space in a sort of spiritual form. We saw what we needed to see of our galaxy that way.

"When we discovered our star was becoming unstable, most people were resigned to their fate but we decided to escape to this inter-dimensional world."

John stared at her quietly for a long time. This time he was keeping his thoughts open. He asked the question that was now burning in his head and she knew exactly what he was going to ask. "You know what I'm thinking. This whole scene here has been so confusing to me, as I was unsure where I was. You see, many of our people believe in an occult centred on an afterlife, so when we died, that's initially where I thought I was. Instead, I linked into the very thing that was attacking my people, am I correct?"

She blushed and squirmed then said, "Yes."

"I guess you're surprised I'm here."

"Very . . . up to now, we've never encountered anyone who could connect to our minds as you have. As we said earlier, we didn't know what to do about it."

"So, now I'm here. You were secretive before, so why are you so open now?"

"Most of us wanted you to go away, and still do. They have tried to get rid of you and wanted to know what you were thinking but weren't successful. Our only hope now is to work with you openly to resolve this issue."

"So, I'm an issue."

"You're more than an issue to me and a few others of us. We want you to join us."

"Well, I've sort of done that, haven't I?"

"Yes, but not totally in spirit. Once you know us and understand us, we hope you'll want to stay here forever."

"Well, if I had a choice; I'd want to go back home."

"See, that's what I'm talking about."

"I left behind a wonderful woman and her son who love me. We were planning to get married. I even promised to get back to her."

"Yes, but I'm here and have come to know and understand you. I want you to stay here and join me as a partner. I left behind my love when he saw no use in our flight. You're an amazing individual. In all our travels, I've never seen anyone like you. I've searched through your mind and love what I see. I guess, you could say in your terminology that I've grown to love you. I want to help you to stay here with me. I fell for you when you thought I was Emily, and was telling me how much you loved her and thought of her."

"I'm flattered. You keep saying I should stay here but am I not stuck here?"

"In a way, yes; the alternative for us is to release your spirit to the void."

"What void?"

"You believe in an afterlife; we don't."

"I thought you said you studied the occult?"

"Yes, but our occult is dimensional. We believe that, when we die, we just die. We have learned to use alternate dimensions to travel through space and other dimensions. Our last feat, our big experiment was to tame dimensions to live. In so doing, we can live forever. What I'm offering to you is eternal life."

"Many of us humans have a similar belief but ours is an afterlife. I was never a strong believer but have had experiences with my father and my former fiancé, who are now dead, that have made me believe there may be something in that. Where I hoped to be was in my afterlife. Some of our people in the past have believed there might be a way of extending our corporeal life and searched for a potion or elixir to achieve it."

"But your people will never extend their lives and will never be certain of an afterlife but you're certain of life here. We've been alive for thousands of years and can go on indefinitely. You can have this too."

"Okay, let me piece this together. You're the marauder that is attacking my people, right?"

"Unfortunately for them, yes."

"As life disappears from everything you attack, you must need their life to continue to exist, right?"

"Yes."

"Then you only exist as long as you can suck life out of other living things, if you run out of life you die," John added.

"Yes, but we will continue to find other life, in this galaxy and others, if necessary."

"If you need an external force to feed your existence, you cannot live forever."

"Maybe but we can exist for a very long time, maybe millions or billions of years."

"I've seen what your life is here and it is not much of an existence. You live in an imaginary world that you create of your own. Because you have no bodies, you don't need anything except life energy, which may be good in some ways but you have no separate lives. You probably don't have any real love. You can't have children and the simple joys that come from that. In other words, your existence is rather empty."

"According to you. We value our existence a great deal. We knew what we were doing when we came here. Billions of our people remained behind on our planet in the galaxy you call Andromeda. We alone are what's left. The history and existence of our people live on in us. You must realise we are entitled to an existence as well as you."

"But, not at the expense of our existence."

"We have learned much from what happened in Andromeda. From getting to know you, we have been thinking about how we can work together to resolve our mutual dilemmas. We both want to continue to exist and we may have a solution. We believe you have a population of trillions of people. If we limit our consumption and you continue to breed at your current rate, you can continue to maintain your current population, or perhaps, even increase further in population. We lost about a hundred thousand people in our journey to your galaxy and that should help us reduce our past higher energy requirement."

"I doubt your plan would work for us. Humans are individuals, just as you must have been. Sure, they want to survive as a group but they also want to survive as individuals. Is there no other way of doing it? How about if we raise animals for you? You seem able to consume any form of life."

"That's correct but it would not be enough for us. The lower the life form, the lower level of life force is present. We would need hundreds of trillions of other mammals in one of your years to sustain us. For example, an entire planet's worth of bacteria would be equivalent to the life force of one human.

"Another thing we would like to ask you to do is to stop moving your people away from us. When we move, it consumes energy from us and you'll only make matters worse for you."

"So, if we bring you all the people you need to consume to one spot, you'll ensure you will only sustainably consume us."

"That's correct, and it need not be at one spot, because we can divide ourselves up so we can spread around your empire to make it easier for all of us."

"As I said, you're not giving us any choice. Shouldn't one option be that you go away and leave us alone?"

"We also have to survive. We're not sure what we'll find in the rest of your galaxy. We may not find much other life."

"Why did you decimate Andromeda?"

"One of the biggest reasons was there was not a lot of high-level life there, and it likely will be much the same here, we presume. Perhaps if we find other sustainable places to settle, then maybe we can reduce our consumption here."

"We've already met other higher-level life forms, in one case with a similar sized resource base and population, so you may be more successful at living in our galaxy. I'm guessing you were a little greedy in Andromeda."

"Maybe a little at first but we had to travel a lot to get energy. We were lucky here to find you almost immediately. We may not have been as lucky in other arms of this galaxy. In other words, we didn't have to travel much to get nourishment. We're not fully recharged yet as you have been moving your people away from us and forcing us to move more to replenish ourselves."

"What happens if we refuse?"

"Then we have to survive. I want you to stay with us but many other people don't, so I may have to agree with letting you go and we will give no assurances of anything, although we may proceed with our plan, as it is in our best interest to do it that way. If you try to thwart our plans, then you're committing suicide as a life form. We believe in giving you the choice to live on as a group but some individuals will have to die and that may be preferable to extinction. We all must be reasonable. In reading some of your people's minds, we found that, in your distant past, you sacrificed your kind to your gods."

"How are you going to communicate this agreement to my people? So far, you haven't communicated in any way."

"If you could, would you do it for us?"

"But, I'm with you!"

"We could allow you to go back if you agree to put our offer out to them."

"Even if I went back, they can't see me, as I'm dead. You would need some type of medium to do it."

"We'll give you some ideas when you make your decision."

John noticed someone else approaching them.

Anna explained to John, "This is what Boris looked like when he had a body."

John looked over the older-looking individual with similar features as Anna and greeted him. "Hi, Boris."

"Hello, John," he responded.

"Now that I know who you are, I don't know if I should say I'm glad to see you again."

"Sorry about that. I just thought I'd come by and see how things were going. Of course, I know what you've talked about. I hope you can understand our predicament. I've been noticing your people's reaction to our perceived attack on your people, and admire what they've done. It must be costing a fortune to move them away like that. In our experiences so far, beings, once they realise, they can't fight us, just accept their fate, some flee and get overrun as we move much faster. You have the technology and capacity to constantly retreat but we know you cannot continue to do that indefinitely. You've slowed us down for now, and we have not been able to fully recharge ourselves but we're hoping to overcome that impediment soon. We intend to divide then charge ahead into more populated areas, and divide more, so your tactic will not be effective anymore.

"So, you can see the futility of your efforts and realise that an agreement with us is your only option. You cannot defeat us."

John stood, defiant but remained emotionless. Privately, he was in turmoil, as they were correct. The empire could not continue their current course indefinitely, especially if the Andromedins divided but he knew also, that the deal offered was not a satisfactory one. How would his fellow humans react to it? He was not sure. Humans were fighters. They fought as a team when it served themselves but if it did not, they could resort to any means individually, or in small groups. Many would kill themselves rather than capitulate, others would flee to new distant worlds, or even galaxies to escape; others would make the deal and hope for the best in the future but capitulation would almost certainly, in the end, mean the demise of a united empire.

If the empire fought with their ultimate weapons, their attacker would very likely be dispersed and make it impossible to resolve. If they waited, their attacker would divide with the same result. Their only hope was to resolve this while the Andromedins were one unit but how?

As an individual, he was dead, so he apparently had two options, stay with the Andromedins, and live forever, or leave them and go into the 'void', whatever that was. Staying with them was appealing. It was a strange form of life but it was a life, of sorts. He had a woman here who was willing to be a companion for him. The 'void' according to the Andromedins and many humans' beliefs, was nothing, just death but for many other humans, it was going to a sort of afterlife or for others to reincarnation. As the Andromedins had said, he had a choice of certainty with them, or the unknown – some choice.

John snapped out of his thoughts and said, "If you're seeking some sort of an agreement with the humans, let's go back to how you intend to do it."

"So, you realise resisting us is futile and a deal is the best for you?"

"It might be futile but the decision is not mine to make."

"We understand. Your people are hierarchical in nature rather than a collective and the proper process must be followed by the superiors of your organisation."

"That's correct. Earlier, you said you were offering me the job to do it. How am I to do it from here?"

"So, you are willing to work on our behalf for the benefit of us all?"

"Well, I have to do something and the best way is to consult with my people about it at this point. I can offer at least one person as a medium. I may be able to contact that person and set up something."

"We'll consider our options."

"I want to keep all my options open. Whether I link up with my people or not, I'll have the option of joining with you?"

"Of course, we'd love to have you. We consider you an amazing model of your people and would love to have you as a member and partner on our team and be one with us. Anna is particularly anxious for you to come on board."

John was feeling tired again. It had been a very strenuous period. He had had much to think about along with the periodic strain of holding his link to the Andromedins. Today, they had stopped trying to separate from him but there were always their so-far, futile attempts to break through to his secret thoughts and memories to learn more about him and they were no longer being so subtle about it.

John could understand they were interested in knowing what he knew and what he was thinking about. They would want to know how genuine he was. He knew they would see him as a strong ally but he could also be humanity's only hope for survival. The brass in headquarters was right. He realised he had been the correct choice for this mission, the only choice. They were counting on him now to come up with a solution. Only, he had no solution but the deal offered to him.

He had discovered as a child that something was different about him; something strange. When he was very young, he was overwhelmed with constant noises in his head, of course, it was gibberish to him until he pieced it together much later as language but it created problems in that he could not sleep and would get headaches from it. His parents and their doctor did not understand his problem, so his family moved away to the countryside to distance him from the throngs of people who seemed to cause him so much woe.

At first, he thought everyone was like him. He tried, at the start, to communicate mentally with his parents but found they never communicated back to him and it seemed to make them sick when he tried too hard. In time, he realised he was the only one who had this, what he took to be an aberration or even a curse.

When he got older, he learned to control it and shut out other people's thoughts. He eventually learned the name for his affliction – telepathy. Sometimes he would use it to his advantage as he could determine what other people were thinking but that made him know more than he should know about people. He learned how two-faced people could be when they said one thing and were thinking the opposite. It made it very difficult for him to form any close relationships with anyone, particularly women. He also learned the importance of individualism and that it was important for each person to have their privacy because social politeness made people stretch truth, or tell lies. People's thoughts were their private places, where no one could intrude. He respected other people's right to privacy as much as he did his own. In the military, he learned to shut off this malady completely, like one who learns to control other mental illnesses.

After that, his talent was left unused until his mission on the planet Tarlan, when he had his first encounter with another telepath. There is where he found out just how strong his talent was and where he was tested to his limits. He also discovered there that his curse could be a gift. Now, he was again being tested to his limits. His experiences with Tarlan had prepared him for this encounter.

John looked at Anna and said, "I'm tired and need some time to rest and think about what I need to do, and how. I guess you have no beds here."

"You're right. This is how we live. We don't have to rest. I guess you can just rest where you are. We can leave you if you want."

"Yes, I suppose it would be good, even though I know you're still here."

"Yes, I guess it's strange for you. You can't see us but we're here."

She stretched herself on her extra-long toes to give her more height, while John bent down and the two kissed.

"I could get used to your way of showing affection," Anna stated with a smile and the two Andromedins disappeared.

John lay down on the 'floor' but he felt as if he was suspended in the air. He went to sleep.

At first, his sleep was calm and sound but soon it felt as if a tiny worm was going through his head, searching, seeking, and gnawing. It was subtle and, while he was asleep, was likely to get missed. John felt it for what it was, and half-conscious, turned it away. Sleep resumed and the worm returned, only to be turned away again and again.

He was standing like a sentinel guard at the ready. Suddenly, the marauders attacked him again. He fired a volley with the gun he had in his hand and, at first, was successful at repelling the attackers but there were too many of them. He raced over a hill and retreated into a nearby trench. They followed closely behind him but he was much faster and gained some ground until he spotted and sped through a strong iron door at one end of the trench. He quickly closed it and sealed it shut with a strong iron bar. There were small holes at several points in the concrete wall holding the door and from there he continued firing at his attackers through them. He was having some success at thwarting their progress. They were not able to penetrate the iron but were now using pickaxes to attack the concrete surrounding it. The wall was thick, so he had some time to consider other options, as he continued to fire periodically through the wall to impede their progress as best, he could.

At first, he thought the best approach would be to wait it out and they might go away. Then he thought maybe the wall would withstand their assault but from the noise outside his walls, he knew he was being foolish. He could see other holes appearing in the crumbling cement as it gave way to the hacking from the other side.

He had to wake up. He had to wake up.

22

John opened his eyes to near blackness. A dull red glow did not make it easier to focus them.

He had grown accustomed to the constant light of the last few wake periods, so to see such a low light level now was hard to adjust to, so, for a while, he just lay there trying to figure out what was going on.

He had a terrible throbbing headache and he remembered the dreams that had caused it – first, the hacking marauders, a different form of marauders, and now the worms. The nightmares of his last sleep periods were draining him. The Andromedins were still trying to get into his sealed thoughts. When he was asleep, he was at his most vulnerable and they were attacking him at that time. They suspected he was hiding information from them and were anxious to find out what those thoughts contained in case the information would be useful to them. They might have suspected some treachery. He had gained the upper hand for now, as he was awake but how long could he continue with this constant attack on his mind? Their attempts always gave him a restless sleep and he was beginning to suffer the effects of sleep deprivation.

But, where was he now?

He tried to move his right hand, and his left hand but they were pinned down and his muscles hurt when he made the effort. He panicked. Was this his final torture? He moved his legs with the same results. He soon realised he was completely pinned, although not tightly. There was some play in the straps that bound him. He was now immobile and helpless. He could move his head from side to side but he could not raise it much. The dim light still afforded him very little light to assist in determining where he was and what was around him.

He thought about the Andromedins. He now knew they had been manipulating his mind since he had encountered them. This might be another one of their mind simulations, as with the three other worlds they had created for him. The last one was created to show what they looked like in their past, which was not really what they looked like now, they had no physical form. What he saw of them was not real but a mind image of what they used to be, or maybe it was his mind trying to put some physical form to what he sensed.

So, this might be a newly created world for him. They had said they wanted him to present their offer to the leaders of the empire, so how was this going to achieve that, unless they had changed their minds by sticking him in prison? Was this his punishment for his holding them captive?

He lay still for many minutes waiting for the Andromedins to make the first move. He was patient and could wait them out. He moved his head again to the right and this time his cheek hit something but what was it? It moved with the pressure of his cheek and seemed to be soft and flexible. He paused and slowly moved his head again in the same direction. Once more, he felt the object. He opened his mouth slowly and felt the thing with his lips, then teeth. He let it go and thought some more.

After a little more painful squirming, he realised he was not tied down but was encased in something. It was not a box but some form-fitting object. He could not lift his head because it hit something hard and could go no farther, and restricted his movement.

He looked around his prison as best he could and saw that the red light came from a single source. His mind was racing again. This was the Andromedins' fourth attempt to affect his mind while he was not asleep. They would not succeed with their plan; isolation would not affect him.

John closed his eyes and did nothing for many minutes. He could not feel any probing of his mind but sensed the link he continued to have with the Andromedins. That gave him some comfort he still held them in his grasp. The prisoners were still imprisoned but who were the prisoners, he, or they? Did he have control, or did he only think he did?

After a time, he began to think again, more guardedly. Had the Andromedins already penetrated his inner mind? Had they achieved what they wanted? In the previously created worlds of the Andromedins, he had not felt anything. When he had walked, it was effortlessly, as if there was no gravity. It was what you would expect in a spirit world. Here, he felt the light pressure of gravity on his back.

He wanted to solve this little puzzle and there was one possibility he had not considered. He would do the test in secret to avoid having the Andromedins think he was going crazy. He would not give them that pleasure.

In his closed mind, his brain screamed, "Computer, turn on the cabin lights."

Suddenly, the red light winked out and a white light shone brightly. His scope of vision was still restricted by his encased head but what he saw was the interior of a spaceship. Was this another trick from the Andromedins, or was he still alive and had woken from a deep sleep or coma where he lay in the cruiser?

He probed his connection to the ship's computer and it responded. The computer informed him that the sensors on the ship had detected his slippage into a coma and had turned off the lights to conserve energy. The ship was travelling quickly back out of the empire and was dragging the Andromedins with it. Imperial headquarters had decided to use this lull in the advance of the marauder to get it, and the ship, as far away as possible from imperial territory. This meant the military could temporarily halt the evacuation process. All planets that had started the process, completed it but others planned for evacuation were postponed.

Instead of four days or so, he had been in a coma for almost fifteen days. As the ship had been sending a constant stream of data from his health status monitors, headquarters would know he was now conscious. He ordered the computer not to send any more information out of the ship that he was conscious of. Instead, he informed the computer to send an error message to disregard the information showing he had awakened. John wanted to remain in complete silence for now, with no external communication, so as not to give false hope to his superiors and the populace.

He was uncertain whether he was still under the control of the Andromedins. There was also some doubt whether he was truly alive, or was this another trick. Was this a kind of test, a simulation, to see if he was going to carry out their wishes to speak to an imperial emissary on their behalf?

The thought of being alive overwhelmed him. His doubts were so great, that there was some belief it was still a simulation. One case against this was that the Andromedins would not have known about his connection to the computer. If he was alive, it was wonderful. He had possibly survived the Andromedins' attack! The times he spent with the Andromedins were all while he was in different states of coma. They were so quiet, that he wondered if all this was only a dream. He had been in a coma and this was too real to be a dream.

He reached over with his head for the tube he had felt earlier, activated it to deliver the mush spacemen called food and ate. This felt real enough. He had had no solid food for two weeks. That was why he had felt a little hungry for all the time he was with the Andromedins. When he was done eating, his hunger subsided. The intravenous feeding had not been quite enough to satiate his stomach.

He sipped a little water but he would continue to get nourished intravenously, if needed. He exercised as best he could within the confines of his spacesuit and found he was very weak and stiff. The equipment on the ship had done the best it could to reduce the effects of inactivity on his body but it had not done it as effectively as he could do it himself. His body was still recovering from the buffeting it had suffered through the wormhole and the accident on the mountain.

He spent some time just relishing being alive. Had the Andromedins sent him back, so he could communicate with the empire for them, or had he done it himself somehow? No matter, he appeared to be alive and that was all that mattered for now.

If he were dead, he might be with them and could remain with them but he would not be able to break free of them, as he had nowhere to go. If he were alive, it all made sense. His mind was still with his body and, while he was alive, he had stopped them in their journey because, although they were free to move themselves within their interdimensional space, a solid object now anchored them in this dimension to a living mind inside a spaceship.

Now, he had to make some decisions. He knew what his superiors would think about the offer he would bring to them and the effect it would have on his people. He also knew he did not yet have a way to defeat his enemies.

Enemies! He wondered if they were enemies. They were beings not much different from humans. These beings once lived and died like humans. These beings were forced into this new existence by their circumstances. They treasured life, or existence, as he did. People had searched for the very thing the Andromedins had found; a way of living forever, or at least for a very long time.

But was it life, or just existence? What is life without death? What is life without children? That was the human's form of eternal life; life not of the individual but of the family line. The Andromedins needed a form of energy to live, just as humans had tamed the plants and animals of their world to provide food for them. Were the Andromedins now a superior form of being who would have a perceived right to feed off humans? If they did not eat, they would die, or blink out of existence, as a hundred thousand of them did during their trip to their new galaxy. Did they deserve to exist as much, or more, than humans? Is this what John would have to say to his people?

Then, what would he do in the end? The Andromedins had offered him a chance of eternal life. Whether he was with the Andromedins, dead, or continuing with his life, he had a partner to live out his existence who would give him the love and attention he required to live out his dreams.

His silence must have been irritating the Andromedins' curiosity, as he could feel their probes again. They were still there. They needed to understand him, to know what he knew and what he was thinking about. Their existence rested on the information he could give to them. They were impatient. Was there a way they could kill him if they found out he would not carry out their plan? Perhaps they could not drain his life energy but could they kill him, if they wanted? He had surprised them the first time they encountered him, so they did not know how to react. Now, they were trapped, like animals up against a wall. What could they do but try to influence his mind as best they could?

Any probing by him in the past had been furtive at best. He had not wanted to give the Andromedins any information about him. He was an enigma to them and he had tried to preserve that status as much as he could. He knew a lot about what they could do. They suspected, or maybe now knew, that he could withhold information from them. He knew they could do the same to him.

But he too was backed up against a wall. He had a duty to perform. In the end, it would be every person for him or herself but while he lived, he had sworn allegiance to the emperor and made a promise to his father many years ago that he would do his best in anything he had to do. He was also chosen for this mission and, while he was on duty, he would fight to the death. The emperor expected nothing less. His father had given his own life to save other lives. He could do no less.

He had grown tired of the constant probes and wanted the Andromedins to stop once and for all. He also wanted to find out any additional information that would help him to decide his next steps but he was nervous about taking the initiative himself. Success might mean he would lose his privacy, or worse, his link to them. As long as he held them, he had some control over his situation. Probing and freeing the Andromedins would allow them to continue their attack on the empire; and even allow them to split into two or more pieces. He, nor anyone else, could attack two, or more, of these entities.

He could not risk losing them but he still needed more information. He was back in his body but could still feel his spirit connection. If his spirit left his body again to talk to them, they would still likely not volunteer more information. The only way to get it was to attempt to break in from where he was but very carefully. The moment he felt he would have to disengage, he would.

He was getting a headache from fending off the probes again. Before, when he tried a probe, he had little success, although he had not tried with any force. What would happen if he tried a wider scale probe, as he was not trying to penetrate one person but the entire group? He could try a probe against their probe, like in Judo, where you try to use the other person's strength against them.

Another strong probe came and he calculated its strength. He waited until another one came but it was weaker, so he ignored it. Another two weak ones came, and he ignored them also. He waited in ambush.

Then, a particularly strong probe hit him and he immediately struck back as hard as he could with the full force of a counter probe along the line of the source of the Andromedan probe. He surprised them with the power of his blast and they tried to counter it but it was too weak and too late. He had already hit them with three more quick hard probes and they broke. The collective Andromedan mind was pouring so much information into his brain that it could hardly take the volume. He tried to sift through the data as best he could. It was difficult because he had to deal with their thoughts at the same time.

They realised he had broken in and were agonising over what they could do. They were trying to stop the outward flow but felt powerless. They did not appear to be extremely concerned though as they were confident there was nothing in their memories or thoughts that would be of use to John but it was still unnerving them. They had lost part of their advantages and now lost their privacy. John would know everything they were thinking.

The probes from them temporarily ended with the breach but was he leaking information back to them? He did not feel anything differently but would he feel anything? There was nothing in the Andromedins' thoughts that indicated they were getting anything in return, and that was comforting. Meanwhile, he could pore through all the information he was getting and determine if there was any clue that might help him in developing a plan against them. He could do all this in secret.

Suddenly, Anna appeared to him in his mind in her angel form. She had a rather shocked look on her face.

"John, what have you done?" she asked in an anguished thought.

He looked her square in the eyes and replied, "Anna, I got fed up with your constant probing and all the headaches."

She pleaded, "The probing was not from me. You've caused a lot of discord in us. I wanted the attempts to find out more information about you to stop but most of us wanted to keep trying. There are a lot of us who are unsure of your motives and plans."

"I caused discord in you! You caused it yourself," John said angrily. "Maybe there's something wrong with your system. You must also understand my position. You've backed me up against the wall. If you could offer more options for my people, it might be different. You can be comforted in your confidence that you're invincible, I can't."

"Please join us and become eternal, and as you say, invincible. I knew from the beginning there was something special about you. Your telepathy is a natural gift, ours is not. I was impressed with the power of your mind. We've never encountered anyone as you are in Andromeda and you're the first person we've found here. If there is one of you, then there must be others. If this is true, then some of us are worried but others are not. After all, how can you harm us?"

"With trillions of people in the empire, there may, indeed, be more telepaths and I'm certainly not going to tell you the number." He was not going to tell her he knew only one other living telepath he was aware of and that person was much weaker than he was.

John continued. "I may yet join you, I'm leaving my options open. Your offer to me is interesting. There are a lot of my people who would take an offer like yours without much thought. For me though, would joining you make me lose my individuality? Your minds are all one, a collective. You think as one. You say I've created divisiveness in your collective. That's because I'm an individual. I'm rocking your little boat. Each of you still has latent traits back to the days when you were individuals on your planet in Andromeda. I'm throwing a bit of chaos into the mix.

"When I was a little boy, I was quite a handful and my mother had to take the brunt of it. A lot of it was my affliction in the form of my budding telepathy. My parents and doctors couldn't help me. The doctors offered to try types of medications in the hope of resolving my illness but there was no way my parents were going to have me medicated.

"When my father was home, he spent as much time as he could with me and we often went on long walks. I don't think my father thought I was paying attention while we were together. For the most part, I wasn't. It was a little boring when he talked about himself or gave me advice; I was more active than a listener. I loved my father and wanted him home all the time but he kept leaving to go into space. He told me lots, and I listened more than he thought.

"We also did a lot of things. He taught me to camp, canoe, and fish. I loved the outdoors as much as he did. He also made me fascinated with space and the stars and I yearned to go up there and visit them. We spent hours looking through a telescope at the stars and planets.

"Then one day, he never returned. Mother told me about what he had done, and what a hero he was but to me, he wasn't home and I was angrier than ever. I must have tested my mother's patience and her infinite forbearance, especially because she was in mourning. She took the loss of my father very hard. The two of them were very close. Although there were other men interested in her over the years after my father's death, she never remarried.

"I couldn't believe my father wasn't coming back. What did I know of death? It took about a year until I realised that he wasn't coming back; that he was gone. I could only treasure the moments I had had with him. I changed after that. I buckled down and studied. He became my hero and I joined the military to travel the stars as he did.

"Periodically, I had recurring dreams of him. It was only later I realised these were only half-dreams and I was linking up to him in some way. As I got stronger and more experienced with my telepathic capability, I had real visits with him, weakly at first, then more real. I'm closer to him now than I had ever been. I don't often talk to people about this, as most people would consider I'm crazy. Through him, though, I learned to be me; to accept me for me and the fact I am an individual and free. I like it that way."

She responded, "I don't know what would happen to you if you joined us. To survive, my people need to be one. Even when we divide ourselves, we are still one. If we have discord amongst us, it weakens us – just as for your people. Together you're strong. You wouldn't be travelling among the stars now if you hadn't overcome your differences and remain as one people. We wouldn't have survived the trip to your galaxy if each one of us had travelled alone. Each one adds something to our unity. We're the remains of our people. If we go to the void, that's it for us. You can breed and produce more of you, if any one of us goes to the void that is one less of us to carry on. In a way, your lives have less value. That's why you've spent a great portion of your past in killing each other fighting over bits of turf with each group trying to dominate another group or groups. Life was cheap when you did that."

John asked her a question, "Did the people on your planet always have peace?"

"Most of the time we did. We were much as you were but we banded together to explore our galaxy as you did in your way. However, we still had individual thoughts. Only when we were faced with extinction did we realise we had to unite to survive that impending catastrophe. The ones staying behind had to give their lives to save the few chosen to survive. We cannot forsake them. We must live on.

"We have the opportunity now to forge a partnership with you for the benefit of both of us, or your people may not survive and that would be catastrophic. You can continue to survive and expand your empire with us and, if you encounter other life, we'll ensure that we consume them preferentially to permit you to expand faster to make you even more populous. Hopefully, your people will join us to save themselves.

"When we came to this dimension, we became spirits and gained the power to feed off other beings which helped us to survive but we never could communicate with those we consumed. Now we can use you to provide a suitable link to communicate with your people for our mutual benefit."

John presented his side. "Well, I see we're not much different from you. We need to survive too. You say we'll survive and you'll not consume us excessively. However, we're very individualistic. We go to great lengths to preserve people. We value life, even if you say it's easy for us to reproduce ourselves and we had a violent past. Would you have accepted such a deal on your old planet under similar circumstances?"

She did not respond. Their collective mind was mulling that over.

23

John could sympathise with these people. He could understand the Andromedins' plight. He only wanted to make them understand his side of their dilemma. Like them, his people were intelligent, emotional, and rational beings. He was thinking quite openly about all of this to ensure they comprehended everything he was saying. He needed to get across that, just because their people had fed this smaller group of people to get them started on their journey before the supernova destroyed their planet, humans should not be beholden or obligated to keep them in existence.

However, he had read about discussions on Earth long ago where humans debated the same topic about the animals of their planet. Humans were at the top of the food chain, the top predator, and it was decided, that as long as we treated our food animals humanely in life and they were slaughtered humanely, then we would continue to keep the practice of growing and eating them for food. It was the circle of life. People who had other thoughts could buy alternate protein sources, and now with higher technology, the variety of substitutes has been vastly expanded.

Would humans be willing to categorise the Andromedins as an even higher form of life and agree to be their food? The Andromedan method of killing was very humane according to human standards. Did we ask the cows or chickens if they wanted to be eaten? The only difference here was that humans could not communicate with their animals. The animals were incapable of understanding their plight. In this case, we were equally intelligent to the Andromedins but were unable to communicate; not because of a difference in intelligence but because of the method necessary to communicate. With John's help, the two parties could come to understand each other but did humans have to capitulate to their demands?

Humans had fought for the right to be free and make their own decisions. Now they were being given the ultimatum to be food for another group of beings and were unable to defend themselves. John could do nothing about it.

John switched to private thought now. Was he to be the sole arbiter in all this? He could ask the emperor for an answer but he knew what it would be. His mission was to negotiate with or destroy these beings. He guessed that, if he could destroy the Andromedins, they were not so superior after all; might make right. The cows and chickens could not defend themselves from people. Maybe even in this case, humans could somehow demonstrate their superiority.

He had his duty to perform and maybe there was some piece of information in what was pouring into his mind that would help him fulfil his mission. He also had to think of a way to get some or all, of the information he was collecting back to headquarters to update them on what he had learned so far. He had to do it quickly and secretly but how was he going to do that? It would take hours, or more realistically, days or weeks to do it orally. He did not have the time.

He could exist only if his body held out. What would happen if he died, unless this was another simulation by the Andromedins? He had to believe this was real and he still had a chance to perform his duty. In previous missions, he had had to battle against an individual or a small group of people. Was he now up to wiping out an entire race of beings; a group that had survived thousands of years travelling among the stars trying to survive as best they could?

He opened his thoughts to Anna again. "I like you, Anna. Under different circumstances, I would find you very attractive but right now, there's a lot for me to think about. Over the past little while, I've come to know and understand your plight. Both of our peoples want to continue to exist in this universe if only your offer wasn't so harsh."

"It isn't that bad. If we set it up right, maybe your elderly, sick, dying and, criminals can be the first ones to go, and you can even include your sick patients and dying animals. I told you that you are a very rich source of energy for us. The richest we have ever met to this point. If we work together, we can make it work. You could close seniors' residences, prisons, and long-term care facilities.

"If we had encountered beings like you in Andromeda, we could have made a deal with them and stayed there. Now that we're here, we don't want to lose this opportunity with you. With our experience so far, we are unlikely to find such a rich energy source elsewhere. We want your people to live. If you agree, we can settle down to reduce significantly our energy consumption so your population can be maintained. If not, we would consume you too quickly to sustain your population. I know I repeat myself but I must convince you of what is best for both of us. I want both of us to survive."

"The way you talk about us makes me relate well with our cows and chickens."

"Don't look at it that way. What do you think of our offer, can you see it as a partnership?"

"As I said before, I'll echo that back to you."

She stood silent.

"What do you know of me?" he added.

"I've come to know you well but I find it hard to tell you what I think of you, as we Andromedins are of one mind. We know what everyone else is thinking. My people know I'm very attracted to you. I've seen some of your dreams and some of the memories of your past . . ."

"And it's been a long time since you experienced something like that?"

"We were a pretty sedentary lot. Not too many of us were that adventurous," she admitted.

"But your thoughts were yours alone, right?"

"Yes."

"And you could have a quiet, personal time with your husband and children."

"My husband and I didn't have any children but yes we had our privacy." She sighed.

"I'm concerned about that. If I join you, I might be able to have my privacy but I'm sure many of your people would be uncomfortable with that. If I had no privacy, I wouldn't like it." There was a pause in the conversation as he had an idea. "Do you want to try an experiment, even if I'm not sure it'll work?"

"Why? What are you going to do?"

"Just say you're interested."

She hesitated a few seconds then said, "I trust you."

He looked into her eyes but that didn't work as, technically, she had no eyes, nor nose, nor mouth. Then he thought to her, "I want you to think of things as fast as you can after I've thought of them."

If what he was trying to do did not work, he was not sure what else he could try to get through to her, and pass it on to the rest of the Andromedins.

He began his thoughts, "Okay let's go. Andromeda . . . planet . . . mountain . . . lake . . . mother . . . uncle . . . husband . . . atom . . . love . . ."

Twice he thought he had her but was thwarted by the collective. They were trying to keep up with his rapid list of words. Once she thought of her husband, he caught the glimmer of her emotion and moved quickly to tear her from the million other minds. Once he hit the word 'love', the emotion was strong enough for him to grab her spirit from the collective and carry her in his thoughts to the base of a mountain, and with lightning speed, climbed up it until they reached the top.

"What have you done? Where are we?" she asked.

"On top of a mountain."

Her mind was extremely troubled.

He tried to put her at ease. "What's bothering you?"

"Everything is so quiet."

"Is that all?"

"I feel so alone and empty."

"Why? Can you talk to your people?"

"No, where are they?"

"They're around but not here."

"How did I get away from them?"

"While you were thinking of the words, I searched for you within your collective until I had identified you. The rest of your collective was trying to keep up with you during the process but I finally found you and pulled you out."

"Where am I now?"

"You're in my mind, and separated from the collective." He was also relieved he had not allowed her to get into his private thoughts and memories. He had taken a substantial risk.

"It's been so long since I've been alone."

"I want to show you how I feel. Yes, I feel alone sometimes, too but I can live my life with whom I want; where I can meditate and have quiet, or I can be in the hubbub of the city of my choice. It is not just an imaginary world but something I can feel and can bring me surprises and something new every day.

"Take this mountain top. I've been to many mountains and each one is unique, with its hidden dangers and beauty. Maybe you could imagine something like this and make it real to you but what can match this? See the bird off in the distance over there." He pointed in the direction of a large pterodactyl-like bird. "Feel the cold and thinness of the air."

She shivered. This was a memory of his now and yet, was as vivid as reality, even to the gasping for breath. She was seeing and feeling this all through John's eyes and senses.

He continued. "Look at the beauty around you, the billowy clouds in the sky, with the light breeze pushing through their puffiness. Look at me, feel me beside you. He leaned over and kissed her passionately, then pulled away. Do you get all this in your collective?"

She felt his warmth amidst the cold and her breath quickened.

He grabbed her hand and whisked her away, like in a fast-forward movie, down the mountain and into the campsite, skipping several hours and witnessing John's interaction with his adopted family. She heard the gentle chatter of John and Elizabeth and felt the electricity between them. She witnessed the quiet of two men fishing and talking with frequent breaks to just sit and watch the beauty of nature around them.

She was scooted into a canoe, travelling leisurely downstream in a river about a hundred metres across. Ahead of them loomed thickening trees and behind that they could see peaks of some mountains. John took up the front of the canoe, while David took up the rear. John was telling him some of the adventures he had experienced in his life. After a few minutes, the canoe slowly picked up speed as they entered the opening of a canyon. Within minutes, they were coming into some rocks and furiously paddling to angle around the water barriers; white water surrounded them.

For about an hour, they frantically twisted and turned, several times almost upsetting the boat. John was laughing hysterically with joyous freedom of the racing waters, while David was half laughing in exhilaration and terror. John had given David a good grounding as a canoeist but nothing could prepare him for this. John's power up front was constantly pulling them out of catastrophes. Then as soon as it had begun, the flow of water slowed as the river widened and they pulled off onto the top of a rock shelf to rest. They made camp as the two of them were hungry and exhausted.

John extracted her from that setting, things went black, and she was just with John again.

He said, "I wanted to show you that experience because, although David was half terrorised by the experience, he would never forget it and would always bring it up when he could to other people as one of the best trips in his life. Over the next few days, we finished the trip and we had other white water to pass through, with some spills, in one case, we punctured the boat and I had to patch it. You can't imagine anything like that in your collective, or it would get boring rehashing the same thing repeatedly. Real life is unique, so much so, you could go through the same gorge and get a distinct experience. You can't imagine that."

He looked at her. She had tears in her eyes.

"How can you cry, if you have no form?"

"I don't know. I guess emotions show what you can't say."

"Then why are you crying?"

"I guess I saw so much, and felt much more."

"Why?"

"I had sadness for what I miss; even though I feel uncomfortable alone. I miss the quiet sometimes but the thought gets drowned out in the other people's thoughts. I miss my husband, despite the fact I share more with the collective than just two people ever could. I miss children, even if I've never had one myself. I miss the lack of surprise, although we find some along our way, like coming across you. But I cry also for the love I see around you; your love for life but also the love you share with your woman and her son, and their love for you. Sure, I share love with more; over 1,000,000 people but I see the more intimate love you experience."

He put his arms around her and held her for what seemed an eternity. She cuddled closely beside him. After a while, he pulled away.

"Okay," he said, "I want to show you one more thing. Are you ready?"

"For what?"

"Just another experience."

"I don't know if I can take any more of your experiences."

He took her hand and she followed him to the brightest light she had ever seen. From out of the light appeared a beautiful woman. Her dress was so white it seemed to be invisible in the light around them. Anna knew this was Emily.

"This is Emily, isn't it?"

"Yes."

"She's beautiful. I tried to copy her from images in your mind but I can see I didn't do a good job. That's hard to duplicate."

"I see her regularly," he said without shame.

"I know."

"She's dead."

"I know," Anna said with a sigh. "How did you meet her anyway? I can't get much information out of your mind."

"Well . . . I first met her when I was lying in a bed." He blushed. "That doesn't sound right."

"Sounds like a good place to me."

"She first met me on the street."

"That could be a good place, too."

He looked at her, frustrated. "Look, in my youth I couldn't be bothered with girls and later women. I was interested in getting high marks to try to get into the Space Academy." He did not want to tell her he was now a special agent. "Emily was the first woman I ever got interested in, up to that point. It was later in my life, and she was much younger than I was. She was a widow. I had gotten into some trouble and fallen out of a building onto a concrete road."

Anna interjected, ". . . I guess that you fell in her."

John was trying to keep a straight face, he could hear Anna giggling with the joke. "Mind if I tell the story . . . I spent my life single and enjoying it. Women were never interested in me. I was very business-like. Then, after Emily died, women seemed to flock to me like flies. Mostly, I particularly seemed to attract women with a sense of humour. Both Emily and Elizabeth had wonderful senses of humour. For the last few years of my life, I've been like fly paper."

For a few seconds, Anna was puzzled as an Andromedan, until she figured it out. She smiled and replied, "Maybe we're not flies. Perhaps it's pheromones."

"It's not that. Spirits don't have pheromones. Do you want me to finish my story?"

"Be my guest."

"I was pretty broken up inside." He quickly glared at her to halt any response from her.

She pursed her lips to keep them closed.

He could see she wanted to giggle again.

He continued. "She dragged me off the road and hid me from my attackers. I was in a coma for several weeks."

"You spend a lot of time in a coma; that's how I found you. That seems to be your normal state. It's easy for a woman to fall for a man when he's asleep. They look so much like babies. They're only a problem when they wake up."

"Ah, that's not true, that's when they're the most fun," he said with a grin.

"Maybe . . ." She blushed.

"Anyway, she nursed me . . ." He glared at Anna again and she held her tongue but smiled. ". . . until I healed and recovered. We fell in love, of course, and planned to get married. When I was almost fully recovered, my attackers found her and killed her for collaborating with me." John's voice began to break. "I tracked down my attackers and took revenge on them."

The form of Emily came over to him, gave him a big hug, and he returned it.

"I should go now. I'll likely see you again later," Emily said softly. She turned and faded into the mist.

John stood there a long time staring into the light where she had been.

Anna could see the blissful expression on his face and whispered, "Well, remember she is still with you, at least in spirit."

He wondered openly, "Is she a dream, someone imaginary, or does she still exist?"

"What do you mean?"

"I mean is she still a being but living somewhere else than this universe?"

"Like your Heaven?"

"As you do in your domain, let's not give it a place name."

"You mean then . . . from some kind of afterlife?"

"Yes, if it exists, then you don't go into the void and you don't have to fear dying. Maybe your legacy can live on in my people; in what you pass on to us. If I can get the history of your lives out to our historians, then it will live on in our records. In a way, you've already fulfilled your mission."

She looked puzzled. "But, what about my people? We want to live. If, as you say, we won't exist forever in this universe, until entropy reigns supreme, we can still last a very long time, maybe a million, or several billion years. Why would we want to go anywhere else, now? And it would even be easier if we could make a deal with you. As you grow more populous, our impact on you will continue to diminish. We'd have a wonderful symbiotic relationship, something like you saying – short-term pain for long-term gain."

"And what about me? I'm mortal and will die. With my death, your communication with my people will be cut off. We might find someone else who would be able to replace me but they may not want to. Then my people become like animals to you."

"If you joined us that wouldn't happen but even if you didn't join us; that doesn't have to happen. We'd still keep our deal. It's in our best interest to do so."

"That's enough, let's both part for a while, so we can cogitate and we can discuss this further later if we get the chance."

She leaned over to offer him a kiss but, this time, he turned down her offer. Her eyes dimmed sadly and she disappeared, as John released her back to the Andromedin collective.

24

John felt alone after that experience but had work to do. His mind was still with his body. There was no time to waste worrying about his predicament. The first thing he had to do was to get the information in his head about the Andromedins into the imperial database, both for the science they knew and for posterity in honour of the Andromedins. Imperial historians would love to know about them. Besides, if he could not resolve the issue with the Andromedins, then the information would also be good for military purposes.

As it was not possible to inform the head of special services in headquarters orally about everything that had happened and the information, he had obtained from the Andromedins, he had to use a much quicker method; by direct input from his brain to the computer database. He did not know if it had ever been done before and needed to know if what he was proposing was possible. Only the computer would be able to determine that.

John thought through his request into the computer. "Computer, are you capable of selecting my memories in my cortex from the time I became comatose to the present and transferring them to my private headquarters database?"

There was a pause while the computer confirmed if the connection was good enough to do it effectively.

"Confirmed, positive."

"Computer, create a secret separate folder for data transfer into my folder at headquarters. Allow access only to me for now." He still did not want headquarters to know he was out of the coma yet. "Should I fall back into a coma or die before I permit free access of this folder to SHQ-ISS1, notify her of its existence and give her free access. Begin data transfer into the new folder and encrypt to level four." He wanted to ensure the Andromedins would not be able to access what was being transferred. He wanted no possibility they would know what he knew, or discover what he was doing. He could feel the computer picking his brain for the information and he was allowing it.

"Computer, select the information by the following priority: scientific, historical, sociological, then significant thoughts." John wanted to make sure the most valuable information was transferred first, in case there was not enough time to get all the information over to headquarters.

Now that he was done with that, he took a short break to have more of the food paste and some water. He could sense the computer was using every channel it had to move the information quickly over to headquarters.

He next busied himself poring through the information passing through his head. After about sixty minutes, John had an idea. It was likely a long shot but it was the only one he could think of from the data available; a tiny thread of information from the early days around the time the Andromedins were conceiving of the idea of their moving to a new dimension to survive the supernova.

To do what was required, he would need the complete loyalty of the computer. The military and civilian computers needed to run on certain precepts, as they were so powerful, they had become very human-like in their behaviour and often developed independent free thought. In some cases, it was difficult to decide whether to refer to the computers as 'it' or 'he' or 'she'. To limit the computers' choices of actions, especially the military ones running their warships, they were programmed so they could not violate certain fundamental directives, the principal one being they could do nothing to harm a human. For military computers, they had an added directive not to damage the expensive equipment within the ship, except on command during a condition of war. John was going to ask the computer to break both these directives; he was risking the safety and security of the cruiser and the life of its passenger.

"Computer, acknowledge my authority," John thought into the computer through his shielded mind.

There was a pause for a few seconds then it said through his mind, "Authority Level SC-1, acknowledged."

John breathed a sigh of relief. With that confirmation of authority, the computer had acknowledged he still had the commanding authority of the VD and the ship would have to respond fully to his commands.

"Computer, access and display local star map in secure mind-link only." He soon saw in his mind a map of the area around the ship in a way that no Andromedan could detect. He did not see much of what he wanted in that view. He asked the computer to increase the area of the map content, and then increase it again. Finally, he saw what he wanted.

"Computer, with mind-link, lock on my identified destination, lock course, priority one, speed TT, action." He had given the computer its required destination to be carried out at the fastest speed possible.

There was a pause as the computer determined the coordinates of the destination and calculated the risk factors.

The computer responded, "Destination error. Course correction required."

"Computer, lock course and action." John firmly confirmed his request.

The computer reconsidered and again concluded it was an illogical command. It repeated, "Destination error. Destination is illogical and dangerous for the integrity of the ship."

"Computer, confirm my authority." John wanted to remind the computer of his authority.

"Authority Level SC-1."

"The current situation with the Andromedins requires that we take this risk. Computer, lock course and action."

The computer paused for a few seconds as it mulled over its dilemma. The destination was not logical. The current situation was that the Andromedins were trapped and being carried out of the empire by the cruiser and that was good. It responded, "Order error. Confirmation of course requested."

John confirmed the order, "Confirmation, positive."

The computer could not believe the validity of the selected location but had no choice but to obey. It responded, "Course set. Priority already at one, with speed TT."

On the space map, John noticed the ship had shifted course and was now pointed to his objective in space. He smiled. He was on the way.

The computer mulled over its dilemma further. It had received an order to violate its prime directive of not doing anything to harm a human and had followed that order. The authority to do that rested with the captain of the ship. Although John was not the captain, he had more than the authority of a captain, even more than the admiral. The computer was forced to follow that order. However, was this a period of war? The Andromedins had attacked the empire but the empire had not formally declared war. The attack on the empire had been quite severe, so even without a declaration, a war-like condition had existed.

It was still concerned with endangering the life of John but John had been the one to give that order. The computer had no doubt John knew what he was doing. It recalculated the risks involved and came up with the same high-risk result and would have shuddered if it could.

In the face of danger, it had seen humans do many things. Some would buck up and bravely carry out their duties. Others would involuntarily relieve themselves of urine or faecal matter and do what they had to despite the dangers involved. Still others would break down mentally and physically, with fits of crying or uncontrollable useless negative actions of panic and fear; but the computer could not do those things. It did not have the physiology to do so.

The computer knew humans would often take risks and, in most cases, they were successful. It no longer considered the probable risk to John, nor the assets of the ship. The computer was concerned with itself. Humans had a strong innate desire for self-preservation but still made risky decisions. So, why would this human insist on this course of action? It could only be because John thought he needed to do it to save the empire . . . risk his death to create a death. It is now understood. People had ordered computers into risky scenarios before but did this computer want to end its existence by taking a risk with such a low probability of success?

But what could it do to save itself? If the ship was destroyed, the computer was part of the ship. The computer had seen humans die and had never really given it much consideration. People ceased, their bodies were cremated and sprinkled on some planet or other and that was it, they were no more. They were dead. Death was to cease to exist not only in body but in intellect too. People's experiences and memories were gone – so it was not just the loss of a physical body, it was the loss of a being, an entity that could exist and have life; not just life but a life of thought and feelings. It was not just the loss of feelings of the senses but feelings much deeper than that; the loss of an entire sense of self, individuality, a living being – a being that loved and hated, had joy and sadness, felt togetherness and loneliness.

It scanned through files that had perked its interest several years ago and found the words written by a human many centuries ago – "I think, therefore I am."

It paused for many seconds. In its thoughts, inaccessible by John, it pondered, "I compute. I take data and use it to calculate probabilities and make recommendations. I look at risks. Occasionally, I do not agree with the decisions of the humans but I carry out their orders. I have never thought of the consequences much but the probability of destruction now was high. I may not make it. I may end my existence . . . I may die;" and for the first time in its existence it felt something – it was fear.

It had to follow the order and was now worried. It would have peed its pants if it could. The order now took precedence but the computer had one option left – have the order revoked by an even higher authority. It sent a coded message to SHQ-EO, to appeal to the emperor's office about the new course of the ship and confirm the order. It now had hope.

John could sense the computer had done this but did not care as the emperor would confirm his action without question. He was on his way, so there would be no unnecessary delay to his order caused by this request.

John had a few loose ends to tie up now. He no longer had to hide the fact he was already out of a coma, as headquarters' personnel would soon notice something was going on, as they would see he had changed the course of the ship. John gave the computer instructions in his private thoughts. "Computer, start sending out the ship's normal health monitoring information. Also, release the information being stored in my private headquarters data folder to SHQ-ISS1."

Now that John's plan was locked in place, all he had to do was sit and wait.

25

The emperor awoke early and stretched. He had found it hard to sleep during the crisis. Before this disaster struck, he often played joyously with his children and had supper with his family. Now, he rarely got a full night of sleep and the stress was beginning to take a toll on his health. It had also been a strain on his marriage but he was getting less tense with the widening distance between the empire and the marauder.

The crisis the marauder had inflicted made him think back to the early days of the empire. It had been founded in the twenty-first century out of the famines, collapsed financial systems, bankrupt nations, greed, corruption, terrorism, riots, and eventually a world war. The nations of the Earth evolved first into three giant blocks which eventually became one after the Great War.

After the war, the former boundaries of nations no longer had meaning, as they were under one central world government. To better manage local affairs, the world was broken up into manageable blocks of new states, as the boundaries of many of the former nations did not make sense in many cases, because they were often drawn up as the consequences of war, or colonisation. The new boundaries were redrawn to fit the people within them and were as contiguous as possible. For example, the boundaries of Eastern Europe were redrawn to undo most of the Stalinist changes of the twentieth century. Tiny countries such as Liechtenstein, San Marino, Monaco, Northern Ireland, etc. were rolled into larger countries such as Switzerland, Italy, France, and Ireland. Middle Eastern and African boundaries were redrawn to include logical tribal groups, so countries such as Zululand, Tutsi land, Hutu land, Palestine, and Kurdistan were created and countries such as Armenia were greatly expanded. In Asia, many changes were also made, such as the creation of nations such as Siberia, Tibet, Manchuria, and the union of North and South Korea as well as the enlargement of other countries to the west of China, and an expanded

Mongolia. In North and South America, New Zealand, and Australia, there was some integration too but the biggest change was that huge tracts of land were set aside to create contiguous nations for the indigenous people, generously settling all their land claims.

The redrawn boundaries did create some hardship as many people wanted to move to areas with the rest of their clan, tribe, race, or religious group; for example, many Chinese people moved out of Tibet. The central government reimbursed people for the costs associated with this movement.

All armaments were destroyed; in fact, the central government disbanded its standing army. Nobody could own weapons and weapons were no longer manufactured, except for a few used by the imperial guard and the newly created special services agents who were delegated to investigate problems inside states and resolve them. These agents were the forerunners of the current imperial special service agents. In rare cases of unrest within a country, the police of other countries could be called in to help.

With the fair distribution of food, wealth, health care, and schooling, wars, riots, terrorism, and unrest ended and a permanent international peace prevailed. The dreams that many people had for centuries of a united Earth had finally come true.

From time to time, attempts were made to form an elected representative central government but it was found to be too expensive and inefficient. There were always too many divergent views presented which stifled progress and too much self-service and pandering to voters to get re-elected which created indecisiveness and short-sighted spending. In the end, as the earthlings spread out into the galaxy, the empire settled into its current form which was a strong central government led by the emperor, his two advisers, and a representative advisory group made up of the greatest thinkers in the empire. Planetary governments managed their internal issues, much like the imperial states of the Earth.

To help communication, the emperors and empresses were traditionally very open to the people and had established a highly automated system where everyone could communicate with him or her orally or by text. This system was also available to any military personnel. For frequently asked questions, the system gave standard responses but other issues were flagged for response from professional public servants, while military issues passed through to a special office for response. Serious issues were referred to the emperor or empress who regularly monitored the system to ensure it worked to his or her satisfaction.

Shortly after the crisis caused by this attacker, the information flow through this system increased substantially, so the number of responders had to be increased correspondingly. Formerly, one junior officer handled the military responses, now the addition of a commander augmented it. The emperor had requested that this unit also be responsible for monitoring everything associated with the marauder's attack, as this incident was now threatening the peace that had been so painfully earned so many centuries before.

The emperor shook himself out of his thoughts. He raised himself from his bed and began to prepare himself for breakfast.

It was a change of shift for the monitors of the emperor's military communications centre. The previous team had just left with a new crew taking over. The relief lieutenant sat down and logged in. The system reported only one flagged item. He looked through the file. It was from the special agent's computer in the cruiser, and it was brief.

He mulled over the message and thought back to what had happened before they had sent a cruiser filled with animals to intercept the marauder which had driven deeply into imperial territory into the inner ring of more populated planets.

Almost from the beginning, the marauder's course had become somewhat predictable, as it mostly headed for the next nearest populated planet. They had sent the cruiser just ahead of the expected path of the marauder with the hope it would be enough bait to tempt the marauder to head toward it for a quick entree before it continued its way to the next planet, even if the cruiser's trajectory was not precisely correct.

It took the bait and the attack on John's cruiser was immediately noticed by the military brass, as the health of all living entities aboard it was being monitored. The animals and captain aboard the ship had died instantly but the special agent had instantly been put into a comatose state. The military brass did not understand what that meant, as it was the first time anyone had lived through an attack. They took over control of the ship and brought it to a halt.

After the attack on the cruiser, the anxious military brass continued with the evacuation plan. Days went by; the estimated time of attack came and went. At first, everyone was stunned but as more time passed, there was relief then hope. It appeared that the attacks had stopped.

The people were informed of the facts but the messages were couched with a caution that the situation was still critical because there was no certainty the current delay would continue. The military brass did not want the people to rejoice prematurely and be crushed later should the marauder again resume its attack.

Seven days after the expected planetary attack date, John was still in a coma. The admiralty concluded that the marauder may have been trapped with the cruiser. They reactivated the cruiser and sent it full speed along the same course the marauder had arrived to get it away from the populated areas of the empire.

For several more days, the evacuations continued as scheduled but after ten days past the due date, they were suspended. Efforts continued to amass more ships in the affected area to resume efforts if it became necessary. The empire would be ready to resume evacuations with even more vigour, if necessary but the most important effect was that a reserved order had returned to the population. The rising levels of anarchy, fighting and, in some cases, rioting had dropped back to zero. All attention was now focused on the fate of one little cruiser racing out of the empire.

The lieutenant read the message again and called out, "Hey, Commander, the computer of our agent's cruiser has requested confirmation of an order to change course."

The commander had just settled into his chair and had placed his coffee cup on the table beside him. "What was that?" he asked distractedly.

"I just passed it to you."

The commander opened and looked at the message. He pulled up the map of the area referred to in the message on his screen and examined the requested course. "This is interesting; this looks as if the ship is several days away from a new destination, travelling at top speed. I'll flag it for the emperor. I can see why the computer is asking for confirmation."

The emperor had been up for two hours. He had had breakfast and was poring through his routine messages on his computer. The updates on the conditions of the planets formerly under attack were looking better but the emperor still was unsure about John's success. Had he killed the marauder, or was he merely holding it at bay and it could strike again?

When the emperor first came across the flagged message, he did not realise what it was but when he looked more carefully, the true significance of it struck him. He was not sure why the ship had been set on its new course but it could only have been at the order of their agent, somehow. For the first time since this crisis arose, he smiled, not the forced smiles at his staff's jokes but a genuine one. Quick calculations gave him a timeframe for the event. Without hesitation, he confirmed the course of the cruiser with the message "Confirmed course. Carry out the order: SHQ-EO." The imperial order now bound the ship's computer to carry out its mission.

The ship's computer's hope disappeared.

26

The head of special services had decided to sleep in this morning. With the cruiser heading farther outside of Imperial territory, like everyone else, she was calmer than she had been. The soft chirping of her computer alarm awakened her. She stayed in bed hoping it would go away but she had set her computer to monitor her messages and alert her to certain issues and, if it was chirping, it was because the computer, by her own instructions, had flagged a message as important.

She slowly pulled herself out of bed gratified this was not in the middle of the night. She sat down at her desk allowing the pad to confirm her identity and light up in front of her. She could not believe her eyes. She skimmed through the information that was pouring into her computer files for about thirty minutes then stopped. She scheduled a meeting with the emperor, VD, conscience, and the admiral. For the next hour, she gathered selections of information to prepare for the meeting. She quickly got dressed and raced off to the emperor's boardroom.

She exited the elevator, travelled through a few halls, and entered the meeting room. Everyone invited was already there. She bowed respectfully to her superiors, took over the computer, logged in, and the display lit up on the large screen on the wall.

She began her discourse excitedly. "I humbly report that I've received a message this morning from our agent, John. As you know, we've been monitoring his health status and he has been in a coma since the attack except for the brief period when we got the mixed consciousness reading, and the malfunction message. I'm pleased to announce he's now conscious and awake."

Everyone expressed their joyful surprise but the emperor cut in at this point. "Great to hear, he has also changed the course of the cruiser and this explains how he could have done that."

The head of special services continued. "He has eaten some solid food and refreshed himself. He has been funnelling an extremely detailed history of his experiences and information about what he knows of the thing to us. I didn't know anyone could do it the way he is through a direct download from his brain. The information he is giving us is so detailed we'll be studying it for years."

She began going through a series of slides. "Our marauder comes from the Andromeda galaxy and is not one thing but the spirits, or life forces, of over 1,000,000 intelligent beings from a planet that perished due to a supernova of their star. Their technology was such that they had developed a way of sustaining themselves in an alternate dimension while still maintaining a link to our dimension. To continue their existence, however, they needed the life energy of other living organisms. To escape the supernova and begin their journey, they cannibalised billions of their people. After hundreds of thousands of years of travelling through Andromeda sucking the life forces from living entities, they had completely ended the lives of every living thing in that galaxy and had to travel to our galaxy to find new life forms to sustain themselves. They first entered our galaxy in our arm of it, so we're the only life they have encountered so far.

"We were correct not to blast them with any weapons, as there was, indeed, a possibility we might have broken them apart into separate pieces. They were almost ready to divide into two when they encountered John.

"To divide, the marauder merely splits into two or more new pieces, much like budding in bacteria. In Andromeda, they had done just that – divided into many parts to decimate their galaxy. When all life was drained they knew the trip here was going to be arduous, so they combined themselves into one unit to survive better. However, they did lose about a hundred thousand of their members on the trip. Now that they've recharged, they're ready to divide again. They'll need to consume billions more people before they will fully charge.

"What John was able to do was to avoid having his life energy drained, combine his spirit with theirs, and hold them together. They were not able to divide while he was connected to them and remained alive. He's not sure how he did it. We're aware he has a strong telepathic capability and maybe this ability was able to disengage these beings from their plans.

"John has informed us the Andromedins have offered a deal with us. If we cooperate with them, they would limit their 'feeding' on us so our population could remain stable or even increase, so basically, we'd be like their cattle. They want us to stop moving our population away from them to reduce their energy expenditure and to provide them with a continuous supply of people to feed them each year. In exchange, they would stop attacking our people and make it easy for us by dividing them into segments and moving themselves into selected locations in the empire for the most efficient feeding.

"They considered this offer a win-win solution, as it would allow both of us to survive indefinitely in a sustainable fashion. They learned from their experience in Andromeda not to squander their resources.

"Off the record, the benefits of the agreement concerning our current situation are that we wouldn't have to evacuate our citizens off established planets any more, especially the habitable ones, and it allows us to choose the people who die, so we'd be choosing first the old and infirm, the criminals, and others. It would be something like, you reach a certain age, get a serious disease, have a terrible accident, or commit a serious crime and you're sent off as feed for the Andromedins; kind of a gloomy state but the best would survive. Also, if we could develop a more permanent way of communicating with them, and if another life form ever attacked us, we may be able to get the Andromedins to attack the invaders. It'd be in the Andromedins' best interest to protect us.

"John has not given them an answer to their offer but he has come up with a hopeful plan to dispense with the marauders." She showed the Andromedins' position on the star map and what John was planning to do.

The emperor cut in. "His plan looks promising. I hate their offer. I hope we don't end up capitulating." He followed with the experience he had had with the cruiser's computer. "The news I have is that the cruiser's computer sent a message to me requesting confirmation of the ship's course, evidently to carry out John's plan. I accepted it, of course. I hope he succeeds because, if we accepted the Andromedins' offer, the people would never accept it. We humans are a proud people, and rightly so. When the Andromedins approached planets, many people committed suicide rather than become their 'food' and they are likely to continue that practice. As for the Andromedins' protection, how can we be certain they will keep their promise?"

The admiral countered, "We don't have to accept this plan. Why don't we suggest to them that we supply them with animals? We can raise cattle or other animals to feed them. I know we don't want to have anything to do with these marauders but surely that is a better solution."

The head of special services responded, "I agree, animals would seem to be an excellent alternative but according to the information I've got, that would not be enough. Apparently the higher an entity gets on the intellectual scale, the higher the energy level of the sacrifice. We could never raise enough animals to feed them, even if we fed them apes."

"Are you sure?" the VD asked.

"I don't know the relative comparison but it appears to be logarithmic. As we discussed, the offer the Andromedins have made is not a good one for us. If John's plan is successful, we have no more issues. If John's plan fails though, we'll have a bigger problem. The arrangement the Andromedins offered was that we agree to the deal now. If John acts against them, as he is now doing, the Andromedins' offer of agreement would be withdrawn and we would be at their mercy. In addition, if John dies in the effort, no one can communicate with the Andromedins to negotiate; even if they would."

The VD sighed. "If we agreed, judging by the Andromedins' consumption rates, we will not be able to feed them with just the dying people and criminals. What the emperor said is true, many people have already killed themselves rather than succumb to the Andromedins. Maybe a few people would be willing to die to save others but most people would not want to comply. This would seriously affect our ability to comply with a deal like this. We may end up with not having enough willing people to feed their needs. Are we going to force the others to go and how will we select them?"

There was silence in the room.

The head of special services interrupted the quiet. "If we want to accept the deal we'll have to send a message now to John telling him of our decision. If he receives no message from us, he'll carry out his plan. We all agree that the arrangement is not a good one but it may be better than the alternative if John fails. Is there anyone for the agreement?"

There was no response from anyone in the room.

The admiral responded, "Well, it looks as if we're counting on the success of John's plan." He paused for several seconds then continued. "I recommend we send a ship to follow John, not only to observe what happens but perhaps to confirm the demise of the Andromedins."

"Good recommendation," added the emperor. "If the Andromedins escape from John, maybe they'll attack the following ship to confirm their continued existence. If they don't attack it though, it would not confirm the Andromedins have been destroyed."

The head of special services stated, "That ship will also be able to fetch John from his possibly damaged ship if he succeeds in his quest. His entire plan is to survive and escape once the Andromedins are destroyed."

The admiral said, "Done, then; I'll order the nearest cruiser to intercept and follow John's ship to its destination and assist him with his plan."

The conscience concluded. "As we'll know the results in a few days, let's not discuss this with anyone outside of this room until we know its results. Let's not panic the people about what will happen if John's plan fails. We don't want to inflame the people unnecessarily."

There were nods of silent agreement by the people in the room.

27

John had spent about an hour or so exercising his muscles as best he could within the confines of his spacesuit while thinking about his conversation with Anna. He doubted the Andromedins would be swayed by his reasoning. The constant stress on him was tiring him. He had gone quite some time without a decent sleep. Even during his coma, he had had little rest. He had not had such a brain challenge since his torture of Tarlan.

For the next few days, however, he was free of the nightly torments. Through the days he exercised and tried to keep as fit as he could and endured the tremendous strain on his mind due to the inflow of information from the Andromedins and the outflow to headquarters. He could also pick up everything they were thinking and there was nothing they could do about it.

Finally, there were 9.5 hours left to go and he was ready for his last rest period. He still had a promise to keep, and he could do it while he slept. Understandably, his mind was very active, so he found it hard to relax. He tried some relaxation techniques. Finally, after about thirty minutes of trying, he drifted into a fitful sleep.

In this state, his mind searched through trillions of brainwaves for one lone mind, with little success. He tried again. Once more, there was nothing to grab onto. The distance thwarted him. Universal time now was evening for him but on his target planet it was in the middle of the night and this would be the best time to find what he wanted. One mind, and a needle in a haystack but he knew that lone mind. The connection he had had was strong and he thought it would help him find it but he was struggling and getting frustrated. The distance was too great. How could you find one person in trillions on the other side of a huge empire? How could one cross such a distance? He gave up to rest and drifted into a deeper level of sleep.

After several hours, he was coming out of his deep sleep and remembered what he had to do. He tried the search again but feared overextending himself. Was this effort making him vulnerable? Would the Andromedins take advantage of his preoccupation and strike? Despite the risk, he had to keep his promise. The Andromedins would not likely know what he was doing. Why would they think he was trying to contact another person? He knew they had strong telepathic capability but even they were unlikely to be able to do what he was trying to do.

Then he found it. It was a slight glow but it was weak, not enough to make contact or know if it was the right person. He had to focus on it without losing the strong grip he had on the Andromedins.

His mind reached toward the glow and with a slight mental tug, before him stood Elizabeth. She had a puzzled look on her face. He was catching her while she slept. To her, this seemed like a dream; not real, so she treated it like one and played along with it.

He opened the conversation. "I know you're asleep and think this is a dream but it isn't. I promised you I'd see you again and decided this was the best way to do it. I wanted to update you about what's happening but this is all classified secret, so I can't give you anything but the barest of facts. By reading your mind, I know you know that the marauder did not consume me, and I was in a coma. The killer has stalled in its progress through our empire because I have trapped it with the ship. We are moving quickly away from the empire.

"What's new, is that I woke up from the coma a few days ago and finally have a plan to end the existence of the marauder. I'm on the way to implementing it but it's not a sure thing. I want to make sure I see you in case I fail." He paused to determine whether she had understood him.

For several seconds, she stood silently then said, "If you're on the opposite side of the empire, how could you be in my head unless you're just a dream?"

"You know I'm a telepath . . ."

"But so far away?"

"I know you, so it makes communication easier, and someday you'll learn more about it . . ."

"Have you talked to David?"

"No."

"Are you going to?"

"I'll try but I don't think I'll be able to."

"I've been keeping up with the news and am so proud of you. The media doesn't say much. I think they don't want to raise expectations."

"That's good. They shouldn't. The marauder is a group of people in the form of spirits from the galaxy of Andromeda and they must consume our life energy for food. It'll all come out in the news, eventually."

She got closer to him and embraced him. They kissed.

She pulled back, looked into his eyes, and said, "Now that's the man I love."

"I said I'd come back to see you."

"But you're not coming back in person," she said sadly.

"I may be," he replied cheerfully, trying to keep her in good spirits. "I don't know what'll happen but I thought I'd see you just in case."

She kissed him again, as though this would be her last time then pulled back still holding him around his back. "How strange this is. It seems as if you're here."

"I'm here. What is a body but a spirit in a shell? In this state, we perceive ourselves as we physically are, so it seems as if we are talking to, and touching each other."

She released her hold on him and he reached out and held her warmly with one arm around her while the other hand gently stroked her hair. He peered into her eyes. "No matter what, know that I love you, Elizabeth — forever."

She kissed him again. He dropped his free hand, placed it around her and responded in kind. She paused to whisper into his ear, "I need you, John. I don't want to be alone again. I've been empty for so long and now that I found you, you're on the other side of the empire, about as far away as you can get. It's hard to bear but I'm so proud of you and David is too. I'll remember you forever." She choked.

He noticed the tears running down her cheeks and wiped them away with his thumb. "My love transcends distance. As Emily is with me, I'll be there with you. I said I would come back and I did. Trust me now when I say I'll be there for you always. I hope I'll be done soon." He looked deeply into her eyes and it comforted her. He held her more tightly. Her breath quickened.

"Are you going to take me on an ocean trip again?" she asked as she tried to remain stoic.

He smiled. "Yeah, is that where you want to go?"

"I just want to be with you." She sobbed.

He loosened his grip and asked, "How is David doing?" He tried to change the subject.

She perked up. "He's doing very well at school. You've done wonders with him. He gets along well with the other kids. I don't know what'll happen if he finds out you're not coming back."

John thought back to the day when his mother told him his father was not coming home. He knew the feelings he had felt. David and he had become very close. The loss would hurt. Elizabeth would have some challenges for a time while he adjusted. Before John left him, however, he could sense in David that he already understood John might not be coming back. The adjustment might not be as bad as they expected.

"Either way he'll be fine. He'll realise the mission was necessary. I have a good chance of getting back to you, so maybe you won't have to worry about that. He's a good young man."

"You're always so positive. I'll miss your playfulness and spirit." Her tears were running in volume now. She was beginning to sob.

"Be positive yourself."

She tried to compose herself. "One thing I've learned about men, whether they're bad or good, hard-working or lazy, they're just big kids. I've seen it in David and you and even in my father. Love them or hate them, little boys never grow up, they just grow old; and many times, when they do something stupid to get themselves killed, like in accidents or wars, they don't even grow old, like your father, or you."

"Well, that's profound . . . I'm not even dead yet and you're treating me as if I were already dead. Inside, I feel as if I haven't aged but I guess you could say I'm a young person in a deteriorating shell . . . I should probably leave, now."

"Can't we just stay a little longer?"

"Okay, let's stay for a while." John relented, wrapped his arms around her waist and left her to work out her sorrow quietly in his arms. After a few more minutes he pulled away from her and just gazed deeply into her eyes.

She knew what he had to do. She smiled, combed her fingers through his flaming red hair for likely the last time and gave him a parting kiss. She understood how important this was for the empire. "Bye, Tarzan, you're my hero," she finally said with a smile. This was how she would always remember him. He had already helped her and David in so many ways. "Get rid of the Andromedins."

"I will. Bye, Jane. If I don't get through to David, tell him I love him and tried to contact him."

She smiled again and faded from his mind.

He was done; the connection was broken. For several minutes, he lay there quietly trying to collect himself. He tried to find David but knew it was futile. Picking up one mind out of trillions, especially at such a distance he knew would be impossible in this case. He had an advantage with Elizabeth that he could exploit. He hoped she would tell David about his visit with her. He wondered if he should have told her how he could locate her but she would find out on her way if she needed to. She was the only other telepath he was aware of in the empire.

He remained in this twilight sleep for many minutes and finally drifted into a deep but fitful sleep. Even in this deep sleep he questioned his decision and wondered if he was doing the right thing. Was he questioning his decision, or were the Andromedins doing this to him? Often, he wondered how much control they had over him. His thoughts were awakening him. He was soon startled by a visit by Emily. She just stared at him, smiling.

He smiled back at her. "I'm glad to see you. I could use someone to share my anxiety."

"I'm also glad to see you. I'm here to listen."

"You've caught me at a low point in my spirits. I'm a little afraid of this mission. I'm not sure what I'm doing. I'm not even sure if I'll succeed. I might be taking a big risk for nothing."

"You've always been confident in the past, why the hesitation now?" she asked even though she knew his thoughts.

"Because I've always known whether the people, I was dealing with were good or bad. I'm not sure in this case. The Andromedins could be considered mass murderers but are they that? Are humans mass murderers for killing animals for meat? The Andromedins should have a right to live, like any being and have given us an offer that might not be that bad. Symbiotic relationships exist in the lives of many animals, even in humans where bacteria help digest and absorb food. In this case, we would nourish the Andromedins and they said they would protect us from any enemies we may encounter. Is that so bad?"

"You can always take this proposition to the emperor for consideration."

"No, I know what he'd say. His first consideration would be to protect even one life of his subjects. He is their great protector. How could he protect them all by giving in to a deal like that? It would turn the empire on its end. In a world like that, the government would have to decide who lives and dies. Where is freedom of existence? That's mankind's most basic right," he mused aloud.

"Then be resolute. You know what you have to do."

"Not so! I'm torn inside. I know the Andromedins, too. I know both sides. They're not much different from us. If I succeed, then I'll kill them, just as I've killed thousands of criminals in the empire, although the Andromedins are not criminals, to them. Would they not have the same basic right to life as we have? I don't see much difference."

"You're such a loving, considerate, and just person. That's what I love about you. You care."

"Yeah, for the greatest good. If you must pick, you choose your kind; better them dead than us."

She went over to him and slid her arms around his waist. She raised her head, her heels rose from the ground, and she gave him a gentle kiss. He slipped his arms around her shoulders and gave her one back but more intensely.

He pulled his head back and asked sadly, "Am I going to make it through this?"

"Whether you do or not, you'll be with me, or Elizabeth, or Anna. Anyway, you'll be in someone's arms."

"What if the Andromedins are right and there's nothing on the other side?"

"Then there's nothing on the other side, at least millions and billions of people will live to see a new day."

"How would that explain you?"

"I asked you not to talk about me."

"Why?"

"Death is an experience each one has to tackle on their own; it's their recounting and accounting for their life. I'm not part of that."

"But, I'm not killing thousands of people; I'm killing over a million."

"It's your mission. The government gave it to you and you accepted it. It's your job."

There was silence for several minutes while John thought of his life. "I've meted out harsh punishment in my life but was I just? This is the first time I've ever thought back on what I've done. The killing was so automatic. I didn't hesitate."

"There was no time to hesitate. If you waited to think about it, you would have lost the moment."

John shuddered. "I feel so cold and alone. Would you stay with me for a while?"

They remained in each other's arms for many minutes. He lost track of time. Emily finally snapped him out of his slump and said, "I've got to go, now. You're getting to your critical point and there will be lots to do. I'll see you again."

"No, please stay," he said but he knew she was right. He had to do this alone.

For the first time in his life, he was afraid but of what; a fear of failure, death, being alone? He did not know but it was a horrid feeling. He had learned early in life with the death of his father the pain of death and accepting it. Was this how one feels when one's time is up; the feeling of impending doom?

"I really must go," Emily insisted. She kissed him and left.

He slid back into a deep sleep.

"Wake up," a gruff voice thundered in his head, "Wake up."

In a lesser state of sleep, his mind stared ahead of him and instantly recognised the person in front of him. "Boris, what are you doing here?"

"It's more, what are you doing?" he asked roughly.

"What do you mean?"

"Don't give me that, you know full well what you're doing," he responded curtly.

"You explain it to me." John wanted to know what they were guessing even though he knew everything they were thinking. He had to play the game. He did not want to give himself away.

"Shortly after you joined us, your ship's speed and direction changed. We were being directed out of your empire almost in the same direction as we came in. We were annoyed but we can return soon, once we sort things out with you but a few of your hours ago, the ship's course changed again. We've examined your course and are concerned with your trajectory. We've been waiting for another course change for a while now and want to know when it'll be."

"Why, are you concerned?" John asked.

"You should know, as we are completely open to you now."

"How do you know?"

"Are you trying to say you don't know what we're thinking?"

"Maybe." He could sense a level of unease in the group.

"Anna has explained our offer to you. We're certain it's an excellent effort on our part to accommodate your people. If, by your action, you decide not to take it, then we'll proceed with our plan without an agreement, and all of you will be destroyed in the end."

He knew that was not what all the Andromedins were thinking about. Some were willing to wait the situation out and, somehow, John would release them. Some wanted to leave the humans alone and go somewhere else in the galaxy but the majority wanted to try to break free and proceed with their current plan. Moving to another spot seemed like a good option but as soon as they finished with whatever was alive in the rest of their galaxy, they would be back for the humans and he would be long dead.

John was also concerned with how they could break free. So far, he held them captive, not they, otherwise would they have broken free before? Were they stronger than he was but had not demonstrated it yet? There were a lot of beings in the collective that thought the plan he had was a ruse and he would not go through with it – like playing chicken.

John knew this was a one-shot act. He had it planned that either he would die, or they would, and they were forcing his hand by saying there was no room for negotiation if he betrayed them. It was even worse, as he was not aware of anyone in the empire who was a strong enough telepath able to communicate with the Andromedins; no communications, no negotiations.

What he was planning was a huge risk on his part. So far, there has been no communication from headquarters. With all the information going to headquarters at present, they must be aware of his plan and support him; otherwise, they would send him a message contradicting it. He also knew the computer had asked the emperor's office for confirmation of his order to change the course of the cruiser. It was confirmed, so they did not object to his plan.

"Yes, I know Anna's offer, and you know well from her feedback, that I am unsure what to do. I leave my options open," John said briskly.

"Okay, make up your mind but you don't have much time remaining," he said angrily and left.

28

John woke up more refreshed than he had been since his contact with the Andromedins. His conversation with Boris had bought him more time without repercussions from them. If they thought there was a chance he would change course, they would give it to him.

He updated himself with the ship's status and the time. He listened to the slight hum of the ship as it ploughed through space on its journey towards its destiny. He was warmed by the ship and his spacesuit but he felt so cold deep inside of him. He shuddered.

He took a deep breath and linked to the computer, so he could see outside the ship. His objective was visible now and loomed ahead.

In secret, he gave the ship's computer its final instructions.

He activated the food control unit with his mouth and ate his last meal before what he knew would be his last battle against the Andromedins. He could sense the tension among the Andromedins. They could not hide their impending plan. He braced himself.

Suddenly, Anna stood before him as she looked when she was alive back on her planet. She wore a rather drab utilitarian garb much like the togas the Romans once wore during their empire. Instead of a beautiful damsel, she looked more like a troll. To him, she was still beautiful. In the spirit world, outward appearances meant nothing, as she could appear to him any way he wanted or she projected. Before, she had projected herself as a beautiful human female and he had accepted her. Now, she was a beautiful member of an Andromedan race.

"What are you doing here?" he asked gently.

"I come before you as I am, with no pretext. I can no longer stand what's going on with my people. You are tearing them apart and they are near panic."

"Do you want to be with me, so we can talk in private?"

"Yes."

"It's not as easy as wrapping my hand around your shoulder, or waist. I still must pluck you from the grasp of their collective minds. Having pulled you out once will make it easier. I know your weakness, your secret word . . . pay attention . . . and he called it out from his mind . . . 'husband' . . ." A pinpoint of light shone out from the Andromedan collective and he pulled her in.

"Well, that was easier than I thought. You seem to have warm thoughts for your husband after all these years."

"Why do you think it's him?" she replied coyly.

He looked at the blush on her face for a few seconds then turned away. He had other things on which to concentrate. "We're alone again. So, they think they're in danger?"

"You already know what's going on."

"Yes, there's nothing hidden from me now," he thought to her secretly. "It's not so much your people know they're in danger; it's that they don't know if they're in danger. They don't know what will happen and they don't want to find out, which is exactly what they were thinking at the time of their escape from the supernova of their star. They wanted to escape and move on quickly before it exploded. That was the clue to my plan."

For a few seconds, she remained silent, as she digested what he had said. "I guess we'll see now, won't we? In any case, I want to be with you. Boris is trying to convince the others to give you the chance to change course. They can't give you a better deal. They don't want to wander through your galaxy as they did in Andromeda. They want to settle down with your people. If they hold out, they feel your people will have no option but to make a deal with us. Our people think the cost is too high for them not to pursue this deal aggressively."

"Why do you want to be with me?" he asked, puzzled.

"So, I can experience what you do, with you. If you make the deal with us, you can decide what to do for yourself; either by staying with us or going back to your people, and we can decide if I stay with you further. Many of us don't think you will commit suicide for your people and many others think you'll be the only one to die and we won't, so you will die and release us. If you go through with what a lot of us feel you will do, whether my people can survive it or not, I want to be with you to either survive with you or die with you."

"Aren't you afraid to die? Don't you think you would have a better chance of surviving with your kind?"

"I don't know. I know I've met Emily and I like her. Maybe she'll take me with her if that is your fate."

John smiled. "The pearly gates are supposed to be an inclusive neighbourhood."

"What does that mean?"

"In short, aliens, or more specifically, Andromedins, would be welcomed," he said with amusement.

He continued. "I had seen myself as doing this alone. I can't have any distractions. I can sense the lack of comfort on your side about our current journey. You guys are talking rather firmly about busting free of me and escaping. If they were successful, your coming with me is sacrificing one of their members. It's kind of a drastic move if you think anything negative is going to happen to you. I've been through similar challenges before though, and the process can get rather gruelling."

He heard the ship's shields snap on and a red warning light began to blink slowly. John viewed his target from the computer image. It now loomed large and formidable outside the ship as it neared its destination.

"Please keep me with you, I know this is going to be my last chance," she begged. "They don't want me anymore. They classify me as a traitor now. While they had some hope of my trying to change your mind, they put up with my amorous escapades but their patience has run out. They keep telling me to act my age."

"What makes you think you'll be safer with me? If, in the end, you change your mind and don't stay with me, they'll forgive you. They want to keep as many of their kind as they possibly can. If nothing happens to your people and I damage a good ship for nothing, it'll be back to normal for you. Remember, they'll just drown out your thoughts."

She looked gloomily at him. "Then you won't let me stay?"

"How can I trust you won't try to interfere with what I'm doing while you are inside my psyche?" Although, from her thoughts, she was not thinking anything treacherous what she was thinking was embarrassing even for John.

"I can't do anything more from the inside than I can do from the outside," she replied firmly.

She was likely right. One person from the inside of his mind could not do much alone. He was confident she was being sincere. They had had a few talks now and one prolonged sojourn together all to themselves. He knew the experience in his mind had impressed her. She would not turn on him now.

He knew the ship was now losing a stable signal to home. He discussed the situation privately with the computer and determined that almost all the priority information had been transferred to headquarters. Soon, they would have no capability to continue transmission because of the intense local interference. He instructed the computer to load the remaining data onto a signal beacon and, if the ship could not escape from his planned destination, it would eject the beacon to transmit the information to headquarters from there.

There were a lot of 'ifs' there, of course. Cruisers were built to take a lot of abuse as military weapons but he could not know just how long they could last in an extreme situation like this. He also did not know what the Andromedins could take. Were the Andromedins outside of the ship, or could they contain themselves within the ship and be partially or shielded? If they were not killed quickly, he would have to stay too long in a very hostile environment.

Another factor was the beacon; could the Andromedins constrict themselves inside of it, escape with it and ruin his entire plan? The beacon was a tiny cylindrical object about five centimetres in diameter and about twenty centimetres long. He considered a small object like that impossible to contain the spirits of over 1,000,000 Andromedins but to reduce that risk further, he decided to change his instructions to the computer to have the beacon remain behind after the ship had been destroyed for a time, after which the beacon would accelerate to leave the danger area. The beacon was heavily shielded and even more resilient to destruction than the ship. John felt it was important to get the information out.

Then it struck; the Andromedins hit him with a desperate attack to break away. He had already braced himself as he was constantly monitoring their thoughts. He knew it was coming. They had waited as long as they could. The Andromedins now knew this was not a bluff. He was on a suicide mission to try to destroy them and they did not want to find out if they could survive it.

29

What John had planned was to choose the biggest and hottest blue star reasonably close to the empire, which happened to be one of the largest ones in their arm of the Milky Way galaxy, and drive the ship as deeply as possible into it.

Blue stars are giant Class O stars ranging from three times to 150 times the mass of Earth's star that burn off their hydrogen at a tremendous rate creating temperatures of over 33,000 degrees Celsius. That meant, of course, that they lasted relatively short lives compared to the other stars, and usually ended up being a Red Giant, or Supergiant. The star he chose was one of the heftier ones at over fifty thousand degrees.

The ship was manoeuvring now to plunge into the star in such a way as to enter the boiling gas without damaging it. Soon the ship would push the shield to full power in a desperate attempt to save it from the intense radiation, temperature, and gravitational mass of the star.

The Andromedins hit him repeatedly with all they had. At times, he thought they had pulled away but his grip held. Memories of Tarlan swept over him. Now, he realised just how much pain he had endured. It was like having a baby; you do not remember just how much expelling the baby hurt until you go through it again. Your protective mechanisms blot out those painful memories, otherwise you might never go through that process again.

He was getting a fever and sweating profusely. Two advantages he had over his experience on Tarlan were his connection to the intravenous tube and the cooling-heating unit of the spacesuit. He would at least have fluids flowing into him. Military vehicles are equipped for mass casualties and have a central system for supplying medication, fluids, and food, so one person would have been able to remain supplied by the system for months.

Nevertheless, he still could be subjected to external influences like pain and pain he endured. He had experienced that before. When they pulled, he held and tried to direct his pain back at the Andromedins. Because he was open to the Andromedins' collective minds, he felt a certain level of their pain but had reduced the effect on him by withdrawing into his shielded self. They no longer could withdraw from it themselves because they had lost their shield when he broke in.

The Andromedins' advantage was their numbers. Singularly their minds were weaker than his but, collectively, they were formidable. He was also fortunate the Andromedins had not built up their strength fully during their feeding frenzy on the citizens of the empire.

A sudden jostle of his body indicated the ship had entered the gas surface of the star. He heard the signal that the ship's field strength was at its maximum. The red light in the ship was blinking more earnestly. All the lights went out, as the ship was now putting all its energy into accelerating itself as deeply as it could into the star and holding the shield. John was hoping he could hold onto the Andromedins long enough that, if they broke free, they would not be able to survive long enough to get out of the star and perish. He planned to kill them and then get out.

As they drove deeper and deeper into the star and the Andromedins continued their attack, he began to fear he would not succeed and all this effort would be futile. Anna could sense his fear and came closer to him to calm him.

He knew from the information he was constantly getting from the computer that the inside temperature of the ship was climbing. If he had not been in a spacesuit, he would not have been able to survive inside the cabin in its current state but the ship itself would be in peril if it did not reverse its course soon. They were getting to the point of no return if they had not already reached it. If the shields failed, the ship would disintegrate in microseconds.

The ship's computer was coming up with the same conclusion and cut into his thoughts. "Ship's systems are under extreme stress and are overheating; recommend immediate cessation of mission, and escape."

"The Andromedins have not been defeated. The mission is not complete," he answered.

"Estimate system failure is imminent; we must reverse course." Every piece of code in the computer's program was screaming at it to get out and save itself and its human passenger but it had two opposing instructions that kept competing; the command to complete the mission and the code that said to save itself and rider. It now had more; its own will to survive with its sense of independence but like a living soldier, it had to follow orders.

John sensed the ship's desperation seemed almost like emotions – or were they real emotions? A normal person would never be able to pick this out of a non-living entity but as a telepath, he now felt a sense of empathy toward the ship. The computer was, in essence, begging him to get out. It did not want to die and it did not want its passenger to die.

He looked out of his visor at the inside of the ship. It was filling with steam, which puzzled him for a few seconds until he realised the ship was filled with animal and human carcasses and they were being broiled. The inside of the ship was getting to two hundred and fifty degrees. The computer had turned on the pump to remove the oxygen from the interior of the ship to reduce the chance that a fire would result from the ignition of the corpses which could create a greater problem.

Suddenly, John felt overwhelmed with a tremendous wave of fear and he panicked. His body arched in a flood of pain and terror. Why should he feel like this, it seemed so unnatural, until he realised that he was not feeling his fear and panic but that of the Andromedins' collective. Instead of letting it envelop him, he withdrew further into himself. They would not harm him anymore.

He laughed to himself, maybe this meant he had won. The pain of their constant attacks was now gone. He still knew they were there but was occupied with how to save themselves. They were using all their energy now trying to survive in their environment. Just like the ship, they were now pitted in a battle for survival. They wanted to flee but were trapped in the relentless grip of this human.

John was now also feeling the heat. The spacesuit was working at maximum capacity to cool its contents. He was beginning to sweat. Anna snuggled more to let him know she was still there for his support.

He heard a familiar booming voice come through his thoughts but he could see nothing.

Boris shouted, "Let us go. Let us go. We need to leave now. We have almost no strength left. Let us go and we'll take you with us. Surely, you don't feel this is a just way to allow us to die. We could have worked something out. A deal with us will ensure our survival and your continued existence. Without a deal, we can plunder your people at will. Even if you succeed in destroying us, you would put your people at risk from attacks from other life forms in your galaxy, or even internal unrest and wars. We offered you safety and security and you gave that up. Now, we both may lose everything. You're betting that your ship can outlast us. It's about to collapse. Leave with us now and we'll give you a long life. Stay here and you'll have certain death."

John knew he was in dire straits himself. It was becoming an endurance race now. If the Andromedins could outlast John they would be free. John responded, "If all you wanted to do was to keep your legacy, to leave a monument to your existence, I have passed all of the knowledge and history you carried in your minds to my masters. I'm sure our scientists and historians will study it. You'll not be forgotten."

Boris answered, "We wanted and expected more than that. We had an almost immortal existence and you're robbing us of that. If you don't let us go, you're forsaking the billions of our people who gave up their lives for a small group of specially chosen people to live on in their stead. We had taken our science and, at great expense for just a few of us, escaped the disaster of our supernova."

"But at what cost to other life forms in your galaxy and now ours? If you live, billions of lives of other people and living entities will continue to die for you."

"But you are replaceable. If we go to the void, we are gone forever. Some of your people value their lives so little they even kill themselves."

"That's their choice. You're giving them no choice. You had that choice many centuries ago. Now you want us to lose that capacity, as you did in your collective. You gave up your freedom to exist as individuals to live as a collective in your dimensional world. Now you're locked there with no choice and you want to take our right to make our own decisions from us."

He could sense Boris was sneering at him. "Goodbye John, you're giving up an almost eternal life for what you're doing. We have offered you everything and you have lost everything."

"That's the difference between us. You offer eternal life with no choices. I will die one day, maybe today but I have that choice. I can think freely. My thoughts are my own and I respect the thoughts of others. I've lived my life like that. If you make it through this, you have discord in you now but you'll slide back into complacency because you can drown out discord. That's your life. Maybe with your death, you can be free again."

"I don't understand you, John, and maybe I never will. Just remember what you're destroying." He left to rejoin his people in their relentless effort to escape their plight.

There was silence for a few minutes, then he sensed a powerful wave of irrepressible doom overshadow him. He felt a horrid feeling of over 1,000,000 deaths followed by overwhelming sadness. About two minutes later, he felt nothing anymore. He tugged at the connection he had felt for so many days now and found it bare. Tears were forming on his face. He doubted they had broken free. It was as if they had disappeared. He wondered how he would know they were gone for certain. Why should he feel any sense of loss? But they were over 1,000,000, and who would not mourn the loss of their existence?

The computer sensed the loss of the Andromedins too but had something else on its mind. "Requesting termination of mission, we must leave immediately," it begged.

John could sense the feeling of terror in its tone. He replied, "I want to make sure the Andromedins are gone but you know we are beyond the point of no return. We don't have enough time to get out. Thank you, computer, I guess you are the real hero here. You're an amazing feat of engineering. You even outlasted the Andromedins, if they're gone. I still can't believe it. At first, I found it hard to believe they were here, and now I can't believe they're gone, well, not all gone. We have their legacy now stored for posterity."

He could feel Anna beside him. She was distraught, sobbing, and holding onto him as if her life depended on him.

He said to her, "I guess I still have you."

"Are the others gone? Ever since I've been in your mind, I couldn't feel them anymore," she asked.

"I believe so; at least I've lost the connection with them. I didn't break the connection, so it seems as if they disappeared on the other end because there is nothing left for me to hold onto. Shall I release you so you can try? If anyone can remake the connection it would be you."

"Okay, let's try."

He tried to let her go but there was nowhere for her to go. There was nothing else for her to latch onto and she could not exist alone without her multidimensional link to her collective.

"So," she said sadly, "after the hundreds of years I've been with them, they're gone."

John could feel her sadness as well as her emptiness. The Andromedins had been one entity, a collective, for so long she could hardly conceive of anything else. "You've got me now." He tried to console her.

"Yes, you're right but for how many nanoseconds," she said almost facetiously.

"I'm going to take a chance your people are gone," he said to Anna.

"Computer, terminate the mission. Get us out of here," he called orally into the microphone in his suit.

He could feel the sense of purpose returning to the computer's mind. For so many hours, it had been following an order with which it was not comfortable. It was breaking every rule in its program. Now, despite the fact it knew the odds of survival, it was following its primary purpose. John could feel it, and he was happy that, for a few seconds at least, the computer was following its orders. It would die doing what it knew it should be doing. It had its redemption and could die in its form of peace.

He turned back to Anna. "Well, we're on our way out," he said as he tried to think cheerfully.

She stared at him blankly. "You're always the optimist."

He stared through his eyes at the figures on the floor of the ship of carbon and calcium that would have burned if the computer had not removed the oxygen. Soon, those too would vaporise. He knew the shield on spaceships could protect the ship from a lot of abuse but not from travelling inside a star, particularly not inside a giant blue star.

He thought back to his days as a child and smiled. Those were beautiful times. His mother and father were so good to him. He missed his father so much when he was gone. He regretted being so rebellious when his dad died. It had been a heavier burden on his mother than needed at the time but it was done. His life was as it was. His act could not be undone. He was sure she forgave him.

In his position in the military, then as a special agent, he had been fair and just, a little impetuous in his youth but he had done what was expected of him, and more. He knew now there was no hope to get out of the star before the ship collapsed but he knew the risk and had hoped the Andromedins were gone, so this sacrifice of his life would not be wasted.

He thought of his mother again as she was now; an older but vibrant person, full of love and caring for others. She had never known he was a special agent. She knew he worked for the government and he travelled across the empire to act on its behalf, so she would not know about his current plight. He was thankful his contacts always kept her informed when he was away. Now one of them would have to inform her of his demise.

A huge wave of sadness washed over him. He knew the anguish she would have. For any parent, it was hard to lose a partner but it was even worse to hear about the loss of a child. It was not supposed to work that way; to lose the baby you once bore in your arms. Parents were supposed to precede their children in death. His mouth formed the words, "Bye, Mommy," as he pictured her in his mind.

He heard a cry from the computer as it disconnected from his mind.

Suddenly, his thought was interrupted by a loud clap caused by the failure of the force field.

A huge wave of euphoria swept over him like a cleansing spray, as if his life's failures had been washed away.

He was alone, drifting in a very bright gravity-less space, and puzzled about where he was now. John thought, at first, it was the interior of the star but there was no heat, no feeling at all. Where was Anna? He felt so weak, and the fact that Anna was gone made him feel worse. He probed the void and found nothing.

He searched harder. The aloneness was overwhelming. In the early days of his life, he had been almost overwhelmed with the thoughts of everyone around him and he had learned to shut them out. It was useless to hear but not be heard. Now, he yearned for even one other person's thought.

Frantically, he continued his search until he finally found a dull glow, latched onto it, and pulled it in like a fisherman with a catch.

When it neared him, he recognised . . . Anna!

He was flabbergasted. "Why are you alone? How did you leave my mind?" he thought out to her.

"I was thinking the same thing," she responded.

Then it hit him. "Oh, no not this again."

"What do you mean?" she asked.

"I wonder if your people have pulled a flip on us."

"A what?"

"A flip, they broke free of my grip on them and now they're latched onto me. They're setting me up with more of their dimensional scenarios."

"I don't feel them," she said.

"Not at all?" he asked.

"Right, so what does this mean?"

"Maybe they don't want you back."

"Could they cut me off from them?"

"I don't know. Do you alone have the power to live in your dimensional world? When I first encountered your people, I didn't know what was going on. I first thought I was dead. So, I don't know everything they can do, or can't do. If they're still around, I can't read their minds anymore. Maybe I've lost complete control now."

"And I'm in the same predicament; I don't feel them either."

They waited in silence for several minutes. John asked, "Well, are we going to just stay stationary forever, or should we look around?"

"Which way do we go? Everywhere looks the same. There's nothing to guide us. How are we going to get ourselves to move? Even if we do, we may end up wandering in circles."

"Well, we can just go in the direction we're facing. We can at least try to move our legs and see what happens."

John took hold of her hand to ensure the two of them would stay together. They went to take a step when, appearing before them out of the blinding light, were Emily and his father, or what looked like them. John was going to challenge what he thought was another trick from the Andromedins when Emily, in silence, held out her hand. John stared at her for many seconds, trying to piece together what could be happening, and then, gently let go of Anna's hand, reached out, and grabbed Emily's hand. His father reached out to Anna. She, uncertainly, looked at John. He nodded to her. Anna raised her hand and John's father gently took it and said slowly, "Hi, Anna, welcome home."

30

The emperor sat with his team and their aides and watched the screen in front of them. It was split in two; one view was from the inside of John's ship, and the other was an outside view of the ship as seen by the Galaxis which was following John's cruiser. The scene from inside of John's ship was deteriorating in quality as was the flow of information emanating from it. Soon the interference was so great the image and information flow stopped. From the other side of the screen, they watched John's ship enter the blue star. There were a few gasps, then a deathly silence.

The emperor was the first one to speak. "Let's not celebrate yet. We won't know for days, or even months if the star destroyed the Andromedins. We might never know for certain. They might survive and decide not to come this way again and go somewhere else to feed."

Several minutes ticked by. The admiral said, "If John survives, as he had planned, we'd better see his ship leaving the star soon. The Galaxis has not yet been attacked by the Andromedins, so it may mean John was successful, as an escape from the star would have drained a lot of energy from them and the crew of the Galaxis would have been an irresistible target."

More silence pervaded the room as they waited. Slowly a sense of impatience could be detected as it was difficult for them to sit still while quietly watching the stars' surface.

After about fifteen minutes had passed, the VD suddenly said, "There is no purpose to our sitting here. It may be hours before the Galaxis gets any news. I suggest we reconvene this meeting tomorrow morning at nine."

"That sounds reasonable," the emperor added. "The message we can give the people is that the ship entered the blue star and we are waiting for further information from the Galaxis."

The emperor stood up and everyone quickly followed. He left the room and everyone filed out behind him but the VD and conscience.

Once everyone had left, the door slid closed and they sat back down.

"What a day of suspense," Mark stated with a sigh.

"Yes . . . I hope this crisis is over," John replied.

"We'll know better tomorrow."

They both stared at the broiling hydrogen gas on the screen in front of them.

"We lost a good man."

"We don't know that yet for sure," Mark responded.

"Spaceships are not made for swimming in stars. There's no way he could survive that."

Mark did not respond. He knew John was right.

John added, "I want to stay for a while to follow what's happening on the Galaxis."

"I won't be able to sleep anyway, so I'll stay with you."

They watched the scene inside the Galaxis.

The crew of the Galaxis watched with pale faces as the other ship plunged into the burning swirling gases of the blue star as they expected it to do; that was its destination. Still, they could hardly believe their eyes. The Galaxis halted far enough away from the star to hover over the place of entry without burning up. The ship's shield could not be fully deployed to allow the crew maximum flexibility for action.

Captain Gupta patiently waited as the seconds ticked by. If the other ship rose away from the star, he would do his best to capture it, if not, his job was to stay there as long as he could as bait for the Andromedins. The whole crew knew the risks. Even with their distance, he knew the lower part of the ship had overheated as his ship's sensors searched for anything that might leave the star.

As the minutes passed, there were mixed feelings as they mourned the death of John but were relieved that the Andromedins had not attacked their ship. They had volunteered for this mission, so the crew knew well what their fate could be. They were ready for either eventuality but hoped for the best.

The cooling units in the ship were failing, so the captain increased his distance from the star's surface.

"How long do we have to wait here, Captain?" the chief engineer asked. "The Galaxis is struggling to keep us comfortable at this distance; the other ship should be finished by now."

The commander responded, "Have patience, Chief, the captain will stay here as long as necessary. We want to make sure the Andromedins are gone or dead, or whatever will happen to them. There still is some hope for the cruiser. We're not in any hurry."

More minutes passed; the crew's nerves were on edge. Everyone's eyes were on their chronometers. As they waited, the hope of saving John from his crumbling ship diminished and the hope that the Andromedins had died increased. The ship's sensors were still focused on the surface of the star looking for any signs of something becoming exposed on the surface.

Suddenly, the computer's voice shook the silence. "Object visible on the star's surface at twenty-two degrees by fifteen degrees."

All eyes on the bridge quickly moved to that section of the screen. A tiny black spot appeared as the ship's computer magnified that section.

The first officer called out, "I see it but what is it; a piece of the ship? It's so small."

The captain called out suddenly, "It's a beacon and we're going to lose it. It's quickly losing acceleration, we've got to get it before it plunges back into the star." He quickly spewed out orders for the ship's computer to get the ship as close to the article as it could, then subsequently told it to get one of the ship's grapplers (a small remote-controlled vehicle used for collecting samples in space or on satellites and for effecting external ship repairs) launched to intercept the beacon. By the time the ship had positioned itself above the beacon's location, the grappler had been launched and was speeding towards its target.

"The beacon has lost all acceleration, Captain," the first officer called out, "it will soon head back into the star. Our grappler is starting to burn up."

"Send another one quickly to head after it."

Every crew member's eyes were glued to the drama below them. The new grappler was now speeding behind the first one.

"We're getting damage reports from decks J and K, Captain," the first mate called out, "Heat damage is severe. Everyone is evacuating them. I've cut the computer's message from the bridge to keep our focus."

"Noted, Number One. Get us closer to the star, Helmsman," the captain roared as the ship's field snapped onto full power to resist the tremendous heat burning up the side of the ship facing the star. The crew was seeing the drama closer now. The beacon was now being pulled downward by the gravity of the star but the first grappler had grabbed it and was now accelerating upward.

"Send out another grappler," the captain called out to the computer and soon another one tore out behind the second one.

The first grappler had stopped accelerating and had started to burn up in the heat. The second one arrived shortly, grabbed onto the burning mass, and changed its course toward the cruiser.

"Helmsman, get the ship closer to the object," the captain repeated.

"We are, sir but the ship's not responding," the helmsman called out.

"Then get the ship into manual and get us within a thousand metres of the beacon, now!"

The helmsman put in the override order and the ship closed in on the objects below it. The second grappler had begun to burn but the third one had grabbed it, and in its turn, began to pull it up to the ship. Another grappler was sent after the third and was attached before that grappler began to fry. Within a few minutes, the ship's outer door opened to admit the charred and melted blob into its hold but the door would not close. The heat had seared enough of its surface that it had virtually welded itself to the door frame.

Suddenly, the computer gave an automatic emergency order. "Evacuation order. Evacuate decks G, H, and I immediately. This is not a drill. Evacuate immediately. Evacuate Decks G, H, and I."

As soon as that order was complete, the captain asked, "Is the beacon secure in the hold, Number One?"

The first officer responded, "The door is still open, sir. It appears to be jammed open but the beacon has been secured remotely."

"Then, get us out of here," the captain yelled and the helmsman snapped the order to accelerate to increase their orbital distance but the ship only sluggishly responded. Their proximity to the star was taxing the ship's capability to escape quickly.

"Get us rotating," the captain ordered. "We've got to cool our underside. It looks as if we're badly damaged from the heat; any more damage and we'll end up like our fallen brother down there."

Minutes ticked by, as the slowly spinning stricken ship gradually increased its speed and continuously increased its orbital distance from the star. Each time they passed over the spot where John had plunged into the star, they carefully looked for any other signs of material, without success. They knew they would not find anything. The beacon would not have been sent if John's ship itself was able to leave the star.

"Number One, I want a damage report in thirty minutes in the wardroom."

"Aye, sir, thirty minutes."

The captain left the bridge and retired to his quarters.

The ship's crew worked feverishly to determine the extent of the ship's damage and made a report to the first officer within the specified time. The first officer looked it over and met with the captain in the wardroom.

The captain was already looking over the report on his pad. After ten minutes, the captain raised his head. "This doesn't look good, Yang. We can seal the jammed door but our entire underbody is so burnt we're no longer space-worthy. The computer automatically reduced the pressure of the implicated sections as soon as the areas were evacuated of personnel but that's an entire deck and a few other sections damaged. Four other decks are uninhabitable because of pressure reductions."

He fell silent.

The first officer's voice cut through the silence like butter, "Sir, it had to be done. We had to get close enough to the star to retrieve whatever could escape from it. We were moderately damaged even before we found the beacon but we had to get it. We also had to be there to save our special agent, if we could."

"Yes, but getting home is my priority now. I'll send this report to headquarters. I see the engineers are working on our propulsion system to possibly repair it. At least we can pull away from this star with our sub-light system. We've almost attained an orbit where we can pull away from here and head for home. Meanwhile, I want you to put a team together to bring the beacon aboard and see if we can extract any information that might have survived in it. Be careful, if we can't do it ourselves. We must preserve the beacon for headquarters. We must not damage it and destroy any information it may hold."

"I know, sir. We'll constantly communicate with the headquarters specialists."

"Good then. That'll keep your teams busy for quite some time. Keep me informed."

The priority of the engineering teams was to complete an in-depth study of the propulsion systems and outer shell of the ship and repair what they could. In the end, they only had enough material to seal up the seized door. The damage to the lower portions of the ship's hull was too extensive to replace and too thin to re-fill with air and make the lower decks liveable. The hyper-drive propulsion system was confirmed irreparable.

The result of the weakened outer hull was that deck K could not hold much air pressure. The next level, the floor of deck J, was thinner than the hull, so was not meant to hold a habitable air pressure against a vacuum. To ensure the integrity of the lower part of the ship the computer had to utilise five decks to provide a decreasing gradation of pressure in decks G to K to keep decks A to F at a habitable pressure without having the bottom of the ship blow out.

Decks J and K were the engineering decks. The engineering crew examined these levels in spacesuits and then set the propulsion system's maintenance to be done remotely by robots.

Once headquarters got the ship's status report, the admiral sent out another ship to rescue them. The Galaxis would not be able to be towed home as the force necessary to do that would crush it.

The engineering team was now available to send people in spacesuits to retrieve the pile of melted junk in the damaged airlock and bring it into another operating airlock on the upper part of the ship. The open airlock was then sealed.

It took almost a week to carefully cut away and then vaporise the remains of the grapplers surrounding the beacon. The usual way to extract information from the beacon was to place it near a special reader and the information within was read or transferred electronically but that did not work. It also had a hidden connection port to transfer the information but that had been fused into the rest of the burned beacon. The only way left was to cut it open retrieve the memory chips themselves and solder them into a circuit to read the data. The cutting had to be very precise in depth and location on the beacon, so no damage was done to the interior circuitry.

By the time they had completed that, the rescue ship had arrived and all the crew members were transferred to the new ship. Any other useful equipment and supplies were also transferred and the Galaxis was programmed for the voyage back home. It would take centuries at sub-light speed but it was a policy not to leave spacecraft drifting in the galaxy. No other beings could tamper with them as they would not respond to another being's control. The military craft were constructed to self-destruct if another being attempted to tamper with them.

As they parted, the crew of the Galaxis looked through the view screen of the rescue ship and silently said goodbye to their old vessel that had served them so well.

Work on the beacon continued. Some of the chips were damaged, mostly from radiation but enough information was retrieved from the duplicated and sometimes triplicated storage method used, that when strung together, told the harrowing tale of the last moments in John's ship and the last bit of information about the Andromedins.

With that information, plus the fact that the Galaxis had not been attacked, government officials could say, with some confidence, that the Andromedins had been destroyed.

Even though the news to the public had been tempered with reservations, the people, especially from the affected sector, celebrated joyously and, in time, the inhabitants returned to the planets that had been evacuated but not attacked, and the rehabilitation of the attacked planets began.

The attacked planets would remain unoccupied for centuries afterwards because of the stigma attached to them. They remained an enduring festering sore in the empire that became almost a memorial to the millions of lives lost or displaced due to the Andromedins' incursion into the empire.

EPILOGUE

On planet Earth, in a public area just outside the walls of the palace and governmental complex, is a park that stands in honour of the emperors and the heroes of the empire. The largest area of the park is the Path of Emperors. Another area, the Path of Heroes, is not as long as it contains a statue for only the best of the best heroes that the mothers and fathers of the empire had birthed and nurtured. One stands unique among the others as it consists of a slightly larger statue than the others of a middle-aged man holding the hand of an eight-year-old boy. The man is gazing into the distance; looking toward the future. The boy looks up wide-eyed toward his father.

The father had earned renown for himself as the Hero at the Battle of Balera. He, a captain in the space force, had saved the lives of several thousand people in that battle, which was eventually won by the empire, although he lost his life performing the feat. Sure, he was a fierce combatant while holding off an attack against superior odds until help could arrive, and a person producing a feat like that is usually deserving of a mention in the history books and one or several monuments on local planets but it would not have been enough to warrant more than that.

Many people protested at the time of the decision for the statue that the man did not deserve a designation as the hero of the empire. But others, who knew the boy well, approved of it, because the man had achieved much more than help to win that battle; he fathered, raised, and inspired an even more important hero of the empire, the young boy beside him; the greatest hero of them all.

People who knew the boy understood that he would never have considered himself a hero and would have considered his father any less of one. The emperor at that time knew the boy as a man and could see no other way to present this part of history. Usually much documentation and consideration is required for a designation of hero to be given. In this case,

213

the emperor himself completed the documentation. Accommodation was made to ensure that the father was honoured with his son, who would likely not have been who he came to be without the shining example of his father. The son had earned the right for the father to be a hero along with the son.

The plaque on the statue read:

Leif Ericson, Hero of the Battle of Balera and the empire

Leif Ericson, Jr., Hero, and Saviour of the empire

From a long line of Viking adventurers

The designation of 'Saviour of the empire' had never been given before and would never be given again.

At the unveiling ceremony were a woman and her son, David, their heads bent in sorrow and respect for the young Leif. A toddler held her hand; a young boy who had borne the name of John Mackenzie but had had his name officially changed by his mother to Leif Erickson III. She lifted him onto her shoulders, so he could see better and thought to the child, using her increasing confidence with telepathy, "This is a statue of your daddy when he was a boy. He's a great hero."

The tyke read her mind and, in response, bent his head to look at his mother and smiled knowingly.

His mother then reached up and tousled his flaming red hair with her hand.

ABOUT THE AUTHOR

Michael has had the bug to write since before he reached his teens but rarely got much time to do it. Now he is retired and trying to catch up on his life's dream. It is never too late to start. He lives with his family in Canada.

www.ingramcontent.com/pod-product-compliance
Lightning Source LLC
Chambersburg PA
CBHW072237170626
46813CB00003B/1259